8 - 2011

This book is dedicated with all my love to my beautiful daughters,
Ashley Abriana Ziman and Michele Samantha Ziman.

PART ONE

CHAPTER 1

"Go back to bed," he commanded. "Don't move an inch." The timbre of his voice, deep with intensity, demanding obedience. The light from the hallway made it impossible for her to distinguish his features, but she remembered his form blocking the entire doorway, he appeared so big.

She covered her head with the blanket, knowing she would never forget the guttural sound that echoed in her ears.

An agonizing cry . . . A body crashing on the landing . . . Footsteps of someone running . . . Then silence. Broken by the sound of ambulance sirens.

The little girl rolled off the bed and crawled to the door, pushed it open. Her eyes pulled in some light from the hall window.

On the floor, a black puddle.

"Mama?" She reached out a finger and touched the liquid. It was warm and sticky. Her mind screamed, but her throat was mute. A nightmare. But the blood was real. She inched forward and laid her head on her mother's unmoving stomach.

Commotion. Paramedics. Pairs of white shoes. Needles penetrating her skin. A warm wave enveloping her. She was falling, falling down. Sleep, deep and lovely . . .

"Kelly? Kelly?"

Her body jerked slightly as she came back into the present.

"Kelly? Five minutes, honey. You're on in five minutes."

"Thanks, Candi. My mind was a thousand miles away, I guess!" Kelly said with a self-deprecating smile.

The ten o'clock show on Monday nights was usually dead, but from behind the curtain, Kelly could hear a lively, boozy murmur overlaid by the metallic trill of the betting machines. She took a deep breath and held it, closing her eyes. Her last performance. She scrolled through the next few hours in her mind, scene by scene, as if fast-forwarding through a DVD. Finish the show. Visit Porter at his suite at the Venetian. Say a quick good-bye. Then make a run for it. Her bags were in the car. Her kids were ready, as she instructed Betty, her usual nanny, when she called her before rehearsals. Only one person could complicate her plan, and she prayed, as she did every night, that this wouldn't be the night he would show up.

The lights dimmed and the drummer tapped a syncopated beat. Kelly tugged at her wig and whispered to herself, "I am Marilyn. He can't see me." Taking a last look in the backstage mirror, she saw once again that the costume was perfect. A dark-brown beauty mark rode the crest of her Ferrari-red lips. A platinum blonde curl fell across her forehead. Her dress plunged between her breasts, slid around her hips, and dropped into a pool of red satin over her stiletto heels.

All of a sudden the curtain was drawn and Kelly moved into the spotlight, taking the mike in her black satin gloves. For a suspended instant, the audience sat hushed as if mesmerized. She heard a woman's voice murmur, ". . . looks just like Marilyn."

Kelly was pleased by the effect. She began to sing, keeping her voice soft and sultry and training her eyes on the floor. For the first few bars of Cole Porter's "My Heart Belongs to Daddy," she moved her hips just barely with the beat. Once her eyes had adjusted to the spotlight, she peered up through her false lashes and scanned the audience.

The usual. Salesmen, a few tourists, locals. The convention nerds were easy to spot, with plastic name tags hanging from their necks. Two women—ex-showgirls or hookers—sat at the end of the bar, chatting, their eyes following Kelly.

At the dark fringes of the audience, two men each sat alone. One was football-player huge, slumped back in his chair, appreciatively taking her in. A few tables away, white-haired and wearing golf clothes, the other man stared at her ravenously, like a dog on a chain eyeing a bone just out of reach.

Then Kelly ended the song, bowing low during the applause.

"Thank you, thank you very much," she breathed into the microphone, glad the first number was over.

But as she straightened up, an icy chill seized her gut.

At the bar stood a tall man with his back to her. His dark suit jacket tapered from broad shoulders to a fit waist. The back of his expensive haircut was flecked with gray.

It can't be him, she told herself, willing the man to turn around, but praying he wouldn't. *You're safe*, she reassured herself. *It's not your husband, not here, not tonight.*

Her eyes darted over to the drummer, whose sticks were raised, waiting for her cue. Impatiently he shrugged, unaware of the danger she was in.

But it's not safe, her instinct insisted. *Leave now.* She took a breath. *But if I leave the stage, that would draw even more attention to me.* Kelly regarded the audience once more, and her eyes fell on a salesman in the second row. His cheeks flushed from drink, his mouth hard, he seemed to challenge her to begin another song. It snapped her back into her persona. Strutting across the stage, she slid a leg through the slit in her dress and sang Cy Coleman and Dorothy Fields's "Big Spender." *I* am *Marilyn*, she thought, *and even if it is him, he can't see the real me.*

The number went on forever as Kelly watched for the man at the bar to turn around.

Then she held the last note, closing her eyes. When she opened them, the man's eyes were locked on hers. He leaned back against the bar, a half smile pulling up one side of his mouth.

Kelly's dread instantly drained away. It wasn't her husband. Relaxing into the next number, she rehearsed her plan again. It was a good one. It would work. She just had to finish this show. When it was over, she'd be only one painful step away from making her final escape from Vegas.

With relief washing through her, Kelly glanced again at the man at the bar and with a jolt realized who he was. What was Jake Brooks doing here? For weeks this man's face had been on TV, making the case for Jeanette Pantelli, the so-called Platinum Widow, as an abused wife. Brooks had managed to paint his client as a damsel in distress rather than a greedy woman who had hired a hit man to kill her husband. With all the publicity, his celebrity was a certainty.

Jake Brooks gave her a full-blown smile. Kelly pulled her gaze away. On TV, the man was handsome; in person, he was magnetic. Even from across the room, Kelly felt a rush. She went through the remainder of her act feeling her performance charged by his attention—until, in the middle of the next-to-last number, she saw Jake Brooks's eyes drop to her feet and move appraisingly up her body, as though cataloguing each part of her. Reaching her eyes, he stared with a challenging, yet questioning, grin. His joke evaporated the magnetism, and Kelly's defenses shot up. *Not in this lifetime,* she thought. *I don't care who you are.* She was one song away from the end of her last show on this stage, just minutes away from the hardest thing she would ever do in her life. Before she quit, she would show this cocky lawyer what she thought of him and his profession.

Kelly cued the drummer for her finale, Marilyn's "Let's Make Love," and stepped off the stage. As she moved through the tables, she noticed that the owner of the nightclub, Shrake—a mobster whose cherubic face masked his cruelty—had taken the barstool next to Brooks. He was speaking urgently, a briefcase open on his lap. Kelly paused at a table of frat boys and poured on the Marilyn, singing to each one as if he were the only man in the room. Running her finger along one guy's lips, she gave his neighbor a shake of her ass. She ruffled the third guy's hair, then slid into the last guy's lap, breathing the lyric, "Let's make love."

She sashayed toward Brooks, and the electricity of his attention intensified, dangerous and predatory. The club owner leaned into Brooks and whispered something, jerking his head toward the briefcase. Without a glance toward the other man, Brooks pushed the briefcase closed with his elbow. Kelly could just hear his cocky, offhand rebuff: "I don't represent bill-collecting hit men." The shorter man scowled, snatched the briefcase, and stalked away.

Kelly slid back up to the stage, timing her arrival to the climax of the song. Jake Brooks was still grinning as though he owned her. With her voice riding the last note, she raised her arm toward her head. As the drummer bashed the last beat, she grabbed a handful of silvery-blonde hair and, in a flash, whipped off the wig and held it in front of her like a severed head. She heard the audience gasp, felt the cool air on her scalp and her own hair slicked back with bobby pins, winked at Brooks, and sauntered unexpectedly along the cat-walk that pierced through the crowd. Moving closer and closer to him, leaning forward until her lips touched his ear.

"It's all an illusion," she whispered.

For a fraction of a second, Brooks just stood there, stunned. Then he threw his head back and—while the audience broke into scattered applause—laughed.

Kelly bowed one last time, calmly exited the stage, and raced to her dressing room, her mind darkening with what was to come.

The final curtain on love! The last time she would let Porter hold her, touch her, let his deep voice reassure her, instill hope in a hopeless fantasy of a world that could never be. The final curtain . . .

*   *   *

Three hours later, Kelly was speeding down the center lane of the southbound state highway. Running again. Everything had gone just as she'd planned it. Everything, that is, except her lover's reaction. Why had Porter fought her so hard? Why couldn't he just accept the inevitability of her leaving? She had planned their last night together so carefully, yet it had taken such a tragic turn. As the miles passed, she replayed the evening moment by moment, combing the memories for ways it could have gone differently.

Kelly checked the rearview mirror. Deep in the coma of sleep, her children were secured snugly in the backseat. She reached back and rubbed Libby's knee. The four-year-old smacked her lips and nuzzled her cheek against the car seat. Six-year-old Kevin was frowning in his sleep, but he seemed in no danger of waking up. Kelly adjusted the heat and glanced down at the dashboard. The gas tank was still half full, and the sky was still dark. Soon it would start to lighten and she'd have to stop for gas. Her hands tightened on the steering wheel as she pushed the Civic down the highway toward Phoenix and beyond. Taking the long route, she had decided, would ensure her successful escape.

The monotonous road ahead reminded Kelly of the many roads, the many places that had been her life. She had always found safety in a world of anonymity. Some people she connected with for a frozen moment. But no one had come so close, so deep, as Porter. In the midst of emptiness they had found each other. Destiny had played the cruelest card of all—the card of love. A love, forbidden, that was dead to her now.

CHAPTER 2

YELLOW TAPE UNFURLED LIKE A PARTY STREAMER—
albeit a ghastly one—as a policewoman ran the spool down the hall
and cordoned off the elevators. CRIME SCENE: DO NOT CROSS, it barked
in authoritative black letters. In the congressman's suite, a dozen cops,
detectives, and crime scene investigators were already at work. One
man vacuumed next to the bed, lifting the curtains out of the way with
a latex-covered finger and thumb. A woman was painting white powder on each of the doorjambs. In the bathroom, another woman pressed
tape around the sink handles. In the bedroom, a man lifted a disk of
putty away from the headboard, then reached for a digital camera.

Sprawled on a sofa in the sitting room was Congressman Porter
Garrett, his head thrown back at an odd angle in a smear of black
blood, his throat cut open.

The lead detective murmured into a cell phone. "Mmm-
hmm. See you then." Detective Cooper snapped the phone shut and
addressed a man next to him.

"They'll be here after noon. They're flying in a team from DC."

The on-duty manager at the Venetian, a fortyish man in a polo shirt and khakis, nodded. "We can arrange a few rooms on this floor at government rates."

The detective ignored the remark and chose, instead, to listen to a familiar squawk from his mobile, detailing new information. He pointed toward the hallway with his free hand.

"You might want to get down to the lobby. Fucking vultures are here already. My guys are trying to keep the satellite truck out of your valet lane, but they may need some help from hotel security before our backup gets here. Might want to check the service entrances, too."

The hotel manager hurried away, eager for something to do—anything that would get him as far away as possible from the gruesome body and the gruff detective. "Fucking media," he grumbled to himself as he shuffled down the hallway. "Fucking way to start the morning. Not even seven o'clock." He couldn't get the picture out of his head: the room, the bloody body, the disheveled bed. Fucking shame about Garrett, though. That guy was going all the way to the White House someday, and he had stayed at this hotel. That could have been worth something—might still be. Would this be good for business or bad? The manager knew never to underestimate the buying power of notoriety or the macabre. He realized that by tomorrow, there could be people calling to reserve that suite, the murder suite. This could work in his favor after all.

He smiled to himself as he strode out of the elevator—just in time to see his chief of security tackle a TV cameraman and shove him through the glass entrance doors.

"Whoa!" cried the manager, running forward alongside two bouncers moving in from the left. They pulled the men apart as two police vans roared up to the curb, sirens blaring, lights flashing. A dozen cops in helmets poured out and barricaded the doors, standing shoulder to shoulder. Against such odds, yet another camera crew ran up to the hotel—the shooter in the lead, trailed by a sound guy holding a mike on a boom and a producer in a baseball cap and sneakers. They tried to shove past the policemen but were bounced back.

"*Eyewitness News!*" shouted the producer. "Channel Five!"

"Let us in, you fat fucks," grunted the cameraman, feinting with his gear in an attempt to fake out the shortest cop in the row.

A taxi wheeled up to the police lines, and a man leaped out before it stopped moving. He was tall, with graying dark hair, and dressed in jeans and a black blazer. His face was set in an angry grimace, his carved cheekbones underlying gray, alert eyes. He sprinted toward the doors.

"Sir! No one comes in or out!" shouted a cop.

"They're expecting me," mumbled the man, trying to step around the barricade.

"It's Jake Brooks!" shouted the TV producer. "Over here! Brooks! What have you heard? Jake! Why are you here?"

"Sir, step away, sir!" the cop yelled, trying to keep his balance amid the jostling.

Brooks whipped out a phone, at the same time shaking his head and turning away from the TV camera in his face.

"Forget it," mumbled the producer, before yelling, "This way!" He took off toward the side of the building and around the corner, his crew following him. The manager raced after them.

"It's okay, officer. He's with me," called a woman's voice from behind the police barricade. The spikes of her striking copper-colored hair poked above the cop's shoulder. "He's part of our team."

"Ma'am. We've got strict orders not to let anyone in or out. Please move back inside."

"Cassie, get someone down here," growled Brooks as he looked at her over the helmeted cop's shoulder.

"Jake, it's awful, he—"

"Get someone down here," Brooks repeated firmly. Cassie's head disappeared from view as she pulled back inside the hotel. Brooks stepped off the curb and walked a few paces down the circular driveway, trying to calm his mind.

He had been asleep when the phone's shrill ring had awakened him, and he was still processing the news. Cassie's strained voice had whispered in his ear. "It's bad news, Jake. Porter's dead. Murdered. Suzanne wants you to . . . if you could identify . . ."

A thousand questions had tumbled through Jake's brain as his body snapped awake, and he must have voiced some of them to Cassie, but his memory hadn't recorded anything beyond that ominous first pronouncement: "It's bad news, Jake. Porter's dead." Somehow he had dressed. Somehow he had hailed a taxi.

"It's alright, Martinez, he can come through."

Jake snapped out of his reverie as another part of his brain caught the officer's declaration, and he watched as the cops opened a small gap in their defense to let him through. Behind him, the break sealed as quickly as it had opened.

Cassie stood in the hotel lobby with a man who had a full mane of nearly white, curly hair. His eyes were pale blue, fringed by almost translucent lashes. He wore jeans and a blue nylon Windbreaker.

"Hey, Cooper," said Jake, taking note of the enmity in the cop's eyes. This wasn't going to be easy.

"I shouldn't even be letting you in here," barked Cooper. "Especially since this doesn't involve a mobster or a corrupt CEO."

Jake held his anger, and calmly said what he knew Cooper already knew. "Suzanne Garrett asked me to come. I'm representing an old family friend." Jake knew there was nothing Cooper could do to keep him out. Off the murder scene at least—the investigation was a different matter.

"I didn't know lawyers like you *had* old friends," muttered Cooper.

"Lawyers like me would surprise you in many ways," replied Jake without smiling.

Cooper glared a moment. "It's this way," he said finally, turning away. "Brace yourself. As they say, it's not pretty."

Jake clenched his teeth on the elevator ride to the twenty-fourth floor, saving his questions until after he'd seen for himself the incomprehensible. Cassie held a tissue to her eyes. Cooper stayed in motion, rocking back and forth on his heels, his hands clasped behind his back.

In the suite, the curtains were open and the early morning sun poured in. Clamp lights positioned around the room gave it the appearance of a photo shoot venue. As he scanned the scene, Jake took in the officer vacuuming, the woman dusting for prints, the photographer shooting bed linen draped on the sofa. Men were on their hands and knees, combing the carpet with gloved hands. He didn't see Porter. The bed was empty, the covers rumpled and thrown over the floor. The chair was covered with papers, and Porter's laptop was open on the desk. A black silk robe lay in a pool on the floor by the window. Jake looked back toward the sitting room. That's when he saw that the photographer wasn't taking pictures of bed linen. It was a body. *Porter's* body.

"He's over here," grunted Cooper. "You want to take a look?"

Jake nodded, trying to appear matter-of-fact, and was relieved when his phone rang. He pulled it out of his jacket and uttered a simple *hello*.

"It's Suzanne. Are you there yet?"

"Just got into the room."

"Is it true, Jake?"

"Suzanne. Can you wait five minutes?" Jake heard Suzanne's voice catch, but then she answered evenly, "I'm here. Call me back."

Jake silenced his phone and slid it into his pocket.

Cooper stood over the body, looking annoyed. Jake forced himself to take two steps closer. The *click-whirr* of the camera shutter seemed louder than normal as it put in freeze-frame what Jake was already experiencing in slow motion.

Click-whirr. It was Porter, no question. His body, naked, was splayed awkwardly—his hips on the sofa, his upper thorax mangled. *Click-whirr*. Like a target. *Like a dismantled hangman,* Jake found himself thinking. *Click-whirr*. Porter's head canted at a right angle to his shoulders, a huge gash from ear to ear severing his neck in a mess of blood. *Click-whirr*. *Click-whirr*. Porter's handsome face in a hideous grimace, one eye open, one closed. His thick, sandy hair matted black with blood. *Click-whirr*. Blood on his hands, both clenched into fists.

Jake had seen enough. He turned away and forced himself to say something.

"What time do you think this happened?" He noticed Cooper gesture impatiently at the photographer, who lowered her camera and moved away toward the windows.

"Between one thirty and three."

"What else?"

"There's no sign of forced entry. It looks like whoever did it was already in the room with him. We've got what appears to be semen on the sheets. Also, long blonde hairs in the bed and on the floor. Probably female, though it could be either sex, at this point, but there's also lipstick on one of the pillowcases. Though that's not conclusive evidence, either, that the companion was female."

Jake covered his mouth with his hand and pretended to be clearing his throat. Porter had had a lover? How had he not known that?

This close to the election, and Porter was having an affair? Or was this a one-night encounter? Or a setup?

"It's definitely female. Porter wasn't gay or bisexual," said Jake.

"You know who it was?" said Cooper, showing the first spark of animation Jake had seen so far.

Jake shook his head.

Cooper snorted. "It's going to be impossible to keep it quiet any longer. Someone's going to have to go feed the beast soon. The cameras are all over this like flies on meat." He glanced at Jake's angry face and, out of respect for the dead, apologized. "Sorry."

"Detective!" called a voice suddenly. "You need to see this."

Jake followed Cooper and the photographer into the bedroom in time to watch one of the investigators pull the bedspread off the floor. Underneath was a platinum blonde wig. The photographer fired off one, two, three, four quick shots in a row. She moved behind the investigator and squeezed off four more frames, then nodded at the investigator. He lifted the wig in his gloved hands and peered inside.

"More blonde hairs," he reported. He put his fist in it and held it up, giving it the distinct shape of a head. The wig was of good quality and appeared to have been cut and styled by a professional.

"Seems like platinum blonde wigs are in style," muttered Jake.

"What?" said Cooper.

"Marilyn Monroe wigs," replied Jake. His eyes narrowed. "I had a very sexy encounter with one last night."

Cooper looked disgusted. "Did it happen here in this suite?"

"Fuck off," grunted Jake. Cooper moved away for a closer look at the wig. Grateful to have a moment to himself, Jake glanced once more into the other room at Porter's body. A different photographer was standing over it with her camera. The irony was hard to miss. As a congressman and, until this morning, a candidate for the U.S.

Senate, Porter Garrett had spent most of his waking moments trying to look good in front of the camera. These would be his last pictures.

For nearly two decades Porter Garrett had been Jake's closest friend. They had met as prosecutors in Las Vegas, fresh out of law school. Young, idealistic, they had been superheroes then, going after the scum of the earth who preyed on the innocent and the good. They had developed a healthy competition with each other, and their friendship was built as much on respect for each other's legal skills as on their mutual desire to rid the world of bad guys.

But they had a core difference in outlook, and inevitably their career paths had diverged. Porter relished the logic of the legal system, believed in its overall fairness and overlooked its flaws in favor of the good it did. Politics for him was a perfect fit, and once he had started running for office, he had never lost. His popularity in the House of Representatives had gotten national attention, and he'd been tapped to run for the Senate, with the implication that he was being groomed for the White House. The campaign was in its final weeks, and Porter had been making impressive gains against his opponent—a crusty old incumbent named Theodore Henckle, who—conventional wisdom had it—was unbeatable.

While Porter had grown more idealistic over the years, however, Jake had grown more cynical. Both men took to victory like a shark to the smell of blood, but after a while Jake had stopped seeing the difference between the criminals he put behind bars and the people whose vast fortunes supported the system he was sworn to protect. Too many times Jake found himself seeing things from the defendant's point of view, understanding the complicated circumstances that led a person to commit a crime—in some cases, a very serious crime. The more he saw of the justice system in action—outside the sterile classrooms of Harvard Law—the more Jake saw the subtleties and started losing his faith.

So he had abruptly given up his practice as a prosecutor in Las Vegas one summer and moved to Los Angeles to become a defense attorney. "A *high-priced* defense attorney," Porter always pointed out, never passing up a chance to tease his friend. It was a testimony to the character and intelligence of both men that they had remained close. The transition had not dented his friendship with Porter Garrett; it had, however, earned him the hatred of just about every cop on the Las Vegas force. The moment he'd seen Cooper at this scene, bringing back the memory of their scorn and derision, Jake had known he would not be welcomed any further into this investigation.

He turned toward the window, away from Porter's horrific body, and fought the urge to throw up. Jake knew one thing for sure: He had to get out of there right away.

* * *

Kelly's eyelids were growing heavy in the overcast, shadowed morning as the headlights of the oncoming cars flickered in a hypnotic dance that threw her back to another ride, another vehicle, back to her teen years.

She forced her mind to focus on the reflection of the beam of headlights passing by as they created a light show on the ceiling of the limousine. They helped to drown out his voice violently pounding in her ear, "You're my wife! You are mine! I can do whatever I want with you!" as he forced himself into her, over and over again. The car lights, dancing to a frantic rhythm, drowned his presence, her cries of pain.

She felt nothing.

Somewhere in her mind, his voice echoed, mashed in with the voices of many other men who had hurt her. A revolving door of strangers, all paid to be there as caregivers in the broken foster care system.

Her present reality awakened her to the fact that she was once again entering the unknown, a zone of comfort where nothing was familiar, and nothing was anticipated, where no emotions were put on the line. Acutely aware of how dangerous love could be, Kelly was certain that leaving Porter had been a must, and that escaping now into the unknown was her only way out.

*   *   *

Jake found Cassie with her phone to her ear, pacing by the elevators near some local agents wearing Nevada FBI Windbreakers. It reminded him to turn his ringer back on. The phone rang immediately, just as Cassie was finishing up her own conversation.

"Brooks," he uttered, and paused, listening. "Howard," he said firmly into the phone, "we'll do a statement. In about an hour. We'll call you."

He felt a movement by his elbow and turned in time to catch Cassie as she fell forward into his shoulder. They hugged awkwardly. She was trying to speak but managing only to force out little sobs of air. Finally she cried hoarsely, "I found him. I had to get security to open the suite, and I saw him . . ."

Jake gripped her shoulders. As Suzanne Garrett's assistant, Cassie was called on to lead a life that revolved entirely around protocol. Unfortunately, and especially in such grim circumstances, she was the quintessential overeducated, under-experienced recent Ivy League graduate who hadn't a clue how to behave. Smart and beautiful, with a childhood as sheltered as a Ferrari in a garage, Cassie was brilliant when things went according to her script; when she had to improvise, she fell apart.

Jake reminded himself that she was young, that he needed to help her pull herself together, back into one piece. And he needed her to be discreet.

"They're all calling," she whined. "The networks, CNN, the wires. K-LAS. They're sniffing for blood—I don't know what to say."

"*You* say nothing. Where's Alana?"

Cassie wiped her eyes with the backs of her hands.

"I think she's on her way here."

"Maybe stuck outside, like I was?"

Cassie's eyes widened. "Oh, shit!"

"Pull yourself together," Jake said gruffly. "Don't open your mouth to anyone. Find Alana." Alana Sutter was the political strategist—campaign manager—for Porter's now-defunct campaign. Jake was surprised she wasn't already on the scene. Cassie nodded at Jake through her tears as she punched the elevator button.

Jake's phone rang again. He held it to his ear and heard Suzanne's voice.

"It's him?"

"Yes. God, I'm sorry, Suzanne."

There was silence on the line. Jake tried to fill it.

"I'll do a statement on behalf of the family, if you want. The FBI is sending backup this afternoon—a special team from DC. I'll be at that meeting." Jake paused. "I'm getting static from the LVPD. I may need your help."

"What are those assholes doing? I'll tell them where to get off." Jake had always admired Suzanne's way of handling hard situations by talking tough. He almost felt valiant, giving her this opportunity to excoriate the local police, so he swallowed his pride.

"That'd be a help, Suzanne. Thanks."

"I won't be at the press conference."

"That's okay. I'll handle it."

"Alana says it's best."

"She's with you?"

"Yes."

That made sense, but still Jake was surprised that Sutter hadn't come to the crime scene.

"Put her on. I want to run the statement by her."

* * *

An hour later, as Jake stood in front of the assembled news media in a hotel conference room, he spoke robotically.

"Congressman Porter Garrett of Nevada was found dead in his Las Vegas hotel room early this morning. He appears to have been a victim of homicide. Congressman Garrett will be deeply missed by his family, his friends—and the American people."

The lights seemed brighter than usual, the cackle of follow-up questions more cacophonous. Jake was more than accustomed to the media as a result of his highly visible—some might say sensational and glory-seeking—court cases. The TV cameras were sometimes his best allies in getting a case to go his way. He was unsentimental about it, having watched the innocent take the rap simply because they weren't photogenic, having seen the guilty escape justice simply because they had star quality. He had long ago learned to view talk shows as pathetic arenas for egomaniacal know-it-alls, wasting a public resource to broadcast their opinions simply because their facial features happened to appeal to the cameras. Yet even as he regarded those cameras as the parasites of humanity, sucking the blood out of people in their most vulnerable moments, Jake knew how to manipulate each and every one he faced. And some part of him had always loved it.

But today was different. Jake realized that he had stood silently just a little too long. The questions were growing louder and louder.

Abruptly, he turned his back on the cameras and left the room. Several staffers tried to follow him, but he waved them off. "Five minutes," he said.

As he stumbled down the hall, his gut balled up as though he'd been kicked. How could Porter's life end so abruptly? Here today, then gone in an instant, a finger snap. And soon enough he would be replaced—erased from everyone's mind. What was left behind? Speeches, important bills, a life of devotion to America? But who was going to remember? Even his children didn't really know the battles their father had fought, the commitments he kept against all odds. How he was always struggling to do the right thing.

The pointlessness of a life taken, especially a life so well lived, made Jake want to punch a fist through the wall. Jake knew people who had touched futility and limped back with a vacant look in their eyes—the look of nothing more to lose. Porter had never been that way. Futility had never been a part of his outlook. But everything Porter had felt deeply about would be tinged with this—a gruesome end in a hotel suite. Porter would leave a dim memory behind—if he was lucky. And a sordid mess if he wasn't.

Jake found an empty stall in the men's room and locked the door. He sank onto the toilet seat and, holding his face in his hands, let the silent sobs pound through his body.

His world had become an instant vacuum. Porter was the brother he'd never had, his conscience, his idol. What was left now? Who could he talk to? Who would listen?

CHAPTER 3

KELLY PASSED A BURGER KING AND TRIED TO HOLD
her breath, but a whiff of cooking grease seeped in through the vents.
With it came another flood of revolting memories.

> Fast-food bags crumpled on the floor of the Cadillac. The per-
> vasive smell of fried food. Knee socks, a tartan skirt, and girl-
> ish underpants around her ankles. Her hair in ponytails.

Kelly accelerated.

> Her thighs spread open as she lay back on the seat. Faces in
> the window.

Kelly swerved around a pickup truck with a gun rack across the back
window.

> A cop tapping on the car window. "Alright, knock it off."
>
> Her husband's grin. "But, officer, this is my wife." Male
> laughter.

Kelly flicked on the radio, found a station playing gospel music. She willed the memory away.

"Mo-om, I'm hungry," whined Kevin from the backseat. She'd been driving for nearly seven hours, stopping only once for gas. As far as she could tell, no one was following her.

"That's why I got off the freeway, honey," Kelly answered in a singsong voice, peering down the row of plastic fast-food signs as they passed by. Finally she found what she was looking for: a diner that held the promise of a burger made with actual meat and a real slice of pie from a tin pie plate. The kids scrambled into a booth, squirrelly and talkative. Kelly pulled crayons and paper out of her purse and hoped they wouldn't get too rambunctious. She'd have to find a playground or park eventually, but first she needed to put more distance between them and Vegas.

While the kids drew, Kelly slipped her Sidekick into her lap. The tiny computer screen snapped into place and, using her thumbs, Kelly navigated through her e-mail. She checked some news sites. Satisfied, she clicked off and put the device back in her purse. Her eyes drifted to a television at the end of the counter, tuned to ESPN. A basketball player spoke into a microphone. The diner was close to the Mexican border and busy with breakfast customers, most of whom were Latino workers and truckers. The waitress—a skinny woman in her thirties, with a distinct smoker's rasp—was friendly, smiling as she brought orange juice and coffee to the table. When Kelly's ham-and-cheese omelet arrived, she took a bite and was shocked to realize she hadn't eaten for almost eighteen hours.

"Are you hungry?"

She hadn't eaten for a day and a half, unless you counted the paper cup of ice she'd managed to get from a McDonald's. Chewing on it had made the hunger pangs subside, but she would have done just about anything for some real food.

She was fifteen—a runaway escaping from the cops, hiding in alleys, sleeping in backyards and in parks. She was used to being shunned or ignored, and she welcomed being invisible. She was not going back to the Gordons' this time. If the cops or social workers caught her, she would refuse to go back to her foster parents. She hadn't figured out how, but she would. When she had slipped out the bathroom window on that last night, she'd known Mr. Gordon's fists would be more unforgiving than usual if he caught her. But he wasn't going to catch her. She was determined to escape. If she stayed, he'd just keep terrorizing her, punching her, and humiliating her. The beatings had been getting worse and worse as it was. Even icing her stomach wasn't helping anymore. She was sure that one of her ribs was broken. She dreaded one more night of such unbearable pain.

From the first day she had moved into the Gordons' home, they had made it clear to her that she was disposable. She was told to expect to eat last, to shower last, to make herself invisible. She learned to look down at her plate during meals. Only once did she dare to ask to watch TV with them. That time, Mr. Gordon's hand came across her face with such speed, she thought her jaw would fly off.

She was left to do the dishes, holding her jaw and crying silently to herself. From that day on, she found solace only when isolated in her bed, where she would pull the covers over her head and whisper to the memories of her mother. Under the covers, she created a world of make-believe people who loved her. She repeated the words "she loves me," "he loves me," "they love me," concocting a family in her mind.

Every day she'd wake up early, eat her allotted breakfast, clean up, and rush out, almost always before Mr. Gordon's alarm went off. School was a safe haven. There, no one beat her. She always chose the last row of seats in the classroom, keeping to herself, yearning to disappear into the background, planning her escape.

During recess and lunch break she retreated to the far side of the football field, alone, thankful to be left to her own thoughts and dreading the bell that signaled the end of the day. She sat, looking out at the park across the street, where mothers pushed infants in swings and toddlers tumbled over the sand and down slides. In the safety of being a voyeur, she allowed herself to remember her own childhood.

Her real life—that's what she called it—had ended abruptly, and the memories had now sifted down to a basic few, which she pulled out and rubbed like beach stones, their contours growing blurrier and softer with each recollection. A ballet recital in which she wore a sea-green tutu. A booth in a restaurant where the waitresses wore little white hats that looked like Kleenex boxes. Riding on her mother's back in someone's swimming pool, as though on a dolphin. A dollhouse with a set of dishes no bigger than buttons. She remembered less of her father, even though she had last seen him when she was the same age. He had died in prison from unknown causes, she'd been told. And this news had snuffed out most of what remained. The two memories she did have— flying across the sidewalk while each parent held a hand, and clinging to his neck on their way out of a movie—didn't bring her any comfort or answers. At the trial, the judge had asked Kelly questions about him. She didn't know what she was supposed to answer, so she had tried to figure out what the judge wanted her to say. Her father had taken her mother away from her. That was what it all came down to. Then he was gone, too, and she went into "protective custody," "foster care"—terms she had heard for so long. An avalanche of strangers, a bottom-less pit of insults, pain, and indifference.

The morning she'd met her husband had been dreary and drizzly. Kelly had crouched in a doorway, shivering, the too-short sleeves on her jean jacket leaving her forearms red and bumpy. Her feet, clad in soaking-wet socks and tennis shoes, were freezing. Dressed in a three-piece suit, the man had approached her cautiously, holding out a big umbrella and offering her a white handkerchief with a monogram embroidered on it.

"You look cold. Are you hungry?"

"MOMMY!"

Kelly jumped.

"Kevin's eating my fries!"

"No, darling, those are not your fries. You're not supposed to have any fries. Let's see what else they have that you might like."

She waved at the waitress to come to their table.

"Do you have any sugarless desserts for a diabetic?"

"Sugar-free Jell-O?"

"That'll be great, thanks." Kelly turned to Libby, saying, "Honey, you'll love it."

The children continued to bicker. Without a word, Kelly breathed on a spoon and pressed it to her nose. It hung on the center of her face, and she waited for them to notice. As she watched their faces, a wave of love enveloped her. It was easy to put aside her memories of his voice that day, nine years ago, asking, "Are you hungry?"

"Mommy!" squealed Libby, instantly forgetting about Kevin's offenses. "I want to do that!"

"It works on your chin, too," said Kelly, demonstrating. Kevin covered his fries with more ketchup as Libby hung her spoon from

various parts of her body and experimented with the different surfaces of the table and the vinyl seat. Kelly took a sip of coffee as the
waitress came over with the Jell-O.

"May I invite you to have lunch with me?" he asked politely,
gentleman that he was.

He pulled Kelly under his umbrella and led her to a warm
restaurant where they studied menus the size of newspapers
in a booth in a back room. In a whisper, Kelly ordered a steak,
a baked potato, and a strawberry shake. She hadn't been in a
restaurant since her mother had been killed, and it was what
her mother had always ordered.

He drank some type of clear alcohol with a twist of lemon
in it, as Kelly recalled, and he simply watched her eat. They
did not speak. Kelly chewed quickly. When she put down her
knife and fork, he slid toward her and, putting his hand over
hers, broke the silence.

"You know, little one, I pride myself on being a real good
judge of character. I can see that you are a good girl. You don't
belong on the streets." His sad eyes moved across her face. "I
have no family. The only people who live in my house work
for me. They can take good care of you," he said in a fatherly
voice. "Come home with me. You can have your own room. I
live in a big house with far too many things for me alone. I can
use the company. I'm tired of eating alone every night. You can
get a puppy or a kitten, whatever new clothes you want. I'm
just like you: all alone in the world."

Kelly had recognized immediately that he was holding out
a way for her to escape the Gordons and the police. Whatever
this man's motives, they seemed far less threatening than Gary
Gordon's fist or juvenile hall. He might be nice for a couple of

days. So Kelly had nodded and wiped her mouth, and when he got up and offered her his hand, she took it and followed him to his car.

His house was set back from the street by a curved driveway. The November trees in the front yard were bare and slick with rain. As he'd promised, the house was large—a mansion, really—and painted white with a gray roof and dormer windows. A portico and two pillars framed the front door, which was painted black.

He punched some buttons on a keypad, and a wrought-iron gate swung open. Kelly stayed very quiet as he led her up the steps and through the front door. The entryway was vast, with black-and-white tiles that stretched away from her like a giant checkerboard. He showed her the game room with the pool table, the screening room with the projection TV and cabinet full of movies, the kitchen with a refrigerator that took up an entire wall, and a walk-in pantry stocked with snack food.

Upstairs was her room, already made up. It contained a bed with a red bedspread. The floor was covered in fluffy white shag. The dresser, vanity, and desk were white.

Looking back on it, as she had done so many times, Kelly wondered why the few things she remembered from that day were so vivid, while huge chunks of time from the rest of her life—before and after her husband—were complete blanks. She did get new clothes, a uniform for school, but couldn't remember how she got them. He must have taken her shopping, or perhaps he brought them to her, afraid the cops would notice them. They ate somehow, but Kelly couldn't remember whether he ordered in or employed a cook. There were so many people that came in and out, cleaning, fixing, serving. She never got a pet. Kelly was pretty sure he didn't touch her at all in those first few weeks except to stroke her hair or hold her hand.

She turned sixteen a couple of months after he had brought her home. The memory was a vivid one.

They had been in the screening room, watching *Pretty Woman*. During the scene when Julia Roberts leans out her window and Richard Gere gets ready to climb up the fire escape, Kelly volunteered, "Today's my birthday."

He stared for a moment, then took her hands in his. "Marry me. Marry me and the courts won't be able to do anything to us. To you."

Kelly didn't even have to think. She'd been surviving on what other people had been offering her since she was six. She grabbed the chance to decide for herself. For that moment, she allowed herself to be Julia Roberts.

"Okay," she said.

She married him three days later in the Houston city hall. She signed the marriage license that said she was eighteen. No one questioned it. The two of them stood alone in front of the judge, but Kelly wore the elaborate white dress and veil he had bought for her. When the judge was finished talking, her new husband lifted her veil and kissed her.

"That does it," he whispered. "Now you're mine forever."

"Yes," she heard herself reply. She looked up at him and saw that his eyes were vacant, impossible to read. "I love you," she said, repeating what she'd heard on commercials and in movies. He smiled and pulled her to the car.

He drove her home and carried her up the stairs. "This is your bed now," he said, draping her on the black comforter in the master suite. "Turn over." Slowly, he undid each of the dozens of pearl buttons running down the back of her dress.

He tore the last few and threw the pile of tulle on the floor. He rolled her onto her back.

"Now touch yourself," he demanded.

More confused than frightened, she reached between her legs. Her husband wiggled out of his suit. Suddenly he smacked her hand, flipped her over, and forced himself into her. Kelly screamed.

"Shut up!" he shouted. "Do you want to go back to the streets?"

She pressed her face into the mattress and refused to let herself cry. When he was done, he rolled her over and kissed her lips gently.

"You're mine," he said with a grimace. "Remember that."

From that moment on, Kelly let him do whatever he wanted, and she performed whatever he dreamed up. And yet, as clear as most of that night was in her mind, the next several years were a blur. Eventually she became an expert at anticipating his moods, for the sake of her survival, just as she had been adept at reading the emotions of her foster parents, but sometimes she misjudged. His rage came unexpectedly and, out of nowhere, he might pinch her nipple until she felt pain in her groin, or, overcome by his own nightmares, he might rip her clothes off and sodomize her.

Kelly looked up suddenly. The diner had gone quiet. Everyone had shifted in their seats to face the television, where the words BREAK-ING NEWS were scrolling across the bottom of the screen. Kevin was drumming on the table with his fingers, lost in his own little world. Libby was eating her Jell-O. The waitress turned up the volume. A man with thick, dark hair and gray eyes spoke. Kelly recognized him immediately from their encounter at the club.

"Congressman Porter Garrett of Nevada was found dead in his Las Vegas hotel room early this morning," said Jake Brooks in a monotone voice. "He appears to have been a victim of homicide. Congressman Garrett will be deeply missed by his family, his friends—and the American people."

The mug fell from Kelly's hand and shattered on the floor. A firework of coffee arced around the shards.

"Mommy, you spilled!" cried Libby.

Kelly fought to control her reaction to the grief and confusion she was forced to tackle. Her mind was spinning. The race was on. It wouldn't be long before they'd trace everything to her.

"Honey, you alright?" said the waitress, bending over with a dustpan. Kelly kept an eye on the TV as the waitress swept up. She saw Porter's wife, supported by two large men, stagger into a limousine. Pictures of an ambulance speeding away, a row of police barricading the hotel, a reporter with a microphone standing in front of some yellow tape. Suddenly, the reporter's face on the screen morphed into the weathered and kind face of Porter. Kelly caught her breath. It was file video, probably from a campaign, and Porter looked comfortable, even heroic, surrounded by bright lights and a crowd of people.

Los Angeles, thought Kelly. *He'll be buried in LA, where his wife always wanted him to stay. And a lot of his big donors will be at the funeral.*

The waitress mopped up the last of the coffee. "Well, you want to know what I think? Politicians can go to hell. When's the last time a politician ever did anything for us?"

Kelly struggled to keep her mouth shut. It was crucial she didn't make herself memorable. She put a twenty on the table, smiled politely, and pulled Kevin and Libby out to the parking lot.

Even before the diner's door shut behind them, she felt a trap closing in on her. It was Kevin who voiced her thoughts for her.

"Mommy, the car's gone!"

"We must have parked it somewhere else," Kelly said, trying to make light of the moment. But even she didn't believe her own words.

"Nope," Kevin responded, shaking his head. "It was parked right over there," he insisted, pointing to the empty spot.

The hairs pricked up on the back of Kelly's neck.

"Maybe someone *stole* it." Kevin sounded excited by that possibility. It was Kelly's turn to shake her head, her heart racing. What should she do? *Get out of the exposed parking lot and into shelter.* She grabbed Kevin and Libby by the hands and pulled them toward the gas station next to the diner. Suddenly Kevin wrenched his hand free and pointed.

"Look, Mom! Over there."

Kelly looked. Behind the diner was the car, parked under a scraggly palm tree that shivered in the hot breeze. Kelly approached the car and looked in the window. On the driver's seat was a piece of paper. Kelly looked closer. Drawn in blue pen was a smiley face. Her husband. He—or someone who worked for him—had done this. Kelly opened the door and snatched it away.

The game was on. The same game he had taunted her with many times before. She was the prey, he was the hunter . . . and the kids were collateral damage.

"What's happening, Mommy?" asked Libby.

"Nothing, honey," answered Kelly, scanning the backseat. "Someone was playing hide-and-seek with our car. Pretty silly, isn't it?"

The children laughed and climbed into the car. Kelly dropped behind the steering wheel, scouring the road to the left and to the right as she pulled back onto the freeway. There were no cars in sight. She didn't even notice the police cruiser parked behind the gas station—or the cop inside it, talking into his radio as she drove away.

Her mind was somewhere else. She kept returning to the encounter with Jake Brooks at the nightclub. She kicked herself for pulling that stunt with the wig. She had let her ego get in the way of all her careful planning.

The net had been cast, and Kelly was on automatic pilot. Only two words echoed in her brain: The first was *run!* The other was his name.

Porter.

CHAPTER 4

"COOPER, WHAT'VE YOU GOT?"

Jake sailed into the investigation headquarters that had been temporarily set up in a suite down the hall from the crime scene. He held a Starbucks cup in one hand, a fistful of attitude in the other. Having pulled himself together after his breakdown following the press conference, he felt the need to direct his emotions elsewhere— to take out his grief over his friend's death on anyone remotely connected to it. He knew what he was doing, but he didn't care. Fuck the seven stages of grieving, or however many there were. He was going to remain at this stage: rage.

Cooper looked up from his phone and motioned for Jake to sit on one of the chairs next to the hotel desk. Jake ignored him and hovered, jangling the change in his pocket and reading the computer screen over Cooper's shoulder. Cooper switched on the screen saver and shuffled a printout back into its manila folder, but Jake caught a glimpse before it was concealed. It was from the FBI.

Jake huffed around. Desks crowded each other where the beds had been. Men and women fingered computers and murmured into phones. Jake tapped impatiently through the e-mails on his Black-Berry while Cooper continued his conversation, the phone balanced between his shoulder and ear. He wrote with a pencil on a notepad. Jake noticed that the old detective was left-handed.

Cooper hung up and swiveled toward Jake, who was rubbing his bloodshot eyes.

"You know, I really don't have to tell you anything," he said.

Jake leaned forward, his jaw muscles tense like pulled sling-shots. "Listen, you bag of bullshit, it was your guys we put on security watch last night. They've got a lot to answer for. And so do you."

Jake watched Cooper's eyes weighing the possibilities. He was almost suspicious when Cooper actually replied.

"Still no weapon," said the detective abruptly, fixing his strange, pale eyes on Jake. "We've got tissue and blood under the congress-man's fingernails. And hair in his fist. A dozen strands, six to eight inches long. Color, medium brown. The blood on his head wasn't just his. All the samples have gone to the lab for DNA work. We're inter-viewing the hotel staff. Most have alibis. We're following up with a few who don't or who we haven't found yet."

"Fingerprints turn up anything?"

"It's only noon."

Jake glared at him.

"Have a few matches already. Colin McDowell. A New York real estate mogul with friends in Colombia. Akira Makihata. He's in Tokyo now, but comes through Las Vegas about once a month. Busi-nessman. He's been linked to the Yakuza." Cooper flicked some but-tons on his computer and continued. "Steven Chasen was in the Peace Corps, that's why his prints were in the database. He owns hotels in Oregon now."

"High rollers?"

"It's a VIP suite." Cooper typed some more. "This was a strange one. Natalie St. Clair. Picked up on shoplifting ten years ago."

"A maid?"

"We checked that. No one by that name on staff."

"Any aliases?"

"Nothing on record."

"What does she look like?"

Cooper turned his computer monitor so Jake could see the image. A young girl, about thirteen or fourteen, stared out sulkily from the screen. Her hair was as black and shiny as shoe polish and hung down straight on both sides of her pale face. Her eyes were outlined with thick black makeup, and her red lips looked swollen.

"You have anything more recent?"

"Nope," said Cooper, swinging the monitor back.

"What else have you got?"

"Nothing on the wig. The hairs are at the lab."

Jake thought a moment, remembering the singer at the club. He dismissed the idea immediately. How many Marilyn wigs were there in Las Vegas? A hundred? A thousand? Ten thousand?

"Those two over there are going over security tapes." Cooper pointed across the room to a man and a woman, each seated in front of a monitor. They were moving through the video, frame by frame. "The camera is positioned over the elevator. We've watched everything from four p.m. to six a.m. Lots of people going in and out, but no blonde wig going up. It could have been part of some ritual or act inside the room, so we're focusing on all the women who go up or down."

Jake felt his blood pressure rise again, his anger at a slow boil. "You planning on coming up with something soon?"

The pair going through the videotape stopped mid-toggle and looked over. Then Jake heard a voice over his shoulder.

"Jake?"

Suzanne Garrett, Porter's widow, glided into the room. She was, as usual, sleek and icy. Her blonde hair sliced down each side of her face as though her hairdresser had used a paper cutter. She put her arms out to hug Jake, but embraced the air between them instead. Though her eyes were red, the rest of her—from her snugly fitted, camel-colored Chanel pantsuit to her flawless manicure—betrayed nothing about what her inner state might be.

"How are you holding up?" murmured Jake.

"Well, you know," whispered Suzanne vaguely.

She was accompanied by Alana Sutter, who was also impeccably dressed—in a dark skirt suit and a blue French blouse. Attractive and tall, with short auburn hair, Sutter was brilliant as a political strategist, but her personality was too restrained for Jake's taste. He tried to picture her wearing a platinum blonde wig. It didn't help.

"Gentlemen," Suzanne said in a loud voice, addressing the room as if she were at a public library benefit. "And ladies," she continued, pointedly staring at several of the female officers. "I appreciate all your hard work so far on this case. As I'm sure you can understand, this is a very difficult time for us, and it means the utmost to my family that we bring the congressman's killer to justice."

Jake noticed the blank stares on the cops' faces, but a few of them nodded politely.

Gesturing toward him, Suzanne went on. "I wanted to make sure all of you know that Jake Brooks is being retained as my personal counsel in this case and, as such, is to be offered every"—she lowered her voice in emphasis—"privilege and access he needs in order to fulfill that duty. I would like to ask each and every one of you to afford him every courtesy you would extend to me or my husband. My . . . late husband."

Jake could practically feel the tension radiating off Cooper.

Jake himself was annoyed by Suzanne's patrician manner, though he had learned through years of hard practice when to keep his ego out of things.

Suzanne's eyes roamed the room, staring down the cops' machismo attitude. When she got to Cooper, she turned on the charm. "Detective, thank you for your diligence. I know I can count on you to help us in any way you can."

"Yes, ma'am," the veteran cop answered with a deference Jake knew he didn't feel.

Suzanne turned to Jake. "I'll be at Porter's office. When you're finished here, could you come by?"

Jake nodded, but as he did so, he noticed Suzanne's eyes harden.

"What are you doing with that?" she spat, pointing to the corner of the room.

The blonde wig, arranged on a stand as if on a head, stood covered by clear plastic on a table.

Cooper answered. "We found it in the room. We think maybe the murderer or someone else—"

Suzanne cut him off. "That's my wig."

Cooper was speechless. He stuttered, "We . . . we found it in the room, Mrs. Garrett."

"I don't care where you found it. That's my wig."

"We found it there this morning. Where were you last night?"

"At a fund-raiser in California. I left it here the night before." Suzanne strode over to the wig stand.

Cooper leaped to her side. "And you left it here?" he asked, incredulous.

"Are you interrogating me?" she snarled.

"Ma'am. It's evidence."

"I want my property back," insisted Suzanne.

"Mrs. Garrett," pleaded Cooper.

Jake knew Cooper didn't want to insult the congressman's widow. He saw his chance. "Suzanne," he said softly. "Let these people do their job. When they realize it's not evidence, they'll give it back to you."

Suzanne's stare was full of hatred, but she acquiesced. As she left the room, her words came out through gritted teeth. "I'll see you in Porter's office as soon as you possibly can, Jake." Sutter stayed behind.

Jake received his gratitude from Cooper in the form of a curt nod. It wasn't much, but you never knew when that sort of thing could be useful. Jake decided to see whether it would already come in handy.

"Anything else you don't want to tell me before I go?"

Cooper rolled his eyes, but lowered his voice so that Jake had to lean forward to hear. "You want to know about the pubic hair we got out of his throat?"

Jake pressed his lips together. He tried to think. *So Porter had been with some girl. Big deal.* But Jake knew that if Porter had been cheating on his wife, it *was* a big deal, especially at this point in the campaign. It meant a long-term affair. Porter never would have risked a one-night stand.

Still, Jake concealed his surprise and glanced at Alana Sutter. The woman was ashen. She opened her mouth as if to say something, then clenched it tight.

"Alana?" Jake started. She shook her head.

Jake sank his coffee cup in Cooper's trash can. "The minute you know something, I want to know it," he growled. "I'm going to see what Suzanne wants. Get this over with."

He turned to walk out with Alana Sutter, but the strategist had disappeared.

* * *

Jake ducked under more yellow police tape to enter Porter Garrett's office. He moved to sit on the familiar white couch where he'd lounged hundreds of times before. Suzanne sat behind Porter's desk, muttering into a cell phone. She held up a finger, leaving Jake waiting awkwardly.

He looked around the office. It seemed deflated now without Porter's big presence. The wide desk was still covered with papers; family photographs stood on a corner. More photos decorated the filing cabinets and bookcases that ran along the wall, too—Ian and Anna, Porter and Suzanne's children, riding horses, sailing, camping.

On the wall opposite the windows hung Porter's collection of Sidney Randolph Maurer paintings. The bold, dynamic depiction of movie stars was classically beautiful; Maurer's uniquely colorful strokes, with many shades of gray, brought sensuality and glamour to Hollywood's biggest celebrities. Porter owned six, four of them instantly recognizable classics: Rita Hayworth, Brigitte Bardot, Humphrey Bogart, and Marilyn Monroe. The other two were of starlets from the 1940s whom Jake had never heard of or seen. The two unknowns had the same sense of drama and were just as beautiful as the stars who had endured. Jake thought about the fickleness of celebrity.

The paintings were hung so that one of the unknown sirens was between Hayworth and Bardot and the other between Bogart and Monroe. Jake wondered why Porter had chosen that arrangement. Maybe it was chronological. Porter had had a knack for arranging things; in the earlier days of his marriage and career, he had been in charge of all the seating plans at dinner functions. Porter had enjoyed the intricate social puzzle of bringing certain people together while meticulously keeping others apart.

"Coffee?" purred Suzanne, snapping her phone shut.

"I'm alright," said Jake.

"You are a dear for being here like this."

Where else would I be? wondered Jake.

Suzanne came around the desk and settled on the sofa, crossing her legs tidily. She fiddled with the hem of her jacket, then smoothed her hair. "Could you believe the trouble they were giving me over that wig? I mean, really . . ." She laughed out of sheer avoidance, a forced bark that fell flat in the room.

Jake stared at her. He felt her sense of guilt, aware that anything he would say could be misunderstood.

"It's none of their business what it's doing there," she continued, "if you know what I mean."

Jake rubbed his eyes with his right hand.

"Oh, relax, Jake, for God's sake. You look awful."

Jake looked closely at Suzanne. In his opinion, she didn't look awful enough.

She continued, "You know, I was talking with Glen this morning . . ."

Glen Green. The governor of Nevada and an old friend of Suzanne and Porter's. Suddenly it clicked for Jake. When a congressman dies during an election, his wife is often asked by the party to run for the seat. Name recognition alone can pull a victory. Come to think of it, even dead politicians had won seats when the public voted for a familiar name instead of the warm body. Given Suzanne's friendship with the governor, his support would be almost guaranteed. Why hadn't Jake thought of that before? It also explained Suzanne's cozy new relationship with Alana Sutter.

Suzanne seemed to notice the shift in Jake's eyes. "So you see, all this wig nonsense is really quite silly, and I'm going to need your help to convince those . . . those *gumshoes* in there."

Typical Suzanne. Distract with charm and then go straight for the jugular. It was both her most endearing and her most irritating trait, depending on which side of it you were on. Jake had done plenty of rearranging facts and calculated overlooking of evidence in his career, but this was another story. This was a plea to suppress evidence in a federal murder case. The murder of his best friend, and *her husband*.

"I'll take that coffee after all," vamped Jake.

"There isn't any coffee," said Suzanne.

"I know." Jake sank onto the couch. He decided to test how serious she was. "You know, they found blonde hairs in the wig."

Suzanne wheeled toward him, her face stormy. Then, in an instant, her features rearranged themselves into a smile. She pointed to her hair. "Blonde," she said.

"*Long* blonde hairs," pressed Jake.

Suddenly Suzanne was standing over him, like a hawk on a mouse.

"Listen," she hissed. "I am not going to have it come out that Porter was with a hooker. Even if she did kill him. Even if it means his murder goes unsolved. He's gone—but I'm still here. Do you understand what I'm saying?"

Jake was surprised to feel a wave of pity for Suzanne. The wig was the least of her problems. Claiming it was hers just complicated matters and made her look like a liar. But he'd faced much more formidable pressure from clients, and he was not going to be intimidated. He laughed.

"Oh, Suzanne" was all he said. He watched as she straightened up, searching his face. As quickly as she had become a bird of prey, she returned to her Blanche DuBois routine.

"It's so hard being left with two children. They're devoted to him, you know." She glided in front of Jake. "Tell me you didn't know," she whispered, resting a hip on the arm of the couch.

"Of course I know they're devoted to him." Jake sat back. He realized that wasn't what she meant, but evading the question was easier than trying to answer it. Besides, he was wrestling with his own feelings of betrayal and didn't feel like getting mired in Suzanne's as well. But there was no getting out of it.

"You're avoiding my question, Guv."

Jake winced to hear the nickname Porter had given him in the earliest days of their friendship.

"Was I the only one in the fucking dark?" she asked.

Jake took a breath. "He never said anything to me, either."

Suzanne's eyes glazed and she turned toward the Maurers, holding a handkerchief to her face.

"You know, they say a wife always knows. But I didn't. I had no fucking clue." For a second Jake glimpsed, in the slight droop of her shoulders and hands, the vulnerability she'd had when the three of them had first met. Over the years she had hardened so much that Jake had been unable to remember what she was like in the first place—and why Porter had married her.

Suzanne patted her mouth with the handkerchief, leaving a ghostly imprint of her lips. "I don't know why, but it helps to know that you were in the dark too," she said sincerely.

Jake nodded. He knew what she meant but still didn't want to become her new best friend—if that were even possible with her. He was, if anything, more loyal to Porter now than ever. Porter must have been shut out by her to even contemplate an affair in the middle of a campaign.

Suddenly Suzanne tacked again. "Say *something,* Jake. It sounds to me like you're protecting someone. An adulterer? A liar? A bitch who knew he had a family?"

They were both silenced by the severity of her words, which hung in the room like a nuclear cloud. Suzanne was fishing; Jake knew that. But he didn't even try to reassure her. He just sat and waited.

Finally she cleared her throat. "We're going to do the service in LA. He was okay with that," she said, somewhat defensively. "I wanted to ask if you would give the eulogy."

"Of course." There was another long silence.

"What's with that fucking wig?" Suzanne spat out suddenly. "Was she a stripper? A hooker? Because I don't know what's worse . . ." Suzanne brought her hand to her mouth. Her shoulders convulsed once.

Stiffly, Jake put a hand on her arm. "No idea," he said, honestly. But there it was again, the wig and a flash to the night before. The triumphant look in the singer's eyes when she'd pulled off the crown of platinum blonde.

Abruptly, Suzanne stepped away. "I'm going back to LA tonight. I'll call you before the service, make sure we're on the same page."

"Are Ian and Anna coming with you?"

"They're meeting me at home." She paused.

For lack of anything better to say, Jake mumbled, "It's going to be okay."

"Sure it is, Guv," replied Suzanne, the sarcasm twisting her mouth. "Maybe when I've got a seat on the appropriations committee and every lobbyist in Washington is standing in line to kiss my ass, I'll thank that hooker. But at the moment what it is"—she took a deep breath—"what it is, is humiliating and dirty and selfish." Before she could see Jake's reaction, she retreated to the bathroom, blotting her eyes.

On his way out, Jake closed the door as quietly as he could.

* * *

Jake had been in the meeting for only three minutes and already he knew it was going to end badly. Cooper was bad enough, with his

provincial thinking and hostility. Plus, Jake couldn't imagine a dim-
mer pair of FBI agents than the ones assigned to Porter's case.

Brewer was a beefy man with a chin that tapered to a rounded
point like the end of a baseball bat. He had gone around the room
handing out his business cards, flicking each one out of the stack like
a magician, offering them with his first two fingers, cigarette-style.

Norris was a thin, weaselly man in a turtleneck and blazer, a
style Jake loathed for its Gallic pretentiousness. He had a thin, bristly
mustache and combed-back hair.

The two spent twenty minutes pissing around the corners of the
investigation, alternately bullying and confusing Cooper as they tried
to establish their dominance. Once Brewer, the more obvious bully,
had that down, Norris took over as the talker.

"What we're probably looking for is some kind of loner.
Working alone. Probably a right-wing extremist. Possibly a white
supremacist."

Jake groaned. Everyone turned in his direction as he said,
"You've gotta be shitting me. That's what you've got? You're here to
tell us *that*?"

Brewer grunted. "Last I checked, you were an ambulance chaser
with an important friend. Are you a detective now?"

"No," Jake answered evenly. "It's just that I was hoping this case,
the murder of a member of the U.S. Congress, would be assigned to
competent investigators. I wasn't expecting Washington to send out
Frick and Frack, waving invisible-ink pens and decoder rings."

Cooper held up two pale hands. "Gentlemen, please. We're on
the same side."

"Except we have badges and he doesn't," said Norris pointedly,
his Adam's apple bulging through his turtleneck.

Jake nearly threw the table over. "This investigation will go
nowhere with these incompetent assholes involved!"

"Easy!" shouted Cooper.

Norris sneered. "And what is this bullshit about the wig? Garrett's wife is claiming it's hers?"

Jake was on his feet, leaning across the table. He spoke as calmly as he could. "Let me remind you that Mrs. Garrett is very likely going to become *Congresswoman* Garrett sometime in the next few weeks. You might want to think about who you're pissing off."

Norris actually stopped in his tracks, standing stock-still. The expression on his face said he hadn't considered this possibility. He blinked at Brewer, who shrugged.

"So, he's protected when the widow's around," said Brewer, not looking up.

"But you're on your own when you're not peeking around her skirt," finished Norris triumphantly.

Jake lost it. "This is bullshit!" he roared.

Materializing as if by magic, Alana Sutter was suddenly at Jake's side. She touched his arm.

"Hang on," she whispered smoothly. "Let's go outside. Just for a minute."

Seething, Jake allowed Sutter to lead him into the hall.

"I'm not going to be squeezed out by a couple of fed pricks," fumed Jake.

"Suzanne wants you involved, and you have my word, too," reassured Sutter. "You won't be shoved out. But you've been through a lot today. I know what Porter meant to you." She looked at Jake intently. "He meant a lot to me, too."

Jake didn't want to get into it. He felt his temper flare again.

"And I know what you meant to him," pressed Sutter. "He trusted you. Don't worry. He's not up there keeping score on what you're doing now."

Jake was still irritated, maybe even more so now. It killed him that Sutter may have known about Porter's affair, may have even been helping him cover it up.

"Seems you've gone from one campaign to another."

Sutter had the decency to look chagrined. "She'll carry on his agenda."

"How could this have happened?" asked Jake, changing the subject.

"Porter asked for a light detail, and I told security to give it to him," said Sutter. "That's what I have to live with."

"Did you know that . . . ? Did you know he was . . . ?"

"Did I know he had a woman on the side?"

Jake nodded. Sutter examined her fingers and then looked at him.

"I'm telling you this because I like you and to show you I mean it about keeping you in the loop—if you lay off those FBI agents. They're annoying little pricks, but they have a job to do, and we need Washington's help with this. Alright?"

Jake nodded again.

"Porter never said anything. But he had been asking for space more and more often lately. I didn't see anything, but I had a feeling something else was going on. I'd also felt him distancing himself. Like . . . a pulling away."

Jake silently exhaled. It sounded like Sutter was covering her ass.

She continued, "Like I said, he asked for a light detail last night, and I gave it to him. That was my mistake, my role in this. Once we get through this investigation, I'll have to make my own amends with that. Until then, we've all got jobs to do."

Jake nodded and returned to the meeting considerably quieter but no less agitated. He had never really liked Sutter, but had always found her accountable. Now he wasn't so sure. Suzanne had always seemed disinterested in Porter's career, yet here she was poised to take it over. The case was being handled by bureaucrats who were trying to shut him out. His best friend had had a terrible secret that may have been what killed him. Jake was feeling as though he couldn't trust anybody—not even the dead.

CHAPTER 5

"MARCO!"

"Polo!"

"Marco!" yelled Kelly and Libby together.

"Polo!" shouted Kevin.

"Let's get him!" cried Kelly, lunging toward Kevin with Libby on her back. Libby shrieked, and Kevin dove for the bottom of the pool. Kelly's hand grazed his foot as he swam by.

"Gotcha!"

Kevin came up laughing in a spray of water droplets that arced through the air like a scattering of diamonds. Kelly watched as the drops seemed to freeze and turn in the sun against the blue sky. A perfect, unrepeatable, irreplaceable moment in time. She spent her life searching for these moments, these suspended instants of joy that shimmered among the despair, fear, hatred, and loneliness. She gazed at her kids, their faces bright with water and sunshine. They were her salvation, her hope, her entire reason for being.

It wasn't an overstatement. If not for them, she would make any number of different choices right now. She would gladly risk her own life to serve the higher purpose of putting her husband in jail. But she would never do anything that would put her son and daughter at risk. And so that meant Plan B. Porter's death—she couldn't bring herself to admit it was murder—changed things in a big way. She had been working out an idea. But first she needed to get some information.

"Okay, kiddos, out of the pool," sang Kelly, sliding out of the water and grabbing two towels. A glass door off the patio surrounding the pool opened directly into their motel room. Kelly showered the chlorine off the kids and set about helping them dress in clean clothes.

Kevin looked up from tying his shoes. "Where are we going, Mom?"

"Library, then dinner. You ready?"

The Nogales, Arizona, library had been recently remodeled with, it appeared, the bulk of the budget going toward a comfortable children's section and computer terminals with Internet access. Kelly had no trouble installing Kevin and Libby on two fat purple pillows, a stack of books next to each of them. She found a computer in an adjacent area where she could watch the children while she searched. Sliding into the chair, she typed *Jake Brooks* in the Google search template.

First things first: Find out more about Jake Brooks, and understand why he was speaking on Porter's behalf. She remembered Porter laughing joyfully when he spoke of Brooks. But she had to get to know him for herself. The first dozen results were transcripts of, and references to, TV appearances: *Entertainment Tonight* and *Larry King Live*, among others. Kelly clicked on one.

Announcer's **voice-over:** Trouble in paradise tonight as the on-again, off-again relationship between British supermodel Alva Mayhill and attorney-to-the-stars Jake Brooks seems to be on the rocks again. The couple was spotted leaving in separate cars after an argument outside a Los Angeles restaurant.

The forty-two-year-old Brooks, who has been voted one of *People* magazine's "Sexiest Men Alive," was recently in the news for his gutsy defense of Julie Groton, the notorious textiles heiress accused of killing her brother. Brooks won the case, called "unwinnable" by many observers.

Mayhill and Brooks met last winter at the Aspen home of Randy Carlen, a Nevada billionaire. Friends say the pair have a fiery relationship but are very much in love.

Kelly checked the date. The transcript was two years old. She lingered on a still picture of Jake, noticing his intense eyes, high cheekbones, and salt-and-pepper hair. He was holding a door open for a beautiful woman who was flashing a dazzling smile at the camera. Jake's expression was more serious than the model's, but it was not shy. Kelly could tell he had a love/hate relationship with attention, but one thing was for sure: He knew his way around the front side of a camera lens.

She opened a dozen more links and scanned the articles. According to them, Jake's mind was "brilliant," "formidable," "razor-sharp," "photographic," "prodigious." He combined "the cunning of a coyote, the guts of a Navy SEAL, the retention of a supercomputer, and the training of a rocket scientist." His face was "rugged" and "handsome"; his eyes "bedroom" and "prescient"; his body "lanky" and "toned by running and riding horses"; and his hair "run-your-hands-through-it thick" and "calculatedly messy, as though he wants you to think he has just rescued a little old lady's kitten from a tree." His personality was described as "elusive," "aloof," and "lone-wolf-ish," although the articles referred to his many friends and clients, and pictures showed him at parties and premieres and on private islands with beautiful women.

Kelly scrolled through a few more references, a pensive look on her face. Then she quit the search and returned to the Google template for the second search she needed to make: a bank. She typed *American Capital Investment Bank* into the prompt box. A corporate-looking website opened when Kelly clicked on it, a boring graphic making the introduction.

> **American Capital Investment Bank: We grow when your money grows.**
>
> For nearly two decades, ACIB has been the safe haven of choice for prudent investors in the United States. Our stellar team of financial advisors combines years of experience in money markets with skilled know-how and shrewd risk-taking. Our new corporate headquarters in Las Vegas's burgeoning commercial center puts us in the heart of the fastest-growing population of investors in the country: the warm desert climates of the Southwest. With branches from Texas to California, and new branches planned for northern California, Oregon, and Washington, ACIB is fast becoming the dominant investment bank in the U.S.A.

The key to our success is our people. We hire only the best and brightest, the friendliest and the fastest-thinking. If you aren't investing your money with us, then we aren't doing our job.

Kelly ran her cursor over the section headings and hovered over OUR PEOPLE. She glanced at Kevin and Libby, who had moved their heads together and were reading from the same book, Libby pointing at the pictures and Kevin following the words with his finger. Kelly's heart gave a tug. She clicked on the chosen link, and a picture of a handsome man filled half the screen. A title next to the photograph read:

Todd Gillis, Founder and President of American Capital Investment Bank.

Todd Gillis's driving passion is making money for the investors in his bank. As president, he has been a tireless advocate for every customer, small or large. His many donations and countless hours given to charities—in particular, the Juvenile Diabetes Research Foundation and Meals on Wheels—show his belief in supporting the community on every level.

After earning an MBA from the Wharton School of Business at the University of Pennsylvania, he pursued a PhD in economics from the Massachusetts Institute of Technology. Mr. Gillis is the recipient of numerous awards and citations, including a Meritorious Achievement Award from the Department of Commerce.

Mr. Gillis and his family live in Houston, Texas.

Kelly studied the photo for a moment, as if memorizing the man's features. Then she closed the window and clicked on BRANCH LOCA-TIONS. Her fingers flew over the keyboard, choosing the information she needed. She plugged in her Sidekick and downloaded a list of ACIB branches in Arizona as well as a list of the branches in Southern California. She downloaded a map to each location. When she was done, she folded up the Sidekick and slid it into her purse.

She glanced at her children. They were still engrossed in their books. She had some time. The third and final search: the mark. Kelly brought out her Sidekick again and Googled *Joan Davis, Beverly Hills.* Three listings came up, and she saved them all. She repeated the search, typing *Los Angeles* in place of *Beverly Hills.* The computer paused, then came up with seven entries. Again Kelly saved them. She snapped the Sidekick shut. Enough for now.

She tiptoed over to the children. "You ready to get something to eat?" she whispered.

"Read to us, Mommy," begged Libby. Kelly glanced around the library, which was quiet and nearly empty. She sighed.

"Okay. But only for a few minutes."

She settled in between the children, sitting so she could see the front door. Then, scanning the entrance and the parking lot beyond every thirty seconds or so, she read aloud for a half hour before setting out to find dinner.

CHAPTER 6

AFTER THE DISASTROUS MEETING WITH THE FBI, Jake had spent the rest of the day wrangling the media, working them like a prostitute works a john—giving only the story he wanted them to hear. Now it was nine o'clock, and he was driving back to the hotel from the NBC affiliate studios. He knew he needed to sleep, but his brain wasn't showing signs of shutting off. He needed something to flick the switch. Not alcohol, though. Nothing that would leave him hungover and blurry.

All day he had been trying to process Suzanne's reaction to this whole mess. She seemed to be so composed—hardly grieving at all. She also appeared to be mad at Porter instead of at the killer. Infidelity or not, was that normal for the circumstances? Maybe. Could she actually be a step ahead of Jake in the grieving department? Jake snorted. Knowing Suzanne, she'd already gotten a diploma in Getting Over Your Husband's Murder, and it was at the frame shop, ready to be picked up. On the other hand, maybe she was just genuinely worried about the world learning about Porter's affair and the effect on his legacy—and hers.

Jake knew the love had been missing from Porter and Suzanne's marriage for some time. Suzanne spent most of her time in Los Angeles, with what she called "her" people. Jake had often wondered why Suzanne had married Porter at all. She was a Southern Californian, born and bred—fifth generation and uselessly proud of the fact. Why she had agreed to give up the smell of eucalyptus and the sight of flammable brown hills to follow him to Nevada and later to Washington was beyond Jake. Through campaign after campaign, they had settled into a certain camaraderie: Porter rarely demanded her presence in DC or at his appearances, and she, appreciative of his light touch, helped him as much as she could tolerate. Eventually they were on their own more than they were together, and what romance they'd had in the past had inevitably cooled. Even so, Jake had never once heard Porter even fantasize about cheating on her.

Jake's phone buzzed.

"Brooks, it's Carlen." Jake tapped the brake as he approached a red light. Randy Carlen had been a faithful and generous donor to Porter's campaign and had hosted the fund-raiser where Porter had given his final speech, the night before the murder. *Last night*, thought Jake, barely believing it. Carlen's fortune had come through his grandmother, who had built a chain of Nevada hotels that doubled as brothels. As the sole remaining heir, Carlen now spent his time managing the hotels and his fortune, proud never to forget a working girl's name. In fact, he loved them all. "Bad girls gone bad," he'd say.

"What can I say?" continued Carlen without waiting for Jake's greeting. "I've been trying to call you." Carlen broke off into an emphysemic hack, ending with an enormous, mucus-clearing gargle. Jake had heard the cough often enough to know that the pause that followed it was Carlen taking another drag on his Cuban cigar. The man was short but stocky, and the lifts in his shoes (as well as the constant halo of smoke around him) gave the impression of his being a much bigger man. "Fucking pisser about Garrett." Jake nodded his agreement, knowing Carlen couldn't see his affirmation but wouldn't be waiting for it anyway. "What can I do to help? Anything, just ask."

Jake hesitated. As with Suzanne, he knew that his frustration with the investigation needed to be played carefully. "You meant a lot to him," Jake said. "Your support meant a hell of a lot." He accelerated out of the intersection when the light turned green. "He'd have wanted you at the funeral."

"I'll be there," drawled Carlen. "I've been talking with Suzie. But you let me know if you need anything else. You hear about anything you need, I'll get it for you."

"I appreciate it," said Jake. "See you in LA."

"Oh, one other thing," pressed Carlen. "I have an associate who's starting out in TV. She's doing a feature about Garrett and says you folks aren't getting back to her. I know it's a busy time, but I'd be much obliged if you could call her, give her a few minutes of your time."

Out of habit, Jake said, "Of course. Have her call me," forgetting that his need for men like Carlen was now virtually nil. It was the sort of favor Porter used to do routinely without complaining. But now that Porter didn't need them, Jake didn't need them.

The phone rang again almost as soon as Jake hung up. Carlen's "associate" introduced herself and begged Jake to come down to the station. Jake cursed to himself for having promised Carlen he'd help out, but agreed to do it.

* * *

The "station" turned out to be the student TV station in the basement of the Theater Arts Department of Las Vegas Community College.

The collection of rooms at the student TV station smelled like a wet dog. The furniture looked as though it had been donated by a homeless shelter: tattered couches in 1970s orange and brown lined a long hallway, their cushions long ago worn shapeless, the varnish rubbed off their wooden arms. Undergraduates were draped across them in assorted stages of sleep and wakefulness, tattoos blossoming across various exposed body parts. The walls were lined with cheaply framed posters of news shows and radio plays.

Jake saw a student heading down the hallway toward him. Purple corduroy jeans hung from her slender hips; a vintage black Kiss T-shirt rode just high enough to offer a juicy slice of her flat belly. Her eyes flickered with recognition.

"Jake Brooks? Well, welcome to our lair. All hell has just broken loose in what the diehards here call the newsroom. Logan asked me to apologize and tell you she'll be here 'shortly.'" The girl drew air quotes around the word. "You can wait in here."

Jake followed her to a dingy room with fluorescent lights and a peeling Formica table. The smell of scorched coffee rose from the belching drip machine in the corner. On the counter sat a plastic dish next to a note card with the words COFFEE—50 CENTS/CUP. ON YOUR HONOR written on it in blue Sharpie.

The girl smiled. "Cup of coffee?"

Jake shrugged and tossed a five-dollar bill into the plastic dish. "Make it a double."

"Big spender. Look out." She poured the thick black fluid into a Styrofoam cup and gave it to Jake. She held out her other hand to shake his. "I'm Morgan. The engineer." Her grip was surprisingly strong. Jake noticed narrow muscles roping up her forearms. She saw him notice. "Yoga. You ever try it?"

"I was doing downward dogs before you were in diapers. I gave it up— inner peace, all that crap. Just give me a few heavy things to lift every once in a while. The occasional horse to ride."

Morgan smiled. "Studio's through here," she said, leading Jake into a room with two old armchairs facing each other in front of a tattered blue curtain. "I'll be right over there." She pointed to the window through which Jake could see a giant mixing board. "If you need anything."

At that moment a tall, blonde woman rushed into the room. "Jake, this is Logan." Morgan grinned.

The reporter also flashed her white teeth at Jake. The woman, clearly Carlen's latest "girlfriend," sat with Jake in front of the cameras and nervously asked polite questions about Porter, leaning forward with what she thought was amiable sympathy.

When the interview was done, Morgan gave Jake a thumbs-up through the window. On his way out, Jake found her and gave her his card.

"You ever need any legal advice, you call me," he said. "Those yoga teachers are torts just waiting to happen."

Morgan checked her watch. "I'm off right now." Her aquamarine eyes were bright and teasing, and she wiped a purple-streaked shank of hair off her forehead. Jake paused. This could be just what he had been looking for, to help him shut off his mind.

"Do you know Olive's at the Venetian?"

"Hate it. How about Opal?"

Jake grinned. "Ten minutes?"

"Twenty."

Opal was poolside on a rooftop, with a view of all Las Vegas shimmering around it. Morgan was late, so Jake ordered a tequila shot and waited on a ruby-red, velvet-cushioned stool. When Morgan ambled up, unapologetic, they had a drink, then decided to skip dinner. The tension between them was mounting pleasurably. Jake followed Morgan's black Jetta back to her apartment. Inside, she opened a bottle of wine and lit about eight dozen candles in the living room. She didn't have a lot of furniture, but there was a long, low table and some scratchy kilims and a huge pile of floor cushions that could have come out of a yurt in Mongolia. Her approach wasn't a bit shy or coy, and when they were naked and fucking on the floor, her toned athletic body moved with confidence. She had beautiful, strong legs and broad shoulders . . . Jake found he needed to fixate on each individual body part just to keep his mind from caving in with thoughts of Porter and Suzanne, of the whole mess of who and why, and of the sordid aftermath of hairs and blood and skin . . .

* * *

"Hey, big spender." Morgan was shaking him.

"What time is it?" Jake mumbled, embarrassed and irritated with himself.

"We dozed off. It's almost two."

"Shit. I've got to go."

"It's okay. I was getting ready to kick you out," Morgan teased, without a trace of guilt or agenda. "Nice job."

"Yeah. You too." Jake dressed quickly. He kissed her cheek, then jogged down the stairs to his car, pushing the remote on his keychain. The Mercedes blinked at him, and he got in behind the wheel. Morgan waved and disappeared behind her door. Jake felt completely dislocated. Morgan had shaken him out of a dream he didn't want to be having—but one he hadn't wanted to wake up from. The songstress from Shrake's nightclub, wearing nothing but the Marilyn wig and black gloves, was singing to him in an empty room. He sat on a chair in the middle of the room. Her gloved hands wrapped around the mike, but instead of singing lyrics into it, she was singing questions that didn't quite make sense: "When did you see Porter?" "Why did you see him?" "Which way did Porter fall?"

And then Jake had noticed that all around the perimeter of the room were television cameras, each operated by someone he knew. Suzanne peered around the eyepiece of hers, mouthing questions. He saw the pig-eyed nightclub owner. Alana Sutter. The FBI agents, Norris and Brewer. Cooper and Randy Carlen were there. The singer-dancer in the platinum wig was moving closer and closer. There was a voyeuristic quality to having an audience, and he was enjoying it. In one fluid movement, the Marilyn look-alike straddled him, and as she leaned forward, breathing, "Hey, big spender . . . ," Morgan had jostled him awake.

A thought suddenly occurred to Jake as he revved the engine and backed out of the parking place. He could just ask the Marilyn dancer a few questions. He was wide-awake now anyway. He steered the car in the direction of the nightclub, secretly pleased to have come up with an official reason (or maybe it was just an excuse) to visit a certain blonde wig. Though he couldn't believe that, after all the horizontal action with Morgan, he was getting aroused by just think-ing about the woman in the red satin dress.

* * *

The man guarding the back door of the club either recognized Jake or wasn't getting paid enough, because he nodded the celebrity attor-ney through with barely a blink as he pocketed his twenty-dollar bill. Jake strode down a backstage hallway, invigorated, suddenly wide-awake with purpose. He found the door he was looking for and threw it open.

"Excuse me, ladies." Half a dozen dancers looked up, bored. Their dressing room was cramped and stuffy, thick with the smell of cigarettes, perfume, and sweat.

"I'm looking for the girl who does the Marilyn act."

"Join the club," droned a tall Asian dancer in a green evening gown. "She left us in the shitter tonight, without a headlining act." She dragged a tube of red lipstick across her mouth and then pushed past Jake. "Excuse me, I'm on." Jake stepped back courteously, and the woman winked as she passed him.

"Kelly didn't show up today," rasped another voice. Jake looked appreciatively at a petite, pale redhead in a black silk kimono. She dangled a cigarette between her fingers and sat back in her chair, her feet up on the makeup counter. "Some of her stuff is still here." The redhead poked her cigarette toward a pile of costumes in the corner, abandoning any sense of concern for privacy or confidentiality.

"Do you mind?" asked Jake, gesturing to the pile. "She might have left me a clue or a note," he added, taking a calculated risk with this falsehood. Perhaps he would be told that Kelly had somebody and it wasn't him—information that could be helpful.

The redhead shrugged. "I don't care."

Jake dug through the dresses, five or six of them, in red and black. Underneath were some high-heeled shoes and gloves. He wasn't sure what he was looking for, but he knew this wasn't it.

"She leave anything else?"

"Nope. Took her makeup kit."

"You could look in here." Another dancer, who appeared to be seventeen at the very most, materialized at Jake's elbow. She smiled at him, and Jake noticed the faintest scar running from between her nostrils to her upper lip. At the end of the room was a closet door. The girl opened it and Jake jolted, then laughed. The closet had four shelves, and on every shelf stood three Styrofoam heads, each wearing a wig. There were red, black, blonde, and brunette wigs, along with three platinum blonde ones. His hunch was completely crazy. Like he'd thought before, how many Marilyn wigs were there in Las Vegas? In less than twenty-four hours, he'd seen at least five.

Jake smiled at the young dancer. "Your big bad boss around?"

"I just saw him at the bar."

"Thanks," said Jake, then whispered, "Get out of this place as soon as you can."

The girl looked at him, surprised. "You mean tonight?" she called after him, confused.

Jake entered the club through a door at the end of the hall and headed for the bar. He could see the owner at a dark table in the back, sitting by a showgirl who looked like Britney Spears. His hand was on her back, and his thumb was worming its way under her halter top.

Shrake was known to be a liar and a cheat, a balding cherub of a man with the unforgiving eyes of a hyena. Their meeting the night before had been less than friendly, as Jake recalled it now. While Brooks had been engrossed in "Marilyn Monroe's" act, Shrake had scurried up to him with a briefcase. He'd opened it on his lap. It was filled with money, of course. Jake had been annoyed.

"You trying to ask me for a favor?" he'd said, jerking his chin at the briefcase.

Shrake had pulled back, feigning injury. Pulling his chubby face into a serious expression, he'd simpered, "I got a pal up on murder one."

"A hit?"

"I'd say, uh, self-defense."

Jake sighed. "What does the DA say?"

"Seems they found fifty G's on my friend."

"You want me to go to all the trouble of seducing a jury and the media for a bill-collecting hit man? I don't think so."

"It's a retainer. Fifty G's, to be exact." Shrake had peered expectantly at Jake's face. Jake's eyes flicked to the briefcase, then back to the singer.

"Well?" pressed Shrake.

"Know what I need more than that? Spiritual balance."

Shrake's jaw twitched. "You could buy a whole bunch of spiritual balance with this."

Jake had tipped the last of his drink into his mouth, keeping his eyes on Marilyn. Then something in Kelly's look caught his attention. While her seduction act was razor-sharp, he noticed a sense of purpose with every movement. She was searching every corner of the room. For a split second, their eyes locked. There was a sudden sense of recognition in her expression. But in an instant a protective shield came across her face.

Who the hell are *you?* he had said to himself. Aloud, he'd replied to the mobster, "Here's where we differ, hombre. You see cash in that briefcase. I see a media circus, grueling, tedious work, and boredom."

Shrake raised his voice. "This guy saved my life once. I promised him I'd convince you to get him off."

"Relax. Lawyers make up eleven percent of the world's population. Seventy percent of those lawyers live here in the U.S. of A. You'll find somebody." Jake had enjoyed pulling statistics from midair and making them sound real. "I don't represent bill-collecting hit men," he had added, noticing the chanteuse just inches away. With his elbow, he had pushed the briefcase closed.

Shrake had scuttled angrily away.

Now, Jake sauntered over to Shrake's table and planted both hands on it as he leaned over the small man.

"What the fuck?" Shrake shouted. The Britney Spears showgirl took a drag on her cigarette.

"I hear your prized possession didn't show up today. I'd like to lay an eye on her again."

"You're right. Bitch isn't here. Those kinds of girls disappear overnight."

"What'd you do, try to rape her?"

"Fuck, man, are you kidding?" whined Shrake. "That one was untouchable. Tough as nails." The girl next to him smirked. Jake smiled at her. "You'll never see her here again."

"I want her address."

Shrake's eyes narrowed. "Well, get in line."

"I can turn you into a quivering mass of snot in the courtroom."

"You're not scaring—"

"The juvenile prostitutes you've got working at your bar. Your friend with the fifty G's. Your needle dick—"

"Alright, alright," the club owner scowled. Jake followed him back to his office, which stank of beer and dirty socks. Shrake undid the combination lock on a small black filing cabinet. Shuffling through a stack of papers, he mumbled to himself, "Fucking lawyers." He threw a page at Jake. "This is what she filled out when she started working here."

Jake looked at the paper. NAME: KELLY JENSEN. AGE: 24. ADDRESS: 2518 MANZANITA LANE. Stapled to the sheet was a Xerox of her driver's license. Jake squinted at the picture. The woman wasn't smiling, but her eyes were intensely focused, set above high cheekbones. Her hair looked sleek and glossy, even in the photocopy. She looked nothing like Marilyn Monroe. But she did look familiar, even without her costume, in a beautiful-showgirl sort of way. Jake folded the papers in half lengthwise and slid them into his inside jacket pocket to keep himself from staring too hard.

Shrake had seen him looking, though.

"That girl thinks her shit don't stink," he said, running the back of his wrist across his nose. "She ain't gonna give you the time of day."

"You know, Shrake, you're the kind of guy who thinks it's raining when someone spits on you."

Shrake grumbled as he put the folder away. "You got what you wanted. Get the fuck out of my club."

*   *   *

Jake's heart pounded as he drove to Kelly Jensen's house. He wasn't sure what he would say if he found her there. It was the middle of the night. He knew this might not go over well.

Reaching Manzanita Lane, a street of circa-1970 tract houses, he slowed. A few of the driveways had boats or RVs in them. Most of the houses, however, appeared to have huddled down, as if shivering in the desert-cold night. Twenty-five-twelve, twenty-five-fourteen, twenty-five-sixteen. Jake drove two houses past Kelly's, shut off the lights and engine, and watched the house in his rearview mirror. It was completely dark. No porch light. Jake reached for the flashlight in his glove box and got out of the car. The street was deserted too. The only sounds were the whoosh of traffic on a nearby boulevard and the crackling of power lines overhead.

Jake crept up to the house, gauging the windows. There were no signs of life. He edged over to a side gate, trying the latch. It opened easily, and he stole along the side of the house. The backyard was overgrown with flowers and decorated with an assortment of scarecrows obviously created by children. A concrete patio covered by a wooden pergola painted red was just outside a sliding-glass door that led inside. On impulse, Jake tried it. To his surprise, it slid open. Fighting logic, he stepped in and closed it behind him.

When his eyes adjusted to the darkened interior, he found himself in a room that seemed entirely beige, from the carpets to the walls to the canvas sofa that looked newly covered. Long, parallel strips of moonlight stretched across the floor, swaying in time with the swinging vertical blinds. Jake flicked on the flashlight and threw some light around the room. He was in a little living area. The front door was directly across from the sliding-glass door he had entered; a hall cut through the room to both the left and the right. The place seemed small and old-fashioned, but clean and freshly painted.

Jake chose the hall to the left and crept lightly across the carpet, stopping every few seconds to listen. Three doors led off the hallway. The first was a bathroom. Jake wiggled his arm up into his shirtsleeve and used the fabric to cover his hand before opening the drawers. He saw about two dozen plastic makeup containers and gobs of assorted skin-colored putty. In contrast, the medicine cabinet was empty.

Jake moved to another room and saw a queen-sized bed stripped of sheets, a dresser, a TV. The dresser was empty except for a lavender sachet in the corner of the top drawer. The closet contained only coat hangers. Jake turned on the TV: MSNBC. He turned it off.

He went through the third door and found two twin beds, also stripped. A poster of van Gogh's *Irises* was on the wall and a basket of dried flowers on a side table. He slid open the closet. It was empty except for some child-sized coat hangers.

Did this woman have kids? Jake's curiosity deepened.

He went back down the hallway and crossed through the living room into the kitchen. It was very clean and, like the other rooms, almost totally empty. A narrow yellow countertop ran underneath a window that overlooked the front yard. Yellow curtains with red cherries on them framed the window. The fridge was yellow too. Inside, it was pretty bare: an old milk carton, some slices of American cheese. A small round table, painted red, stood next to the fridge, along with three chairs. Jake found some empty soup tins in the trash can under the sink.

He wandered back to the living room again, not sure what he was looking for. He turned on the TV. It was tuned to QVC. He turned it off, pushed EJECT on the DVD player. After a whine and a click, a disk slid out: *Sesame Street Dance with Me.* So she did have kids, or at least kids lived here too. Jake sank down on the couch and let his mind wander. What was he really doing here? Breaking into a woman's house to try to get a date?

His thoughts looped back to his original excuse for coming here. A platinum blonde wig had been found in Porter's hotel room. This nightclub singer, Kelly Jensen, had worn a platinum blonde wig on the night of Porter's murder. Jake laughed aloud. Not much of a connection. He pictured a hairstylist being cross-examined into admitting that any number of platinum blonde wigs could be combed into a Monroe style. Even so, he pressed the idea further. Kelly Jensen left her job—and her house—the day after Porter's murder. Still not much of a connection. There had been blonde hairs in Porter's hotel room bed. Kelly Jensen's driver's license said she had blonde hair. It was too ridiculous. Jake knew that even he could never lead a jury to connect those faint dots. So again the question raised itself, why was he here?

A second later, someone was pounding on the front door. Jake flew behind the end of the couch and held his breath.

"Who's in there? I've got a bat." A man's voice. *Boom, boom, boom.* Something heavy, presumably the bat, struck the door. "Open up. We know you're in there."

Jake tried to calculate the time it would take him to open the sliding-glass door, sprint across the weedy backyard, and scale the cinder-block wall.

The front doorknob jiggled.

"We seen your light," came the man's voice. There was some mumbling, and Jake thought he heard a woman's voice, too. Even if he got across the yard and over the fence, he would have to come back for his car. He couldn't risk doing that right away, with the man standing there, but he didn't want to leave it either. Even though it was two houses down, the Mercedes was out of place in this neighborhood.

"What do you mean, you *think* you saw the TV?"

"Well, I thought I saw a flickering."

"Did you or didn't you?"

"I'm almost sure I did."

"Shit, woman. I'm calling the cops." *Boom, boom, boom.* "You hear that? I'm calling the cops." Jake heard more mumbling as footsteps receded off the porch.

He sank even further into the floor until he was sure the people were off the porch. Then he crab-crawled to the sliding-glass door, opened it just enough to squeeze through, and ran like hell for the back wall. It was six feet tall, and he took it like a high jumper, vaulting over it, his body nearly horizontal. He landed in a crouch on the other side and waited. Nothing. No dog. No man with a bat. He raced across the neighbor's backyard, took the next fence, then the next, and eventually exited through a gate.

Knowing that to someone watching through a window, a man running to a car would look more suspicious than one walking, Jake forced himself to saunter out to the Mercedes. He hoped it would look as though he had come out of the house it was parked in front of. He fired the ignition, U-turned, and drove back down Kelly Jensen's street. He saw no sign of the couple with the bat, and he was several streets away when he saw a police cruiser heading toward Manzanita Lane.

Jake drove, his mind and pulse racing. He was too keyed up to go home. He swung his car into a Denny's parking lot and killed the engine. He chose a booth with a view of the door, ordered black coffee, and spread the papers Shrake had given him on the table in front of him, willing the scanty information on the forms to give him a clue. He read and reread her name and address, scouring her handwriting for insight into her personality. He looked at her address and thought again about her house, reviewing every detail one by one for something he might have missed. The coffee took the fuzz off his brain, and he began to twitch his foot absently against the table leg. What was it about this woman?

Then, all of a sudden, he froze. What he saw was so startling, he had to keep himself from shouting out. As Kelly Jensen stared out defiantly from her driver's license photograph, Jake suddenly realized why she was so familiar. He had seen those eyes, that mouth, those cheekbones. Seen them hundreds of times—in Porter's office. One of the Sidney Randolph Maurer portraits.

Jake threw some money on the table and tore out of the restaurant to his car. He steered toward downtown, seething with a mixture of anger, revulsion, and curiosity. When he reached Porter's office building, he was in luck. The police guard at the entrance was a man who owed him a favor from the old days. Jake had gotten his nephew off a drug charge by proving he had been miles away from the scene of the incident. Jake didn't have many friends left in the Las Vegas PD, so this was an especially good time to run into one of the few he had remaining.

"Hey, Miguel," he greeted the guard.

"Mr. Jake Brooks," replied the man and they shook hands.

"Mind if I . . . ?" Jake gestured at the door.

"No one in or out," replied Miguel, holding the door open for Jake. "You know where you're going?"

"Been here hundreds of times," said Jake over his shoulder, holding up the key Porter had given him. He took the stairs to the third floor. The only difficulty now would be if the cops had put a new lock on the door.

The hallway outside Porter's office was still and deserted. The door was unchanged. Jake pulled out his key, pushed aside the yellow police tape, and unlocked the door. He stepped over the threshold, all too aware that he was breaking and entering for a second time in a single night.

Everything was just as it had been earlier during his meeting with Suzanne. Light came in from the street and outlined the objects in the room with a cinematic glow. Jake moved straight for the wall of paintings.

It was unquestionably her.

A younger Kelly Jensen stared him down from within the black frame, her eyes dangerous and intelligent. Her blonde hair was spread over a bare shoulder, a waterfall of bright light contrasting with the shadow of her other shoulder. Jake caught his breath. He had assumed for so long that this was a painting of a dead, unknown starlet from another era. Knowing Kelly Jensen was alive somewhere made it seem to crackle, eerily, with life.

Jake recovered himself and lifted the picture off the wall. With his fingernail, he sliced the backing paper along the edge of the frame, then carefully lifted out the print. The back was signed, SIDNEY RANDOLPH MAURER, 2007. So it was an original. Was Kelly Jensen an actress? Why did Porter have this painting of her?

Just then Jake heard footsteps coming down the hall. Hurriedly he slid the portrait back into the frame and onto the wall.

He was able to get across the room, away from the painting, before he heard a loud whisper at the door.

"Mr. Brooks?"

It was the police guard, Miguel.

"Yeah?"

The guard looked sheepish. "FBI is on its way up here. A guy's downstairs on the phone. You're not really supposed to be here. I understand you're saying good-bye to a friend, but this other guy . . . I don't know."

"Thanks," Jake said sincerely. "I'll take the back stairs."

Jake emerged into the service alley as the glow of daybreak touched the eastern sky. He jogged to his car, fired the engine, and drove toward home, trying to force his brain to make all the pieces fit together.

CHAPTER 7

HIDING IN PLAIN SIGHT, KELLY SAID TO HERSELF AS she looked over at her kids, trying to figure out how they would make themselves invisible in the middle of the Nogales Greyhound Station.

"Let's play Halloween," she said to Libby and Kevin as she led them into the restroom. She took out a brown shoe polish can, one she had often used for disguises in the past, and started to spray their faces.

Soon the kids were having even more fun than she had anticipated, particularly when she began painting her own face.

"Mommy, you look like a Mexican lady," Libby said.

Kelly giggled as she put a scarf around her face and tied it under her chin.

"C'mon, let's go!" said Kevin.

"Wait. Not yet." Kelly held her arm out to stop him. She peeled back a corner of the curtain and peered out. The only vehicles in the diner's parking lot besides her car were a pair of Harleys. She dropped the curtain and smiled at the kids.

"Okay, ready to roll."

As she pulled Libby's arms through the car seat harness, Kelly turned toward Kevin and said quietly, "Buckle up." She glanced up and down the street, saw a stoplight turn red. She closed the driver's door gently and started the motor. A calm in the eye of the storm. No rush of footsteps, no hand over her mouth. The road was practically empty. She drove to the bus station.

Please let this be the right thing to do, she kept repeating in her mind, over and over.

Kelly steered into the Greyhound lot and found a spot in long-term parking. She paid for two weeks.

Inside the depot, while Kevin and Libby watched Nickelodeon on the little TVs attached to their seats, Kelly chewed on her thumbnail and tried to keep from fidgeting.

Her mind wandered to a makeup artist's trailer in the desert, where a movie was being filmed on location. She had drifted onto it as a teen runaway, still clumsy then as an "escape artist" in her own right. But instantly she fit right in to this fantasy world, where everyone belonged yet everyone was a stranger.

She had never forgotten watching the film *The Stunt Man* on AMC, about a criminal escaping into a film set and finding sanctuary within the world of imagination.

And that day in the desert, when the makeup artist had handed her a tray, as though Kelly was meant to be there, she had found her refuge on a movie set. She was fascinated by the many different colors of stage makeup and putties the woman used to change each actor's features, and she let her fingers touch them, knowing that in her hands lay the tools she would have to master—the key to the many escape hatches she envisioned her future must take. She watched each step carefully as the makeup artist worked diligently, and the young actress sitting in front of a mirror aged forty years right in front of her eyes.

A couple of days later the makeup artist was smiling from ear to ear, watching Kelly mimic her technique. Kelly heard the woman utter the words that had remained a mantra in her memory until now: "Remember one thing, honey. You can look like someone else, but you can never *be* someone else."

"Mommy, it's over." Kevin tugged at Kelly's sweatshirt, and she gave each child another quarter. They plugged these into the TVs, and the machines revved back to life. Through the window, Kelly saw a pink sign on the shabby storefront across the street, and her mind drifted again, to other memories.

Pink neon. She almost smiled, remembering. It had been just before she'd met her husband, on one of her escapes from the Gordons, when no one had found her for five nights. The first night she had slept—if you could call it that—in a doorway across from a nightclub called Juicy, its name spelled out in a cursive spool of hot pink. A wash of bass and voices spilled out every time the door opened, and Kelly studied the couples swishing in and out.

The next day, she stole a dress and shoes from a K-mart and made herself up in a gas station bathroom. She waited in the doorway until late, then found the club's kitchen entrance and slipped in. The Mexican prep cooks looked her up and down as she entered, but said nothing. She sneaked into a seat in the back and let the blues rush over her. The singer was exquisite, a small black woman named Kelly Jensen who was able to seduce the audience just by inhaling. Kelly had absorbed the singer's modulation and tone, sponged up her subtle weight shifts and hand movements. When a cocktail waitress came by, Kelly ordered Perrier.

She slipped in the next two nights, too, but on the last night, a few minutes after the waitress took her Perrier order, the manager came to the table and asked Kelly for her ID. She had stood up and left without a word. But she'd had a new identity to aspire to, a new name to take on when she was free. Someday she would become

Kelly Jensen, and she would entertain as unself-consciously as her namesake did.

* * *

After tiring of the Nickelodeon shows, the kids had curled up in their bus depot chairs and fallen asleep.

Kelly gazed out the window at two young girls, obviously immigrants, obviously trafficked, awaiting their tricks. Their pimps were out of sight now, watching from behind the buildings across the street. Kelly felt pangs of hopelessness and compassion for the girls, working at all hours. *Why doesn't anyone care?* she asked herself.

Later, on the bus, the kids mostly slept again, their heads resting on each of her shoulders as mile after mile passed under the wheels—putting distance between them, their car, and their former lives. Kelly, on her Sidekick, went over and over the information she had downloaded at the library in Arizona, feeling the plan start to come together. Finally, she put the smartphone away and let the lurching of the engine work like a hypnotist's pendulum on her exhausted mind.

She jolted awake in her seat as the bus rumbled to a stop at the terminal. Through the window she saw a row of cardboard boxes leaning against a gray cinder-block wall. Various body parts poked out of the cardboard—a bare foot, a hand, a stocking-capped head. The shantytown was heated by a fire in a garbage can.

"Welcome to beautiful downtown Los Angeles, the city of dreams!" the bus driver crowed through the scratchy speakers. Kelly quickly gathered their belongings before waking the children, wondering if she would live long enough to see her dreams come true.

CHAPTER 8

THE DRAGON BAR WAS ONE OF THE MORE SUBDUED clubs on the Strip. Sinewy plaster dragons with jeweled eyes twined around posts and soared along the ceiling, belching smoke. The walls erupted with electronic fireworks, bursts of blue and red and green flashing luridly through the cigarette smoke. Music throbbed from speakers disguised as cauldrons spewing steam. Showgirls slithered through the crowd and posed on the velvet sofas, their sleek hips poured into blue jeans and their breasts billowing out of corset tops. Men in jeans and leather jackets appraised the various body parts as they passed, their eyes clicking like the gears on a slot machine: eyes, hair, shoulders, breasts, midriff, ass, thighs, ankles, toenails. Any time, day or night, the candy store was stocked and open for business.

Alana Sutter's impassive eyes stayed on Jake's. "They've got some mileage out of Natalie St. Clair—the shoplifter whose prints they picked up in Porter's room? This is what they've got so far: When she was six years old, her father offed her mother. The poor kid had to testify. The father got life. No protest from his family. They had dropped him like a hot potato as soon as he was arrested—didn't want to be burdened with a child of a killer. The fastest open-and-shut murder one case Texas had ever witnessed.

"Natalie goes into foster care. For six years, she bounces from family to family. You know much about foster care?"

Jake pulled on his soda water. "I see these kids eventually in court. I know the statistics. Around eighty percent of all inmates in penitentiaries have been in the child welfare system. Et cetera, et cetera."

Porter's former political strategist nodded stiffly. Her conservative dark suit was out of place in the bar.

"Basically. Usually at some point the kids figure out that most foster parents are in it for the money. They get $5,000 a month for kids the system brands as 'difficult.' The more difficult the kid, the more money the families get. Some foster parents confine their toddlers by making them wear helmets all day so that when the helmets are taken off, the toddlers' reactive behavior appears to be a frenzy of uncontrollable movements. And when Child Protective Services makes home visits, they qualify for extra cash."

Sutter jiggled the ice cubes in her Diet Coke. "There was one family—the Gordons; Natalie was with them for a while. Apparently Natalie made accusations that the foster dad beat her while the mom stood by and did nothing. No one pursued the complaint. The checks kept coming from Child Protective Services in Texas. Natalie ran away. Something like twenty times. Once, it took them five weeks to find her. Each time, she was sent back to the Gordons. Once she was booked on shoplifting. But she finally did manage to escape. She got away, and disappeared. Nothing at all on her—until her prints show up all over Porter's suite."

Jake flicked his lighter and stared at the flame for a moment before bringing it to the tip of his cigarette. The burning smell personified his love/hate relationship with smoking. Sutter watched him. Jake took a drag and exhaled, away from Sutter's face. He traced a circle on the lacquered table with the bottom of his water glass.

A year or so before, Porter had suddenly taken up the cause of at-risk children. It had seemed like a sound platform, and one that he had been campaigning on, quite successfully, with Suzanne. Now Jake was suspicious of his motives for choosing this particular area to focus on.

He thought through what he had found out the night before: Kelly Jensen was the Marilyn Monroe showgirl at Shrake's nightclub. A painting of her hung in Porter's office. What were the chances now that the Marilyn wig in Porter's room was *not* Kelly Jensen's? Kelly Jensen's fingerprints had not turned up, but Natalie St. Clair's were everywhere. Jake took a breath. Not telling Sutter—and the rest of the investigators—about Kelly Jensen was withholding information. But telling them meant turning her over to the FBI. Jake felt the watery sensation of betrayal.

Coming clean with what he knew about Kelly meant exposing Suzanne, too. But most of all, it meant handing over Porter himself, erasing every damn good thing he'd ever done and replacing it all with tabloid-style, salacious details of an affair with a nightclub singer. Jake stubbed out his cigarette and made his choice. He changed the subject.

"You going to the funeral?"

Sutter's hand went through her auburn hair, which fell back into shape over her ears. "I've got a lot to hold down here. Mrs. Garrett has her own people there. Cassie's going." She trailed off, seeming uncomfortable with the subject.

Jake was surprised but didn't show it. "I'll poke around when I'm there and see what else I can drag out," he offered.

Sutter nodded and pushed herself out of the booth. As she left,

Jake watched her stride, purposeful and strong, the only woman in the room whose body wasn't the feasting ground for the eyes of the male clientele.

Jake signaled the waitress to bring him another drink. She placed it in front of him, along with a glimpse of her tan breasts, barely held in place by a red velvet bikini top crisscrossed with gold braid—a Las Vegas damsel in distress to go with the bar's dragon theme.

"Anything else?" she purred.

Jake took in a breath, as if to say something, then changed his mind. He shook his head. "No, that's it. Just the check."

Jake reached into his jacket pocket and, for what felt like the thousandth time, pulled out the grainy black-and-white Xerox of Kelly Jensen's driver's license. *Hair: Blonde.* It looked honey-colored even in the picture, glossy and full, cut straight, just below the collarbone. *Eyes: Green.* They were large, set above high cheekbones. *Height: 5'7". Weight: 115.* Jake remembered the body from the Marilyn dress she had worn in her act. That body—leaner but no less curvy than the original—was not messing around. The whole effect had been perfect.

Even if all the recent events hadn't already scrambled his circuits, Jake would have been feeling uneasy. He was starting to believe that Kelly Jensen had something to do with Porter's murder—maybe she even did it. But did that explain his infatuation? *That's how far you've gone*, said a thick voice in his head. *You're the other side of the criminal coin; it's why you understand their motives and defend them. You have more sympathy for criminals than their victims, and that's the reason their crimes don't tear into your conscience. At the core of each case you see an abused child, who has been forsaken and betrayed by a sociopathic or apathetic society. That's how you justify their crimes.*

For the sake of argument, Jake let another voice in his head respond, but when he heard what it said, he wished he'd gagged it:

You've always measured yourself against Porter, and whenever Porter had something you wanted, you managed to steal it. Girlfriends in college. Clerkships in law school. Cases as a young lawyer starting out. You pushed Porter to find things he knew you wouldn't want: Suzanne, politics, Las Vegas. That's why Porter kept Kelly a secret. She had the power to free him from a life he didn't really want. Because somewhere in his subconscious brain, Porter knew you would have wanted Kelly.

Shit. Now he was sounding paranoid even to himself. Porter had loved politics and had loved Suzanne, once. As for Vegas, well, you had to live somewhere.

Jake smoothed his hand over the paper and stared at the picture as if he could make Kelly talk, make her tell him her whereabouts, her likes, her dislikes. She'd told Porter about her past. Immediately Jake felt a slug of depression ooze up from his solar plexus and settle wetly on his heart. Porter had loved this woman—Jake knew this for certain somehow—in spite of everything. In spite of her past, the kind that had produced two kids by the time she was twenty. In spite of her line of work, as a seductress who had perfected the art of arousing dicks. If Porter hadn't loved her, he never would have risked so much for her—his political career, his marriage, his children. The slug pressed down more heavily. He thought of Kelly's portrait hanging, anonymously to the rest of the world but brazenly visible, in Porter's office. Kelly and Porter had the kind of love Jake had never even come close to and, he was slowly coming to realize, never would.

Jake brought his glass to his lips and tried to pour the rest of the water down his throat without swallowing. He got about two-thirds of it in before it trickled out the corners of his mouth. He closed his lips and let the liquid pool under his tongue. Kelly had loved Porter. *Son of a bitch.* Jake recognized the crazy reality: how much he now wanted Kelly to love him, too.

CHAPTER 9

EXCEPT FOR THE STEEP HILLS AND THE OCCASIONAL funeral cortege snaking through the grounds, Forest Lawn Cemetery in Los Angeles could have been a golf course. Vast, lush lawns rolled up and down inclines and across flat expanses. Groves of eucalyptus trees slouched along the perimeter, dangling leaves and scent. The still air was shushed by the 134, the freeway sweeping along the base of the property toward Griffith Park. A fountain in the center of a giant lake at the entrance continually shot a plume of water thirty feet in the air. The few buildings were mock-Gothic, as if a Yale under-grad had won a competition to design them. The graves themselves were virtually invisible, almost an afterthought, marked by small bronze plaques laid flat in the grass.

Jake stood under a white tent beside the open grave. His left arm enveloped Suzanne Garrett, who wept silently into his chest. Jake's right hand rested on the dark head of Ian, Porter's nine-year-old son. Porter's daughter, fourteen-year-old Anna, stood behind her brother and held tightly to Jake's forearm, resting her temple against his bicep, her blonde hair flowing down the back of his arm. Her look of disbelief was mirrored in the faces of the other mourners; distilled on hers, however, it resculpted her adolescent beauty into a portrait of hardened adulthood.

A gospel choir in purple robes covered the silence with their voices. The singers—a multiracial group of children ranging in age from six to sixteen—swayed with the beat and hummed reverently behind the soloist who was belting out "Amazing Grace."

Hundreds of mourners made up a crowd as ethnically diverse as the choir. Suzanne's family and Porter's closest political friends were represented, as well as allies, supporters, donors, and believers. Porter had had an appeal that cut across gender, race, and age. Jake noticed one silver-haired woman, richly dressed in black crepe, moving her toe to the music, although she was off the beat. In the row behind her, a woman bounced a baby in her arms. In the distance, Jake spied a cluster of media vultures, their telescopic lenses trying to capture every tear in the eyes of the immaculately dressed and groomed politicians who were all sunk deep in the act of mourning.

The song finished and the choir shuffled into chairs reserved for them. The priest stepped forward, intoned a few words, and then nodded to Jake. Jake led Porter's family forward, and each tossed a single white rose onto the coffin. The long silence was punctuated by sniffs and the tentative sound of noses being discreetly blown in public. The singers' robes rustled in the breeze while the mourners performed an unchoreographed dance with their hands—dabbing eyes with handkerchiefs, burying whole faces in palms, brushing hair out of eyes and off foreheads. At last Jake led the family back under the tent and helped them into their chairs. The priest gestured, and four workers began filling the grave with dirt.

With the ceremony over, some of the crowd began walking

toward their cars, but most hung around in small groups, hugging each other and talking softly. A few loud voices rang out. A line formed under the tent beside Suzanne, who grasped each hand and air-kissed each cheek that was offered her. Jake stood at her side and murmured that she could get into the car anytime she wanted to, but she replied that she intended to greet every guest and acknowledge the support. As he had many times during the two decades he had known her, Jake marveled at her stoicism, her admirable public face that concealed so much—until he noticed her assistant, Cassie, leading a small posse of reporters and photographers up the hill to the gravesite. He watched Suzanne angle her body in their direction, keeping her eyes earnestly on her well-wishers.

She's campaigning, thought Jake, disgusted and amazed by her gall. But it all made sense. Porter had been neck and neck with Theodore Henckle, his rival in the Senate campaign. With Suzanne's connection to the governor and the Democratic National Committee, she could easily be appointed to Porter's seat in the House. But if she could keep the public's support, she actually stood a chance of winning the Senate seat herself. It had been done before. And the Senate meant real political power.

Jake smiled woodenly as the mourners trooped by and tried to keep his exhaustion out of his face. His mind was clicking through what he had learned since yesterday. After seeing Alana Sutter at the Dragon Bar, he had flown to Los Angeles. On the plane, he'd called Allan Rich, who managed the art of Sidney Randolph Maurer, and arranged to visit Maurer's studio on his way into town from the airport.

Seconds after Jake had rung the doorbell, the heavy door had been opened by a short, bald man with a big round belly and a familiar face. Allan Rich was a fantastic talker, so in addition to hearing everything there was to know about Sidney Randolph Maurer and his career, Jake soon learned his host had been a character actor in the 1950s but, after being blacklisted, had become an art dealer. The peak of his career had been discovering and promoting the famous artist. As he showed Jake around Maurer's studio, Rich told him story after story about the celebrities who used to come there to pose. Finally Jake was able to ask about Kelly. He described the portrait of Kelly's face. Rich said he remembered a man paying a lot of money for Maurer to take a picture of his young wife.

"She was the most beautiful young woman I'd seen in a long time. She had danger in her eyes. Sidney loved that. Although he doesn't usually do private commissions, he made an exception in her case. It was also an exceptional amount of money. The young woman called a while ago, maybe a year or so, and asked if there was a negative and could I make her another print. She was so pleasant, but she also seemed so sad. Something about her made me feel I had to help her."

"Do you remember her name?" asked Jake.

Rich replied without hesitation. "St. Clair. Natalie St. Clair."

Jake had been surprised. Just like that, so easily, he had the link between Natalie St. Clair and Kelly Jensen. But there were other factors: Kelly had a husband? Kelly changed her name? Everything he had seen so far had led him to believe she was a single mom.

Jake was deep in thought when he suddenly heard a voice from behind his shoulder that zoomed him back to the present—the funeral.

"Damn shame, damn loss."

Randy Carlen came up behind Jake and clapped him on the back with his left hand while sliding his other hand down to rest on Suzanne's lower back. It was an oddly intimate pose, territorial and comforting at the same time. Jake was surprised. He didn't know that Carlen and Suzanne had ever even met each other.

Jake stood there awkwardly with Carlen squeezed between Suzanne and him. The smell of cigars wafted up from Carlen's clothes. Suzanne didn't seem to mind.

A woman approached. "My deepest condolences," she quavered in the British-sounding diction of the moneyed classes of another era. "Porter was a wonderful man. His mother and I were friends in Washington. I watched him grow up."

Suzanne accepted the woman's hand. It was the silver-haired woman Jake had noticed moving awkwardly to the music during the service. Behind her blue-tinted sunglasses, her eyes were swollen and red. A wide-brimmed black hat shaded one side of her face.

"Did you come all the way from Washington?" asked Suzanne politely.

"I live here now," the woman replied in her thin voice. "But your husband touched my heart; he was a very special person. I followed his career closely. He would have made a great senator."

"Thank you for your kind words." Suzanne smiled, her gaze already shifting to the next mourner in line.

Carlen muttered his refrain, "Damn shame," and shook the older woman's hand.

"Thank you for coming," murmured Jake. The woman's hand in her black glove felt like a bag of sticks.

"I'm Lydia Haines," she creaked. "Are you family, too?"

Jake cleared his throat. "Jake Brooks. A close friend."

"Well, we all need those."

The woman smiled tightly. She didn't look well. She seemed pale and pained, and Jake noticed her pink lipstick had been applied with a shaky hand.

All heads turned in the direction of a black Mercedes limousine whooshing up the hill and stopping with a crunch of tires. The driver's door opened, and a huge man in a dark suit got out. He loped around to the passenger door and held it open. Another man, tall and lean, emerged.

"Who's that?" Jake murmured to Carlen.

"Todd Gillis."

"Really?" Jake was intrigued. He'd heard of the investment banker and his donations to Porter's campaign. He'd also heard of his arrogance and flash. Jake watched as Gillis approached a group of businessmen, trailed by his hulking bodyguard. Around six-foot-three, with salt-and-pepper hair, Gillis wore a handsomely cut charcoal gray suit. He seemed to be between forty-five and fifty, and he exuded power and control.

"Nice of him to come to the ceremony," Jake muttered dismissively.

"No, you have the wrong idea," answered Carlen. "The guy's a real altruist. The kids singing here today? They're from a group home—what used to be called an orphanage."

"I know what a group home is," Jake growled impatiently.

"Gillis owns this one. His charity runs it. Two hundred kids, staff, psychologists, teachers. Gillis is paying for it all." Carlen looked sheepish. "It makes me feel bad about what I do with all my money." He brightened. "But then I get over it. Hey, whoa—"

Lydia Haines had doubled over. She appeared to be choking. Jake leaped to her side and bent over to look at her face. She held a handkerchief over her nose and mouth.

"Can you talk?" urged Jake.

Lydia Haines waved him off.

"Can you talk?" repeated Jake more forcefully. He moved closer, preparing to perform the Heimlich maneuver if necessary.

"Yes," she croaked. "Please, I'm fine." She coughed some more, still doubled over. "Old age is not for sissies."

"Do you need help?" asked Jake, worried. It wasn't a hot day, so it couldn't be heatstroke. Perhaps standing in line so long had weakened her. "Let me walk you to your car."

"Thank you," whispered the woman. Jake supported her elbow with one hand and wrapped the other around her waist, guiding her gently down the hill. Her high-heeled pumps sank into the lawn with every step. As they approached the road, Jake saw a taxi waiting.

"This is my cab. Thank you for your chivalry." Lydia Haines glanced up at Jake, still holding the handkerchief to her mouth. He helped her into the backseat.

"Are you sure you're alright?" he asked. "I can get you a bottle of water."

She waved him off again. "You've been too kind already. Let's go, please, driver."

Jake shut the door firmly, still worried. He saw the old lady sinking down in her seat as the cab drove away. By the time it was almost out of sight, he couldn't even see the top of her head.

Jake turned back to the tent. There were still a half dozen people waiting to greet Suzanne. Carlen had left her side and now stood with a group of men that included Todd Gillis. Jake watched Gillis for a moment, a kingmaker among kingmakers.

What Carlen had been telling him about group homes wasn't news to Jake. He'd had enough experience as a criminal defender to know a thing or two about them. He didn't doubt Gillis's altruism, but he also knew it wasn't only his money going into the home. For every child ranked at level 11 (very difficult), Gillis—or his foundation—would receive $10,000 to $11,000 per month from the state and federal governments. Most group homes housed such high-ranking kids. Still, it took a certain kind of person to choose to get involved with that kind of charity, and Jake had to admit a grudging respect for what Gillis did.

Jake felt a sudden stab of guilt about his mixed feelings. Porter had never begrudged charity and made giving to others look easy. Jake thought about how Porter had behaved on the campaign trail, clasping hands in his trademark double-handed bear grasp. A born leader, Porter had been unusually skilled at making each person he greeted feel like the only one in the room. Watching him work a room had been a lesson in human dignity. His friend's strong features and rangy presence gave him an all-American appeal. His self-deprecating sense of humor and talent for delivering pithy sound bites had been helping him poll well with both Democrats and Republicans, no mean feat in the polarized political arena. The DNC had been falling all over itself preparing for his presidential bid in four years.

Now, to Jake's amazement, he stood at his friend's grave, watching everyone—those who were overcome by jealousy and had secretly hated him, and those who had loved him—trying to be on their best behavior. The businessmen standing with Carlen chuckled softly. Carlen leaned forward into the group and said something. As the men laughed, Carlen whispered to the man next to him.

Suddenly Jake felt a movement at his side.

"You lost me a rather substantial bet."

Jake turned. Todd Gillis stood beside him.

"I'm sorry to say I bet against you—a spur-of-the-moment whim. You can be sure I won't do that again. It set me back around a million."

In the millisecond before responding, Jake considered his reaction, and every muscle in his face awaited his command. He decided on reserve. One eyebrow lifted. His mouth curled.

"The Pantelli case?" prompted Gillis, not at all put off by Jake's demeanor.

"I'm afraid I can't take the credit," answered Jake. "The jury decided the verdict based on the evidence presented."

"Todd Gillis." Gillis held out his hand.

Jake shook it. "Jake Brooks."

Each man held the grip a second longer than usual.

Gillis grinned. "Tell me something. Was she innocent? The Platinum Widow?"

It seemed to Jake as though the case had been decided years ago, although it had been just a few weeks. Jake had managed to clear the good name of Jeanette Pantelli, the notorious Platinum Widow, saving her from conviction for the murder of her husband, Chubby Pantelli, despite testimony from a hit man claiming that Jeanette had hired him to pull the trigger. Jake had hammered the jury, the television cameras, and Jeanette herself with the message of her innocence—so much so, even she'd ended up believing it. He'd tracked down expert witnesses and dismantled the testimony of prosecution witnesses. The trial had lasted three months. The jury had deliberated for sixteen days, but at last they'd found her not guilty.

In the post-trial publicity, Jake had kept on message: Mrs. Pantelli was not guilty and the justice system had prevailed. Yet privately, Jake couldn't take all the credit for the victory: The jury consultants had been top-notch. The ruling left the widow the sole owner of a dozen lucrative establishments in Las Vegas and Atlantic City, as well as clubs and restaurant chains around the country and even a theme park outside Pittsburgh.

Jake considered Gillis now. His eyes had a playful quality to them, echoed in the lines around his mouth, which looked teasing or amused, depending on your point of view. Everything else about Gillis was polished and sharp. More than he cared to admit, Jake wanted to hate this guy. Still, there was something appealing in Gillis's bluntness.

"Everyone's innocent until proven guilty."

Gillis grinned. "So they say." He softened his voice. "You were a friend of the congressman."

"I knew him a long time. You?"

"I liked what I saw. Straight shooter. Fair. Heart in the right place, for politics anyway."

Gillis's bodyguard shuffled up and whispered something to his boss.

"It's been a pleasure to meet you," declared Gillis abruptly, patting the back of Jake's jacket. "Yes, a pleasure," he repeated. "Let's do it again." Gillis moved quickly down the hill.

Jake realized he needed to get back to Suzanne.

"I'm just about finished here," she whispered when he took his place next to her. Jake led her down to her limousine. As he helped her into the backseat, she bumped her head on the doorframe. She gritted her teeth together until Jake had gotten in the other side and pulled the door shut. Then, like a three-year-old, she burst into tears.

"Jake, I can't handle this," she sobbed. He folded her in his arms, her brittle shoulders heaving in an uncharacteristic moment of honesty. For reasons he didn't care to figure out, it felt good just to hold Suzanne and rock back and forth. She held on even after she stopped sobbing.

"I did know," she whispered. "I knew he was seeing someone." Her shoulders shuddered. "And it hurt like hell."

"It's okay," whispered Jake. "It's okay." Grief held them together, where life never had.

Long before the widow had stopped crying, the gravediggers tossed their shovels into the back of their pickup truck and quietly coasted down the hill.

CHAPTER 10

KELLY CROUCHED IN THE BACKSEAT OF THE TAXI, her hands icy even in the black gloves. Her head was spinning; she could hardly think straight. She had seen the FBI agents staked around the crowd at the funeral, their alert eyes looking for any hints of Porter's murderer. Her heart felt like an out-of-control airplane tumbling through the air as it lurched from feeling to feeling. Porter was dead. She would never love anyone like that again. She had shaken hands with his wife. Big players she recognized from Las Vegas had attended the funeral. The net was closing in on her.

"Please hurry. I need to get back to the hotel," she said in a whispery voice.

The driver looked back in his mirror. "Lady, are you okay?"

Kelly slid farther down in the seat, feeling faint. "Fine," she answered. "Please, just hurry."

"Well, don't puke in my cab," the driver muttered.

Kelly fought to regain control, to force her mind to work like a computer, dispassionately and fast. Typing away on her Sidekick, she did a Google search to locate a pay phone nearby. She sat upright and glanced out the window onto Cahuenga Boulevard. Her eyes searched for the phone booth that should be coming up on the right. She had at last faced up to what she had to do: get her kids some-place safe.

"Driver? Stop here, please," Kelly demanded in a still shaky voice. The driver turned quickly, afraid of some imminent danger to his cab. And as soon as he pulled into the driveway and stopped, she headed for the phone booth—a rare commodity, since just about everyone from bankers to gangbangers now had mobile phones.

There's not much difference in that spectrum anyway, thought Kelly grimly, scooping a handful of coins out of her purse. She dialed a num-ber in Las Vegas and peered around from under her hat, hunched her back in case anyone was watching. She was just old Lydia Haines, on a pay phone because she refused to learn how to use a newfangled cell phone. The line rang, and rang again.

Come on, answer, Kelly prayed.

"Hello?"

"Holly, it's me."

"Sweetheart! Where are you?"

"I can't talk long. But I need your help. Help with the kids. I've got to get them out of here."

"Of course we'll help, honey. We'd love to have them."

"I'll give you the directions. Can you come tonight?" The des-peration in Kelly's voice cut through any rudeness.

"Sure, sweetie. We'll be there. Where are you?"

"Los Angeles."

"Los Angeles?!"

"Please say you'll come." Kelly's voice was thick with pleading.

"Of course we'll come. How do we find you?"

Kelly spoke quickly and hung up the phone. In the cab, as the driver continued toward the hotel, she slid out of view of the rear-view mirror, pulled chunks of putty from her face, and cleaned her makeup off using a wet wipe, keeping her hat on to shield the transformation her face had undergone.

"Pull up here, please," she said, using Lydia's thin voice once more.

She paid the cabbie, rolled up her skirt, and climbed out. She lost the hat when she was crossing the street to the hotel—watched as several cars ran over it.

When she got up to the room, the kids were glued to the Disney channel and the babysitter was flipping through fashion magazines. The girl was doughy and seemed a little dim, but the concierge had assured Kelly that the agency they used did background checks and the sitters were CPR certified. Kelly paid her and shut the door.

Out of necessity as a single mom, Kelly had occasionally had to leave her children with others. She knew the strict rules of Child Protective Services: If the children were found left alone or in incapable hands, even when *she* knew they were safe, they would be taken away from her. Kelly always made sure she had enough cash to stay at hotels that offered proper babysitting arrangements, and she always insisted on the best the agencies had. But leaving the children was always a leap of faith no matter her precautions, and every time she did, she was torn between what she had to do and what she wanted to do. But now she needed something safer and longer term for them. She had to get them out of the city.

Holly had been Kelly's closest friend in Las Vegas over these past two years. They had met through Holly's husband, Frank, who was the bartender at Shrake's club. Holly and Kelly shared the kinship of motherhood, and Holly had pulled Kevin and Libby into her life along with Kelly. She joked that the two kids filled the void left by her son, who had just started college. Kelly and Frank knew that was the truth. Holly was a natural mom, and the kids loved her like an aunt or, Kelly sometimes thought wistfully, a grandmother.

Kelly didn't know that behind her back Holly and Frank talked about how she was the most seductive person they had ever met, which said a lot, coming from two seasoned natives of Las Vegas. Not seductive in a sexual way, they always said, although she was beautiful, and plenty of men and women were attracted to her for that. What made Kelly an exception was more a part of her personal demeanor, the way she made you feel as though she needed you for your unique self, not for what you could do for her. Holly and Frank teased each other that they were both in love with her. But it was a pure kind of love, de-sexualized, like what you might feel for a child or a pet. Indeed, Frank had always seen a hunted animal—perhaps a doe ready to take flight—under the brave façade of Kelly's eyes, and he had felt a need to shelter and protect her.

As for Holly, she just loved Kelly for her directness, her sense of humor, and her clear love of her children. She'd thought a lot about Kelly's looks and their effect on people. An ex-showgirl herself, Holly was beautiful. A little softer around the edges now, but no stranger to the power of beauty and the neuroses that can underlie it. She was most intrigued by how Kelly's beauty didn't alienate other women. Kelly had an equality about her and held other men and women up to equal scrutiny. When they got close, she allowed them equal access to her vulnerabilities and defenses.

With such strong chemistry among the three, they had developed a small extended family together that had been Kelly's main source of emotional support in Las Vegas. There was no one else Kelly would dream of leaving her children with for more than a few hours.

It was past midnight by the time Holly called the hotel room from her car. Kelly had explained to Kevin and Libby that they were going to spend a few days with Holly and Frank in Las Vegas, and they'd get to go on a road trip in their RV. Kelly would join them as soon as she could. It wouldn't be long, just a few days. The two children had protested loudly, as was to be expected, but they perked up at the idea of spending the time in the RV. Kelly had managed to calm them down enough for them to get a few hours' sleep before bundling them downstairs into the underground garage.

She found Holly's car immediately in the prearranged spot, hugged her friends, and let Holly pack the kids in the backseat while she spoke further to Frank about her plans.

"Are you going to be okay?" murmured Frank, his sincere brown eyes moving from Kelly to the sleepy children. "You've never handed over the kids in such a rush. Is he on your trail?"

Kelly smiled a tight smile. "I need a little time to maneuver through a minefield." She lowered her voice to a whisper. "And I just need to have the kids in a safe place for a while."

"So we'll meet at the place we always talked about—unless we hear from you?"

Kelly nodded. She found herself in the strange position of being the one to comfort Frank. "Don't worry. I've got a plan. And they're better off with you for right now."

Holly came up to the two of them. Her voice was firmer than Frank's. "I'm glad you called us for this. You're smart to have a safety hatch for them, and I'm glad we can help. We'll see you in a few days. Keep in touch."

Holly's kind efficiency made Kelly's eyes start to sting. She gripped Holly's shoulders. "Thank you," she said earnestly. Then she leaned into the car. "It won't be long, my true loves," she whispered to her sleepy kids, kissing their temples, between their eyes, the tips of their noses.

Holly squeezed Kelly's hands before getting into the front seat. "We'll take good care of them," she said softly.

Kelly could only nod, holding back the tears she didn't want the kids to see. The car drove away, and she ducked back into the elevator and rode up to her room. She tiptoed into the bathroom, shut the door, and stared at her image in the mirror. Looking pale and unbalanced in the fluorescent lights, she grimaced. One part of her mind was desperately torn away from her, was holding on to her children even as they got farther and farther away. She forced herself to let the other part of her mind take over.

The plan was falling into shape.

CHAPTER 11

THE TEACUP RATTLED IN ITS SAUCER AS CHERYL
Gordon placed it on the coffee table. Jake didn't drink tea, but he was
aware of the social obligation at work here. Mrs. Gordon must have
served a lot of tea to Houston county officials over her years as a foster
parent. There was both a practiced and a guilty air to the ritual.

The large living room was neat, almost obsessively so, although
the furnishings would have looked cluttered in a less orderly environment. The five out-of-date issues of *National Geographic* stacked on
a side table looked as though they had been arranged with a ruler.
All the wooden surfaces in the room gleamed. The room smelled of
strong cleaning fluids overlaid with air freshener.

Mrs. Gordon sat on the edge of a Lambright Comfort Chair.
"You're with Child Protective Services?" she whined. "I've never
seen you before."

"Actually, I'm an attorney with the county council," said Jake, turning the handle of the teacup ninety degrees. "I'm following up on a complaint."

Mrs. Gordon narrowed her eyes.

Jake smiled. "Someone's always complaining. It'll be something dismissible, I'm sure."

Mrs. Gordon regarded him silently. Jake pushed on, hoping she didn't know that a social worker or court-appointed special advocate was supposed to accompany him for this sort of visit.

"Do you remember Natalie St. Clair?" he asked.

Mrs. Gordon sucked on her thin lips. She scratched one thumbnail across the other, pushing the cuticle back. "Yeah, I remember her."

Jake pushed his Xerox of Kelly's driver's license across the table. "Did she look like this?"

Mrs. Gordon squinted. "Could have. I don't really remember. She ran away all the time. She was troubled."

Jake sat back. The woman wasn't meeting his eyes. He held himself back, knowing that when the time came, he would be able to make her tell him what she was hiding. From the way she looked, she had a lot to hide. She was about five-foot-two and weighed around two hundred pounds. The skin on her feet puffed up and around her flip-flops, nearly burying them entirely. Below the hem of her skirt, her calves sagged; her blouse was sleeveless, and her papery arms, bulging with several rolls of flab, wobbled every time she moved. The top had a turtleneck collar around which Mrs. Gordon had tied a scarf that her fingers adjusted and readjusted. It was impossible to tell if her face had once been pretty. It was now swollen with fat and had unnatural dark markings, possibly from bruising, and her suspicious eyes peered out of it with animal fear.

"Why did she run away all the time?" asked Jake.

"She was just one of those out-of-control kids. A real difficult one."

"Did she have any reason to be unhappy here?"

Mrs. Gordon's hands fluttered to the knot on her scarf. "She was always unhappy. Gary used to say she was born a hard case and would never change." Her mind's eye appeared to lock in on Natalie. "She seemed to look at us like a wounded cat on the run."

Startled at her own words, she clenched her teeth to stop herself from uttering any more.

"Does Gary enjoy having foster children?" Jake kept his voice neutral and focused, wondering what angle would draw her out. He was confident one would; he just had to find it.

"He was a great dad. They were lucky to have him. You know, these kids come here like animals. They smell, they're wild, just like animals. Gary is strict. He teaches them values. He gives them discipline they've never had before. They need it."

Jake forced himself to take a sip of tea. "You keep a very orderly home," he said. "It must take a lot of work to maintain it the way you do."

Mrs. Gordon stared at him, judging his flattery. He smiled at her, the way he smiled at juries he needed to sway.

"Mr. Gordon will be home any moment," said Mrs. Gordon. "He's just gone to the market."

"I'm looking forward to meeting him," said Jake politely. "But I'm enjoying talking with you too, ma'am. Do you have any pictures of your foster children?"

Mrs. Gordon touched her throat. "Gary doesn't like it."

Jake kept the polite look on his face. "But you do keep photos?"

Mrs. Gordon's eyes flicked toward the door. "I keep an album in the closet. Do you want to see it?"

Jake tried to conceal his enthusiasm. "How many have you had?"

"Just one."

"Album?"

"Yes."

"I meant foster children."

"Oh. Twenty-five, thirty."

"I'd like to see the album."

As Mrs. Gordon plodded up the stairs, Jake looked around. There was an umbrella stand by the front door with half a dozen canes sticking out of it. A fan tried to move the stale air through the room. Jake loosened his tie.

Mrs. Gordon returned with the album, and Jake dutifully looked at each picture, pushing back his eagerness to find a photograph of Kelly. Each child had a story; Jake noticed that Mrs. Gordon labeled them either as "a good kid" or "a clumsy, troubled kid." He wondered how many had run away from the abuse that was evident by the Band-Aids and bandages that marked the "troubled" ones.

"I don't see any pictures of Natalie. Are you sure she lived here?"

"Of course she lived here. All the children are like my own. Even the bad ones."

"Tell me more about her. What did she look like?"

Cheryl Gordon's face turned sour. "Very pretty. Skinny kid, though, and real wild. She always gave us a lot of trouble. She ran away."

"Why don't you have her photo in the album?"

Mrs. Gordon looked at her hands. Jake asked her again, but she wouldn't meet his eyes.

"How long have you been married?" Jake asked abruptly.

Mrs. Gordon stirred in her chair. "Thirty-one years."

Jake looked surreptitiously at his watch. He had to do this before Gary got home.

"He ever hit you?"

Mrs. Gordon's fingers went to her scarf again, and she looked like she was about to answer, but stopped herself.

"Did you ever try to stop him?"

Mrs. Gordon looked down, her thumbnails working against each other double time.

"Did he hurt you too, when you tried to stop him?"

Mrs. Gordon looked up, her small mouth trembling. "Natalie got it some of the worst," she whispered. "She got to him like no one else did. If she had just stopped resisting, he would have quit on his own. If she had just stayed put, or—" She suddenly clamped her mouth shut. "He's in the driveway."

Jake cursed to himself, and saw through the window a red-faced man getting out of a minivan. Jake spoke urgently.

"Mrs. Gordon, this is critical. You let him ruin her life once. This is your chance to make it up to her. I need to have the information. Whatever it is you're not telling me, I need to know it."

Mrs. Gordon squirmed in her chair. Jake could hear Gary Gordon's shoes crunching on the gravel walkway.

"I never understood why she lived with us. She had an uncle. He always came by to check on her, but he never took her home. I didn't understand that. There didn't seem to be anything wrong with him."

There was a key in the door. Jake held Cheryl Gordon's eyes.

"What was his name?"

"Michael. Michael Young." The front door swung open and in walked Gary Gordon, carrying a bag filled to the brim with cigarette cartons and liquor bottles. He stopped when he saw Jake; his eyes narrowed when he noticed the photo album.

"Gary, this is Jake Brooks," said Cheryl Gordon.

"Mr. Gordon." Jake stood. "I'm with Child Protective Services," he said, hoping Mrs. Gordon would back up his lie. "We're interviewing foster homes in the area to assess the educational assistance our foster children need. There is a national focus on matching academic mentors with our kids."

Gary Gordon grunted, putting the grocery bag down by his feet.

"We're hoping to highlight some of our families who've made a special effort to educate the kids. We think it will get new families involved."

"We're not interested in statistics," said Gordon, his voice surprisingly high-pitched for his size.

Jake pressed on. "We've lost track of some of the children over the years. Do you remember Natalie St. Clair?"

Gordon turned on his wife. "What have you been talking about?" he bellowed. Cheryl Gordon cringed in her chair, her eyes averted.

"Hang on," said Jake, trying to appease him. "I just got here. Your wife had only just gotten out the album. She wanted to wait until you got home."

"Natalie St. Clair was real troubled. Real bad. She's the type of girl that makes people stop fostering."

Mrs. Gordon had dissolved into a fidgeting mound, her hands working overtime on her scarf and fingernails.

"Anything else you could tell me about her would be very use—"

"Nothing else to tell. It's time for you to go."

Jake decided not to push it. He thanked Mrs. Gordon for the tea, but she didn't look up. Jake watched them for an exchange of information. There was none. But as he shut the door behind him, he heard the distinctive sound of skin slapping skin.

CHAPTER 12

SIX LANES WIDE IN SOME PLACES AND SIXTEEN miles long, Wilshire Boulevard unfurled from downtown, in the east, all the way out to the Pacific Ocean, in the west. Its wealthy corridors shimmered in the sun, mirroring the glass high-rise buildings that lined it on both sides. The BMW, Lexus, Mercedes, and Jaguar coupes and convertibles cruised leisurely up and down the perpetually fresh-surfaced asphalt, gliding in and out of spaces between behemoth SUVs.

Kelly pushed an old Rent-A-Wreck Toyota Corolla that she leased for all cash through the traffic, adjusting to the peculiar rhythm of Los Angeles drivers. On the surface, they were unhurried and lazy, moving toward their various destinations just over the speed limit; then, all of a sudden, someone would cut off someone else, or a car would stop for a pedestrian, and a salvo of horn honking and gesturing would assault the driver. The undercurrent of pent-up hostility was notable for its surface calm, and Kelly observed that LA drivers switched back and forth easily between the two roles. She watched a woman in a white Lincoln Navigator lean on her horn, apoplectic because the Volvo station wagon in front of her wouldn't turn left at a red light. A few minutes later, the same woman brought two lanes of traffic to a halt as she herself stopped suddenly and waited for a parking place. As Kelly drove past, she saw the woman chatting amiably on her phone, sucking on a coffee cup, willfully oblivious to the horns and silent screams around her.

Kelly pulled onto a side street a block away from the Bensenhill Rolls-Royce showroom. Stepping out of the car, she caught her reflection in a store window. What she saw was a beautiful redhead, hair long and silky, wearing a black stretch Donna Karan dress and black sandals with high heels as sharp as steak knives.

The showroom was a glass-fronted building situated next door to an art deco–style theater. Inside, it was like an automotive museum. The air-conditioning was turned down to permafrost. The room was quiet but for the faintest drift of Vivaldi. The cars gleamed like hard candies—green, red, yellow, black—under precisely focused spotlights that picked out their salient and expensive features. Kelly's heels clicked on the marble floor as she entered, then stopped as she scanned the room, purposely looking above the heads of the salesmen. They had not approached her but were appraising her out of the corners of their eyes, like a pride of lions that go perfectly still at the scent of prey, even as their ears prick with excitement.

Almost immediately, Kelly knew which man to choose. His brown hair was gelled into place, his Armani suit tailored perfectly both to reveal and to hide his weight-trained muscles. Kelly saw him searching out his own reflection in the mirrored walls of the showroom. This man was obviously obsessed with his image—camouflaging a severe case of self-loathing, no doubt. He could be swayed by flattery. Kelly smiled at him, her eyes scanning his physique appreciatively. He assessed her from head to toe before throwing out a welcoming smile of his own.

"I'm Ali. See anything you like?" he asked, puffing his chest.

Kelly had seen his type again and again in Vegas. She pointed to an exquisite 1968 Corniche convertible.

"This one," she said, smiling unctuously.

The salesman glided over to the Corniche, holding an arm out and selling all the way. He caressed the glossy pearl-colored metal, pausing at the hood, just above the headlight.

"There are only six of these beauties in the entire country," breathed Ali. Kelly noticed the way he was touching the car with just his fingertips, as though stroking a woman's breast.

The thought of him touching any woman's breast wiped the smile off her face. She could easily imagine the lies this man had told woman after woman in the game of sexual conquest to satisfy his ravenous yet fragile ego. Suddenly she felt hugely impatient, and a wave of rage rose against the futility this man represented and the blather he was churning out for her. She kept her eyes on the salesman's and saw a slight hesitation enter them, as if he'd picked up on her mood shift.

Easy, girl, Kelly reprimanded herself. The lessons came back like muscle memory. From within, she heard her husband's voice: "Impatience is the enemy of a successful con." Kelly disciplined her mind and returned the broad smile to her lips. Time to appeal to this man's ego and his greed.

Kelly moved closer so that she could whisper. "Ali. Would you help me convince my husband . . . ? I would give anything to own that car . . ."

"Of course, madam," Ali replied in a low voice. "That's my specialty."

Kelly edged forward to bring Ali closer to the perfume on her satin skin. She assessed her chances. *Couldn't hurt, might help.* "Is there a *private* office that I could use to call him?"

"Yes, of course, madam." The salesman looked around the dealership, then led her to the manager's office. As he stepped around her, his arm brushed her hip, just above her ass. She could see a few pinpricks of sweat on his forehead, and his breath caught just long enough for her to recognize a sexual reaction. Was he attracted to her or to the potential sale?

"Manager's out to lunch," said Ali as he ushered Kelly into the glass-fronted office. Kelly smiled sweetly. She put her hand on the phone as if to lift the receiver, then hesitated for a moment, conveying, "I'm uncomfortable speaking to my husband in front of a stranger." Ali picked up on the hint and left, obsequiously closing the door.

Again Kelly wondered, was it her or the sale? *Who gives a shit,* she thought, and went to work.

As the salesman oozed back to the display floor, Kelly slid into the manager's chair. She punched in the number for Dial-A-Prayer and sat examining her fingernails while the inspirational message played. When it asked if she wanted another selection, she pressed *1* for *Yes* and heard another prayer. This time she pretended to talk to an extremely thrifty husband who couldn't possibly understand why she'd want to trade her Mercedes two-seater for a 1968 Corniche. She shot a look out to the sales floor. Ali was chatting with another salesman. She waited until he glanced over, and then she held up one finger, smiling brightly, drew her mouth into a pout that was worthy of Libby, and slid herself down in the chair like a four-year-old.

Her other hand shot out and went to work like a Nevada desert rattler. She tried the top drawer first. Locked. *Shit.* The next drawer down was filled with files. She riffled through, keeping her mouth moving and her eyes darting back to the salesman. She felt her heart pounding. *Where the fuck are the checkbooks?* Once again she could hear Gillis's voice in her head: "Corporate checkbooks are usually kept in the lowest drawer."

She saw Ali heading back to the glass office. She jumped up and shouted into the phone, "I gave you two babies, right on schedule, lost all the weight, gave up my career! It's my time now!"

The salesman stopped in his tracks and turned back, his hand nervously patting his hair. Still standing, Kelly slid the last desk drawer open with her knee. She peered into it. *Bingo!* Payroll checkbooks. The bank name imprinted on the checks was American Capital Investment.

"Yes!" she hissed, jubilant. She spotted a different salesman looking at her through the glass. Kelly jumped up and down a little, clutching the phone, smiling as if she'd won the lottery. She sat down in the chair behind the desk, lifted the last book of checks onto her lap, and pretending to dig through her purse, carefully pulled out the last twenty pages. She folded them neatly in her purse and replaced the checkbook. She closed the drawer gently.

With a solemn expression on her face, as if being chastised not to spend her $350,000 all in one place, she listened intently to the daily prayer. She was elated to see her salesman had been dispatched to show another poser a car. The anonymous voice on the phone preached: "You are the Lord's child, and to you he listens. Pray to the Lord, my child, and you shall walk your path through life with the Lord's hand upon your shoulder."

"Amen to that," said Kelly and hung up. She left the office, closing the door carefully behind her, and went up to Ali. She put her hand on his arm.

"I did it! He will be here to see the car in a couple of hours." She looked at her watch. "Enough time for a little shopping."

At this, Ali attached himself to her like a tick, indicating to his colleague to take over responsibility for the other customer. He galloped to his desk at the side of the showroom and brought back his card. Beneath his solicitude, Kelly sensed both an attraction and a repulsion to the woman she was portraying. No matter how upscale the environment of his employment, he knew he could never afford this girl. Right now, Kelly was playing the kind of bitch who sniffed out money the way K-9s sniff out drugs. How could he ever get her interested in him? Kelly could practically hear his thoughts: *If I could get her between the sheets, she'd change her mind. They all do.* Ali touched her hand when he handed her his card, and she pulled away.

"What is your husband's name?"

Kelly glanced over at an old issue of *Fortune* on the display desk. On the cover, Baron Hilton smiled a victorious smile. Kelly couldn't resist the irony. Brand names always go over well with salesmen.

"Hilton . . . Baron Hilton, Junior," she responded.

The man's nostrils flared with recognition, but he betrayed nothing in the rest of his body language. Kelly thanked him, promised she'd be back in a couple of hours, and managed to walk out leisurely, looking up at the palm trees and down at the petunias planted in terracotta tubs in front of the showroom. At last she reached the corner where she'd parked the Corolla. She glanced over her shoulder before unlocking the car, then got in and collapsed into the driver's seat.

But she didn't have time to stop now. She drove to the Beverly Center, a mall on the eastern edge of Beverly Hills, and pulled the car into a corner of the vast parking garage. Working quickly, she slipped off her Donna Karan dress and pulled on a pea green pantsuit, blandly tailored, and low black pumps. The red wig came off and Kelly worked some gray-tinted mousse through her own honey mane, then pulled it all back into a bun, with a center part. She frizzed out the sides with a comb. Large, black-rimmed glasses with thick lenses distorted her eyes. A mouthpiece pushed her upper lip forward.

On her Sidekick, she pulled up the screens she had downloaded at the library in Nogales and scrolled through them until she found the one she wanted. After consulting the map, she pulled away from the Beverly Center and headed north, back into residential Beverly Hills, where wide streets lined with palm trees separated the mansions of the rich and famous.

The house she parked in front of was colonnaded and white, like a Southern plantation. A green half-circle of lawn arced around the front like a Christmas tree skirt. A black wrought-iron fence surrounded the property, softened by a square-trimmed hedge.

Even though she had planned this for lunchtime, Kelly knew it could be a long wait. She settled back in her seat and watched the house.

She had called all the Joan Davises on her list the night before from her favorite pay phone—the one next to a restroom in an old Italian restaurant near her hotel. This particular Joan Davis seemed most promising and, unbelievably, her address was listed. Kelly needed her to be white, between fifty and seventy, and, with luck, a combination of wealthy and greedy.

After waiting an hour and a half, Kelly got her chance. The black gates opened and a white Mercedes sports car nosed out into the wide street. Kelly followed surreptitiously.

The car drove straight to Neiman Marcus and stopped at the valet. When the woman got out, Kelly could hardly believe her luck. This Joan Davis was the epitome of a lady who lunches. Every city had them, but the ones in Beverly Hills were the best in the world.

Kelly waited her turn, then handed her car over to the valet. She pulled a black satchel over her shoulder. The pea-green-suit-and-mousy-bun ensemble would be perfect—dowdy enough not to attract the attention of shoppers or salesclerks, respectable enough to put off the watchdogs.

Neiman Marcus at one o'clock on a weekday was a parade of leisure, of women whose compulsion and means had turned them into professional shoppers. The badge of their uniform was a Louis Vuitton, Prada, Chloé, or Chanel handbag, preferably in black, either a shoulder hugger or a clutch.

Kelly easily spotted her mark, air-kissing a friend by the MAC cosmetics counter. The two were carrying identical black Chanel shoulder bags. To an untrained eye, the women were anywhere between thirty-five and fifty, their bodies slim and toned, their hair blonde and tousled, their skin taut and moisturized. From experience, Kelly knew they were probably well into their fifties—and owed their looks more to their plastic surgeons, dermatologists, and masseuses than to the private yoga instructors and personal chefs they employed. These women accepted their role as trophy wives, doing everything in their power to remain perfect and married to their husbands at least past the decade mark, which legally qualified them as "community property" legitimates.

Keeping an eye on the pair, Kelly located the identical black Chanel purse in the handbag department. The saleslady rang up the purchase and started to wrap it in tissue paper, but Kelly shook her head. The woman shrugged, dropped the purse in a large Neiman Marcus bag, and thanked Kelly for shopping at the store. Kelly thanked her too, and resumed stalking the lady shoppers, wondering what possessed women to become walking free advertisements, flashing a designer's logo on everything they wore. Her marks moved slowly through the store—lingering in the scarf section, fingering some sunglasses.

As she followed them up the escalator to the second floor, Kelly sent up a furtive prayer that they would bypass the shoe department. Shoes could take all afternoon. One of the women veered toward a display of Stuart Weitzman boots but was pulled away, laughingly, by the other. Kelly was close enough to hear her say she "had to splash the porcelain first."

Perfect. Kelly followed the women through the swinging doors and stepped into a stall. She hung her satchel on the hook on the back of the door and then took the purse out of the shopping bag. Swiftly, she pulled a new Chanel lipstick, $500 in crisp bills, a sterling silver compact, and a beautifully embroidered handkerchief out of the satchel—enough goodies to encourage a finders-keepers mentality. She slipped them into the Chanel bag. A few seconds later, she heard the toilets flush and the doors click open. Their private business completed, the women went back to bragging to each other about their conquests.

"I bought that Gucci, wore it once, and returned it. They took it back and put it on the reduced rack. I bought it again two days later for seventy-five percent off."

"I love sticking it to them, don't you?" the other responded.

"What's it to them? They *need* us." The two giggled as if they were still in junior high, enjoying the steal. Kelly thought they probably used this method regularly. She took a deep breath and clicked the Chanel bag shut. She flushed the unused toilet and casually walked out to the sink where the ladies were washing their hands, positioning herself at the sink next to Joan Davis and placing her new bag on the countertop. They had lowered their voices, and Kelly waited for them to lean in to each other, probably to whisper about *her outfit*, or *that hair*, or *those glasses*—whatever it was about her that conformed least to their view of fashion.

Choosing her moment carefully and using the mirror as a guide, Kelly waited until they weren't watching. Then she switched her Chanel bag with the one belonging to Joan Davis. Nonchalantly touching up her lipstick, Kelly slipped the purse into her Neiman Marcus bag while the women left the restroom. After a moment, Kelly left too, and within seconds was lost in the crowd of lunchtime shoppers.

CHAPTER 13

HIGH IN A GLEAMING GLASS TOWER ABOVE
Los Angeles's Century City, Jake's office overlooked a development
of skyscrapers. The streets below were named after celestial bodies:
Avenue of the Stars, Constellation Boulevard, Galaxy Way. Built
on what used to be the back lot of Twentieth Century Fox, Century
City continued in the hopes-and-dreams business, housing law firms
and talent agencies, weight-loss conglomerates, and plastic surgeons'
offices.

Jake's domain, a corner suite, was a maze of fastidious untidi-
ness. Law books were grouped into specific areas on the floor, each
stack representing a particular case. Charts were pinned to the walls,
labeled with the names of different cases. The center of his desk
was stacked with city newspapers from all over the country as well
as international papers from Europe and Asia. The perimeter of his
desk was edged with Redweld expandable pockets barely holding on
to their white and yellow innards. Except for one small section, the

width of one cushion, the couch was covered with law journals and popular magazines ranging from the *Atlantic* to *People*. The guest chairs were covered with clippings and notepads, videotapes, DVDs, and CD-ROMs.

The disorderliness belied Jake's genius but also helped it: His gift was an ability to work on several cases simultaneously, and he needed them all in front of him at once to do that. Even with the noticeable chaos, clutter was not what dominated Jake's office. What defined the room, down to its low lighting, was a wall covered in television screens—nine in all, built into the cherry bookcases. Jake swayed in front of them, blowing into a saxophone, watching the news programs terrify their audience with reports on freakish accidents and random violence, then soothe them with features on food and celebrities.

Bread and circus, thought Jake.

He lost himself for a moment in a blues riff, sliding up and around some sweet sorrow, then swooshing through a little gully of misery. The loss of his best friend had penetrated further and further into his gut. For reasons he couldn't explain, he was protecting his best friend's mistress, Kelly Jensen, aka Natalie St. Clair, by freelancing this investigation instead of turning over everything he'd found out about her to the FBI.

On the flight back from Houston after visiting Cheryl Gordon, he had done a Google search on Michael Young. There were many matches from all over the country, of course, but he shortened the list to those in the Houston area. He was waiting for an expanded search from his investigators. He had a feeling . . . Surely finding Michael Young, the mysterious uncle, would be crucial in learning the truth about Kelly Jensen.

The networks flickered to commercial, and Jake's eyes drifted over to Fox News. A token liberal was trying to make her point in the milliseconds in which her flaccid interlocutor paused for breath.

C-SPAN was showing empty Senate chambers to which Senator Mary Landrieu was passionately describing the need to address the epidemic of autism by removing the mercury, Thimerosal, from the MMR and other vaccines; veterans, the elderly, and children, she explained, were falling prey to the needs and desires of the pharmaceutical industry. MSNBC was running a financial segment. It was more corporate corruption than even Jake could handle. The world was falling apart while corporations were continuing to manipulate the system in endless new underhanded ways.

Jake meandered along a new melody, his sax bleating out a questioning tone. What about Suzanne Garrett? She had always seemed so aloof from Porter's political life and aspirations. Jake would never have guessed she had an interest in—much less designs on—his job. Could someone else be pulling her strings? She had a lot of acquaintances who could benefit greatly by having a senator for a friend.

Out of the corner of his eye, Jake saw a light flashing on his office phone. He stopped blowing, mid-riff, and picked up the receiver.

"Yeah?"

His assistant, Joyce Bloom, said in her Brooklyn accent, "Alana Sutter for you."

Jake waited. The phone clicked.

"Jake?"

"Alana. What've you got?"

"I thought you'd be interested in this. You know how the FBI was looking into three-strikes wackos?"

Jake murmured assent, fiddling with the keys on his sax.

"They've actually found someone, based on the DNA in the hair in Porter's fist. There's an interesting twist, though."

"What's that?"

"It's a woman."

Jake's breath caught, and he laid the sax on his desk. *Kelly.* "They think a woman killed Porter?"

"She hasn't covered her tracks well. Her record is a mile long. Foster child in the Houston area." Cheryl Gordon, with her barely hidden bruises, flashed across Jake's mind.

"Joined the Marines after emancipation." *The Marines?*

"Drifted around after being honorably discharged. Settled in Nevada for a while. Did a little time for her first two felonies: stole a car in Laughlin, and a couple years later tried to rob a bank outside Reno. Disappeared around a year ago." Jake thought of Kelly in her Marilyn Monroe getup. It occurred to him that she could disappear into any persona she wanted to.

"What's her name?" He braced himself, both dreading and longing to hear the answer.

"Stacy Steingart."

Jake jerked. "Say that again?"

"Stacy Steingart."

Natalie St. Clair. Kelly Jensen. Now Stacy Steingart.

"The FBI are working every lead they can and are closing in. They're starting to act like they can smell this one."

"Thanks for the update," said Jake.

"I'll let you know when I have more."

Jake hung up the phone and turned to the windows. The blinds were only partially open, and the Hollywood Hills looked hot and dry, uninviting. Every year he forgot about October's heat. Fire season, the Santa Ana wind season. He put his sax to his lips and blew long and loud. He had assigned several of his own private investigators on this case and had feelers out to other police departments. He pictured Kelly the night he'd seen her perform at Shrake's and tried to imagine her in the military. It was hard, but not impossible. The images were different, but Kelly did emit a strength that could have come from surviving boot camp after a miserable childhood with the Gordons.

Jake became aware of a movement to his right and turned. Joyce held up two Evian bottles with one hand. With the other she removed an earplug from each ear.

"Your next meeting," she shouted. "They've been waiting a half hour."

Jake turned and saw two forgettable men wearing gray Armani suits, both squeezing into the small space on his couch. Joyce handed them each a bottle of water and looked at Jake with a *Well?* expression on her face. An East Coast transplant, she moved faster, talked faster, thought faster, and acted faster than anyone in Los Angeles. Jake often said she was his right arm, and she shared her boss's ease with difficult situations and his intolerance of fools—even when the fool, on occasion, was her boss.

Jake turned back to the TV screens and blew a few more bars. This wasn't good. For the first time in his career, he did not feel the tick of excitement about meeting a new client . . . hearing his or her story . . . assessing past, personality, and penchants while the person spoke. Jake just wanted to stare at the televisions, numb his brain, and blow on his sax. He blew a chromatic scale, ending on E-flat, which he put out in several long, low blasts that sounded like a dying rhinoceros. Then he laid the instrument on his desk and turned to his clients.

When they'd gone thirty minutes later, Jake stuck his head out to Joyce's office and said something he'd never said in his life.

"Cancel the rest of my appointments. I'm going home."

CHAPTER 14

HOLLYWOOD BOULEVARD WAS ALIVE WITH FREAKS. Here, the drug addicts and prostitutes so pluckily portrayed in movies were flesh and blood, servicing their clients with real risks. Even from the balcony of her tenth-floor room at the Roosevelt, Kelly could clearly hear the cacophonous symphony below: Trucks roared and clanked and hissed. Bottles rolled and shattered in the alley. Two drunks yelled at each other, then shuffled off to find abandoned couches to pass out on. Cars accelerated in an incessant roar-hush.

Kelly went back through the glass door, picked up the Chanel bag off the desk, and pulled out the wallet. The driver's license identified her mark as Joan Rice Davis. She was fifty-eight. Not an organ donor. Kelly placed the plastic card on the desk and investigated the rest of the wallet. Credit cards, stamps, $116 in cash. The contents of the purse were unremarkable too: bales of Kleenex in various stages of use, Chanel face powder, some coins, a gold-plated pen, a Filofax, half a roll of Certs, and an unused condom. Kelly put everything except the license back in the purse and placed it on the floor, smiling to herself at the evidence of extramarital activities. Joan Davis was an ordinary upper-middle-class woman with common interests to match a common name. An easy identity to steal.

On a white notepad she began gently making strokes with a ball-point pen, practicing loops and curves, circles and dots. Over and over she wrote Joan Davis's signature—quickly, then slowly; methodically, then rushed. She lost herself in the work until the signature was identical to the one on the ID. Kelly put down the pen and stretched her arms over her head.

It was almost nine o'clock—closing time at the department stores. Kelly dialed Neiman Marcus and asked for the Lost and Found.

"Chanel bag? No. Nothing like that here," reported the clerk. "There's a Prada bag, though." Kelly thanked the man and hung up.

"Mrs. Davis, you are one little piggy," she mumbled. She had chosen exactly the type of woman she needed: wealthy yet still greedy, someone to whom $500 in cash still meant something.

Kelly leaned her neck to each side, stretching it gently, then picked up a magnifying glass. She studied the driver's license, scrutinizing Joan Davis's photograph. Using an eyebrow pencil, she drew feature lines on her own face. Next came her eyes. She shadowed the lids until they were sunken, and grayed in a scoop under each eye. Yellow contact lenses turned her green eyes amber. She widened her nose with flesh-colored putty and erased the line with foundation shading and several delicate swipes of a cosmetic sponge. She selected a blonde wig from her bag and, holding it in one hand, combed it until it was a cloud-like swirl. She sprayed it with hairspray, then pulled it over her hair. The metamorphosis was incredible. She was Joan Davis—almost. Kelly squinted into a magnifying mirror. The chin and cheekbones were all wrong. She would have to pay extra attention to those areas tomorrow.

She pulled the wig off and wiped her face. It was past midnight. Keyed up, she drank a glass of water and opened her own wallet. Behind plastic was a picture of Kevin and Libby, taken at a portrait studio. Kevin had been grumpy that day, so his smile was forced. Libby's face was glowing with toddler glee. Kelly kissed her finger and pressed it to each child's face.

Then, with precise movements, she flicked on CNN and pulled her makeup kit to her lap. From the bottom compartment she lifted a small metallic and plastic device, like the machines stores used to use to manually imprint credit cards. It was a check maker, used by banks to authenticate and route checks. Kelly pulled the stolen Bensenhill Rolls-Royce checks from her suitcase, tore one off, and placed it on the desk. She made the check out to Joan Davis in the amount of $9,989.72 and ran it through the machine, which imprinted the sum and dented the paper to make it unique as a payroll check. She slid the check in an envelope, dropped it into the Chanel bag, and repeated the process twelve times.

She looked up as CNN switched to coverage of Porter's murder. An ugly FBI man in a mustard yellow shirt was talking yet saying nothing, with the excuse that he couldn't comment on an "ongoing investigation." Kelly flicked off the TV, disgusted by the lack of information on the news. She set an alarm she knew she wouldn't need and forced herself to go to bed.

But all she saw when she closed her eyes was the image of Jake Brooks talking with Suzanne Garrett at the funeral, and the flickering eyes of the FBI agents all around. She tried to replace them with an image of Porter, but nothing came, not even the outline of his nose or the shape of his eyes.

"Go away," she whispered.

At last she fell asleep, but Jake Brooks came to her again, this time with a smile, gentle and warm. He reached for her, wrapped her in his arms, and grumbled, "Why did you do it?"

Kelly's eyes flew open. She stared at the ceiling and waited again for sleep.

* * *

The next morning Kelly woke before sunrise to reapply Mrs. Davis to her face and body. Giddy with anticipation, she tried to calm her mind. She turned on CNN and applied another layer of her disguise while waiting through a commercial. When the news came back on, she forced herself to watch. A special logo twirled and wrapped itself around a picture of Porter. MURDER OF AN IDEALIST, read the caption. Solemn synthesizer music played, heavy on the horns. The graphic dissolved to an anchorwoman with black hair. She said a few words, then threw it to a reporter standing in front of the Venetian in Las Vegas.

"Investigators are still baffled by this case and say they haven't ruled out terrorism." The reporter talked a little more and then, suddenly, Jake Brooks was on the screen.

"We're working with the FBI, the ATF, and local law enforcement officials," he said levelly, "to see that whoever committed this heinous crime is . . . that he *or she* is brought to justice." Brooks's gray eyes drilled into the camera.

Kelly sucked in her breath. *He or she?* What did Jake Brooks know?

The broadcast moved on to a financial report, the producers already bored by the slow-to-arrive results in the murder investigation. Kelly snapped off the TV and stood in front of the black screen for a few seconds, her body motionless. Then, with swift, sure movements, she finished her disguise. She angled her face in the mirror. It was a good job. She was unrecognizable as herself. Hurriedly, she pulled on her body padding, pantyhose, skirt, and jacket. The last step was the wig. She smoothed it over her head and used her fingers and a comb to get the curls tousled just right.

She checked her watch. Six forty-six. Then she piled the makeup back into the kit, packed everything in her suitcase, slung her purse over her shoulder, and headed for the door. With her hand on the doorknob, she remembered something. She pulled $100 out of her wallet and left the money on the bedside table for the maid. Then, checking the peephole first, she stepped out the door.

By seven fifteen she was merging the Corolla into the river of cars flowing on the 405 freeway, over the Sepulveda Pass. It was a good time to be maneuvering around Los Angeles, and the cars raced over the hill. Kelly tapped the SCAN button on the radio with a long, pearl-pink fingernail at the end of a hand on which she had painted a few age freckles. Several traffic reports buzzed by in succession. Then a man's deep voice emerged from the chatter.

"When children don't have the chance to bond, when they're bounced from foster home to foster home, they are sure to become sociopaths. It's a fact, people. Seventy-eight-point-eight percent of all U.S. inmates in penitentiaries come from the child welfare system . . ." Kelly reached up to stop the scan, but the voice had already morphed into a bouncy mariachi number.

When she had been with the Gordons, the arrival of the Child Protective Services representative was a monthly ritual. A few days afterwards, there'd be a "drive-by" visit by a social worker. Most of the time the woman would pull into the driveway, walk up to the porch, smile at Kelly, chat with the foster parents, and wave goodbye. During those few days, Kelly was spared from the beatings. The

Gordons told her to make faces at the social worker so she would be classified as "unmanageable" and get the foster family a larger check. Kelly once heard them claim she should be moved up to level 8. When she later saw they were receiving $8,000 a month for her, she knew the change had been made.

Kelly pressed the tuner until she found the talk station again.

". . . adoption. It's the best solution to the black hole that is the foster care system. However, a mentor who commits to be a part of a foster child's life for a long time can change his or her life. It just takes someone who cares . . . Most of these kids develop an acute sense of what makes people tick. They can spot a person's most vulnerable push button and use it to their benefit. They learn to excel as manipulators, and ultimately they can become brilliant criminals.

"This is Dennis Prager. We're talking about child welfare and foster care. Let's go to your calls. From Costa Mesa we have Laura. Go ahead, Laura."

"I grew up in foster homes—twelve, to be exact. In ten of them, I was beaten regularly. Most of it was the dads, but sometimes the moms, too. They knew exactly where to hit me to make sure I didn't bruise. For example, you hit someone on the back of the head, you're not going to see the bump."

"You were beaten in ten of your foster homes, Laura?"

There was a pause on the line, then the caller continued, her voice edged with sarcasm that was concealing her true emotion.

"Yes. I'd say around eight of them really thought about where to hit me. At one house they always punched me in the stomach. The lower stomach—you know, below the waistband on your pants? People don't usually see it there."

"What else happened to you?"

"My parents died in an accident when I was five. The first foster home I was taken to forced me to take tranquilizers so that I would appear to be slow. That way I would be worth more money to them each month. I've figured this out since then, of course."

"How are you managing now, Laura?"

"I was raped when I was fourteen. By my foster father. That's when I ran away. Luckily I was picked up by a policewoman who believed me. She decided to become my mentor. A year and a half later she adopted me. That's really rare, though. Every day—I'm not exaggerating—I think about how lucky I am."

"How old are you now?"

"Twenty-one. I'm at UCLA, majoring in psychology. I hope to go into social work and work with other kids like me someday."

"A success story. We're the—"

"But we—"

"Excuse me. Go ahead, Laura."

"I just wanted to say, to remind you and your listeners, that we're—my story—I'm the exception. Most kids who go through what I did don't end up this way. Most don't get adopted."

"Good point, Laura. Thank you. And thank God for people like your mom. You're an inspiration. Please take care. And call us again sometime. Let us know how you do at UCLA. This is Dennis Prager, talking about how it takes just one person to change the life of a child at risk."

> Gary Gordon pulled the blankets off of Kelly with one hand and grabbed her hair with the other. He dragged her across the floor to the bathroom and smashed her head against the wall over and over again. "You want to be a pig?" His voice was rough and croaky.
>
> Cheryl Gordon turned her face away. Her husband grunted as he kicked Kelly in the stomach.
>
> A touch on her face woke her. Mrs. Gordon was stroking

her hair. Kelly, so alone at that moment, started to reach out
and hug the woman. Mrs. Gordon shook her head and walked
out of the room. Kelly knew that she, too, was afraid of him.

Kelly stopped at a red light and watched a pedestrian cross the street
while a caller expounded upon racial inequity in the foster care system.

She rarely allowed her mind to travel down the road of "what
if," but at this instant she couldn't stop imagining herself growing
up in a home surrounded by a white picket fence and a mom baking
something in the kitchen. In her mind's eye she saw the back of this
woman, the adoptive mom she could have had. The woman turned,
and Kelly saw the face of her own mother.

"Shit." Kelly braked and pulled left on the steering wheel in
time to swerve around a white van. She tore a Kleenex out of the box
and blotted her eyes. She flicked off the radio and willed herself to
stop crying. Years of practice had made her able to turn off the tears
just as she would a faucet. She calmed herself by focusing on her driving, turning onto the 101 West and merging with the cars on the other
freeway. Then she took a deep breath and concentrated on becoming
her character.

One of the things she had always noticed when she wore the disguise of an older woman was the anonymity. Drivers did not glance
over; pedestrians barely made way on the sidewalk for her. Each of
her identities had its own difficulties, and each had its particular
charms. The charm of Joan Davis was being able to work almost
entirely unnoticed. The difficulty was not being cut the special slack
that went along with the twin powers of beauty and youth.

Kelly parked in a space in the far corner of the lot of a branch of
American Capital Investment Bank, the bank she had researched at
the library in Arizona. Watching the entrance, she waited. When the
bank opened at eight, she held back until another customer entered,
then slipped out of her car.

As Kelly entered the bank, she noted where the security cameras and guards were positioned. A plainclothes guard stood near the door, scribbling on a deposit slip. Kelly stood in line and waited her turn.

"Next?"

Kelly moved toward the teller's window. She plunked her big bag down on the counter.

"I'd like to cash this check. You see, it's my grandson's birthday tomorrow. I'm going to put some money in his cake."

If there was one way to repulse a bank officer's attention, it was to talk about grandchildren—a habit older people tended to be addicted to.

The teller responded in an ultra-bored voice. "Your identification and account number, please, madam."

"Here it is." Under the bulletproof glass, Kelly slid the Bensenhill Rolls-Royce check, Joan Davis's driver's license, and a strip of paper with a string of numbers on it. Her nerves were steel. The teller was probably in his early twenties, but he looked about seventeen, with pebbly skin, freshly shaved, on his jaw and cheeks. Comb marks raked through his gelled hair. His black-and-red tie reflected the overhead lighting. A nameplate identified him as Eduardo Munoz. He glanced at the driver's license and then up at Kelly, barely lifting his eyelids. He typed some numbers into his terminal, then stamped a receipt.

Eduardo looked up slowly and stared at Kelly for the first time.

"You shouldn't be carrying so much cash, Mrs. Davis. A cashier's check is safer."

Kelly started coughing, a hack that sounded deep and dangerously chronic. She watched Eduardo's reaction. She could practically see his mind weighing the options: the amount of cash this lady wanted versus the hassle he'd have to go through if she got sick, or worse, needed his help during the transaction. Quickly, Eduardo opened his cash drawer and started counting out the $9,989.72. To Kelly, his movements were in slow motion, his fingers meticulously double-checking each bill. Finally, he clinked the pennies on the stack and shuffled the money into an envelope. He was about to slide it under the window when he stopped and peered at her again.

"A cashier's check really would be safer."

Kelly coughed again, pulling another couple of tissues out of her purse.

"That's kind of you, dear. I prefer cash. Checks are just pieces of paper, after all." She smiled thinly and cleared her throat. Eduardo pushed the envelope through. "Have a lovely day," croaked Kelly, and she walked stiffly out of the bank.

She jumped into her car and fired the engine, reviewing the route in her mind. As she pushed along the wide boulevard south through the San Fernando Valley, a smile—her first genuine one in several days—spread across her face. Funny how technology works: All you need is one account in one branch, and you can cash as many checks as you wish in any other branch, and no one will ever know.

Kelly repeated the routine at the Encino branch with no trouble. At the Burbank branch, she approached the teller with another Bensenhill payroll check in her hand.

"I'm moving from Santa Monica to Burbank. Everyone wants to be paid in cash nowadays . . ."

Kelly started the coughing routine again. The teller checked the computer, glanced at the official corporate stamp on the payroll check, and stamped and initialed it. Then she looked up at Kelly, as if wondering what this lady did at a Rolls-Royce showroom.

Kelly picked up on the unspoken curiosity and responded, talking a mile a minute.

"This week was a killer. I had to organize fifteen cars to be shipped all over the country—can you imagine? To top it all off, I'm moving to Burbank, of all places . . . Excuse me, it's cold in here. Could you turn down the air-conditioning?" She coughed some more.

The perfect touch. Now the teller looked as if she just wanted to get rid of Kelly as fast as possible.

"Just one minute, madam." The teller's long fingers swiftly counted out the money. The envelope slid under the window and Kelly took it, silently voicing her relief.

I'm outta here.

Steeling her nerves, Kelly walked out to her car and drove away from the bank. Double-checking the map in her memory, she headed for the 101 freeway again. The next bank was in Santa Monica, then two on the west side, two in Beverly Hills, one downtown, and one in Manhattan Beach.

It took her the rest of the afternoon, but Kelly posing as Mrs. Joan Davis repeated the routine until she had more than $120,000 in cash. She had known the plan would work, but even so, she was relieved that it had gone so well. The banks wouldn't cross-reference the withdrawals until Monday. And she also happened to know that the Joan Davis accounts got special treatment.

* * *

Gathered in the small, glass-enclosed manager's office was the entire sales staff of Bensenhill Rolls-Royce. Ali was sweating, and everyone had the downcast eyes and slumped shoulders of salesmen everywhere who are being ripped a new one.

"Which of you mother*fuckers* sold a car to someone named Joan Davis?"

The men fell over each other denying it. They looked suspiciously at one another, ready to pounce on one of their own.

"Well, she's cashing our checks at the bank. None of you losers will admit to knowing someone named Joan Davis?"

The men shook their heads.

"Well, somehow she got in here and got the checks. Did anyone let a customer in this office in the last day or two?"

Ali felt the blood drain out of his face.

* * *

Just a few blocks away, at the headquarters of American Capital Investment Bank, the president, Todd Gillis, received a phone call. His usually impassive face turned molten with anger.

"The Joan Davis account? Hit? How much?"

He heard the answer and hurled the phone down. In a corner of the room, slumped back in an armchair, his bodyguard, Brigante, sparked to life.

Todd Gillis kept his voice measured. "The Joan Davis accounts have been hit. Go get her."

* * *

Finished with her last bank, Kelly drove slowly through the quiet residential neighborhoods of the small seaside community of Manhattan Beach. She parked on a narrow street called Maple Drive and studied the maps she had saved in her smartphone. There was another bank, in Long Beach, that she hadn't planned on hitting. She glanced at the clock on the dashboard. It was earlier than she had expected. If she hurried, she could just make it. But immediately she decided against it. She had done enough for one day.

Through her window Kelly saw two towheaded children running in their front yard. The scene was like a television commercial:

the late-afternoon light glazing everything gold, the boy teasing the girl, the girl chasing the boy. The door of the house opened, and a young mom called the kids inside. Kelly knew it was time to head back, call Holly, and reunite with her own kids. But as she glanced in her rearview mirror, she froze.

Behind her loomed a hulking black SUV with darkened windows. It hadn't been there when she'd parked. She held her breath. No one got in or out.

As she pulled away from the curb, the SUV moved forward. Kelly accelerated, ready to duck down a parallel street and, hopefully, lose it in an alley. But the black behemoth kept up.

With a sickening realization, Kelly knew what she had to do, where her safest place would be. Gripping the steering wheel, she pushed the car onto the 405 South, toward Long Beach and its branch of American Capital Investment Bank.

* * *

When she finally arrived at the bank, there was a long line. Agitated, Kelly examined the face of everyone in the bank from behind her sunglasses. She had lost the black SUV on the freeway, but she knew that she could trust no one. At last the teller called her to the window.

"I'd like to cash this, please."

The teller glanced at her. Kelly could see her impatience, could tell she was counting the minutes until the bank would be closing.

Kelly passed over one of the payroll checks and the Joan Davis driver's license. "It's my grandson's birthday tomorrow," she explained, struggling through her fatigue to get Joan Davis's voice right.

The clerk smiled noncommittally and examined the check. She turned and typed something on the computer. "That's strange," she muttered.

"What? What is it?" asked Kelly, allowing Joan Davis to sound a little irritated.

"This will only take a moment, ma'am. I just need to check something with my manager."

"I've got to have that money for tomorrow!" cried Kelly. "I'm going to put it in my grandson's cake!" She broke into her hacking cough.

"I'll be right back," said the teller politely. Unseen by Kelly, she pressed the security button under the counter with her knee, then stepped away from her window, taking the check and the driver's license with her.

CHAPTER 15

BUCKLEY'S TAVERN COULD NOT HAVE BEEN A MORE perfect choice. On a dire stretch of Pico Boulevard in West LA, under the shadow of the 405 overpass, the bar was windowless, airless, and brainless. The steak sandwich was gristly and fatty; the bread all but evaporated when Jake dunked it in the dishwaterbrown *jus*. A half-empty beer bottle stood next to a glass. Jake stared into his food.

"Jesus, Jake."

Jake glanced up at Joyce, irritated.

"What?"

"Where the fuck *are* you?" Joyce leaned across the table and rapped Jake on the forehead with her knuckles.

"In Buckley's Tavern," Jake grunted, even more irritated.

There was a moment of silence. Jake swigged his beer and watched the bartender serve a man who had gray hair that grew down to his shoulders. Joyce finished off her bourbon on the rocks.

"Goddamnit, Jake," Joyce said finally. "You snap out of this or I'm quitting. I mean it."

Jake had been hitting a wall the likes of which he had never known before. He needed to find Kelly Jensen but had no idea how. Porter's grave was still fresh, but already Suzanne had launched herself into a full-fledged campaign for the Senate seat. She had retained Alana Sutter but hadn't asked for Jake's help. Jake's emotions were so fried that he hadn't even been able to get enraged over not being asked to do a job he didn't want to do in the first place.

Joyce had never seen Jake this detached. She was the only person in his life who could have suggested he was edging toward depression, but even she hesitated to call his attention to it.

"You can't quit."

"Try me."

"You'd miss my winning personality too much." Jake tried to smile charmingly, but it came out flat.

"You want my honest opinion?" asked Joyce.

"When haven't I?"

Joyce hesitated. "I know you're grieving—"

Jake exhaled, exasperated. "Cut the crap. That's not like you."

"I *am* cutting the crap," Joyce said defensively. "I think you need to give this a rest for a few days. Get your bearings back." She hesitated again. "Maybe back off on the freelancing."

Jake's glare cut through the dank tavern air.

Joyce pressed ahead. "Porter would have wanted you to do what you do best. Not play detective, going off on your own like this."

Jake did not like to admit it, but he knew she was right. He sighed.

"Who is she, Jake? Who's this girl you're looking for?"

Jake opened his mouth to answer, then shut it again. Just then, his BlackBerry jittered sideways across the table. Raising an eyebrow at Joyce, he flipped it open.

"Brooks."

Joyce watched Jake's face change. Whatever he had started to open up about was closing over again.

"You're sure? Surrounded?"

Jake listened for another second. "I'm coming. I can get a chopper."

He flicked his phone shut and stood up. "They've got her surrounded," said Jake over his shoulder. "I've got to get there for the arrest."

*   *   *

Kelly watched the teller go into a back room and shut the door. She tried to act nonchalant, but her eyes ticked nervously around the lobby. She heard a helicopter fly overhead. After about three minutes, Kelly's heart started to pound. What was taking so long? She remembered another one of Todd's phrases from her past: "Timing is everything. An unusual delay means you walk!" Kelly snapped Joan Davis's purse shut and took a step backward. Suddenly she felt a hand on her arm.

"Ma'am," said a man's voice, "could you come with me, please?"

"What is this about?" demanded Kelly, staying in character to keep the liquid fear out of her stomach. The man gripped her arm and led her into the back room. The bank teller was gone. "Please, sit." Kelly obeyed, and the man sat opposite her. He looked directly into her eyes.

Then Kelly bolted for the open door, reaching her hand into her purse.

* * *

Jake leaped out of the helicopter and ran, crouching, toward the police car. An officer knelt behind each of the four open car doors. The SWAT team had surrounded Steingart's desert compound, which consisted of a main house and some crumbling outbuildings. As directed, the FBI agents and other uniformed men held their fire. Two more helicopters thudded overhead, hovering.

Suddenly a voice came out of nowhere—a woman's voice, amplified.

"I . . . AM . . . THE PROTECTOR!"

The captain lifted a megaphone. "Stacy Steingart, you are surrounded. Come out with your hands on your head. There's no other way out of this. Come out here and talk with us. You have nowhere to go."

"You don't scare me with your institutional protocol. I'm an American-made killer. You made me."

Jake's heart thumped. What was she talking about?

"You force us out of our homes, lock up our parents in prisons, institutionalize us from birth until death. You call it 'protective custody.' But instead of protecting, you abuse and neglect us. You turn us into criminals. When we turn eighteen, you throw us out to the streets with no education or choices and nothing in front of us but drugs, prostitution, and crime. We're jailed for the smallest offenses and institutionalized permanently. Our only alternative is to join your military and be trained as killers. Guess which one I chose?"

A blaze of bullets ripped out through a window. Jake dropped behind the left rear bumper of the squad car. The SWAT team shrank against the walls of the building.

"Steingart! Put down your weapon and come out with your hands on your head," barked the captain again through his megaphone. "That's an *order.*"

Steingart's sound system crackled. She was laughing. The sound carried well, as though she had outfitted her home with a public address system, complete with microphone and speakers. As though Steingart had planned this standoff.

"YOU were my parents!" she shouted. "I was a 'ward of the state.' YOU are the state. Every one of you. Senators and congressmen most of all. You are my parents. If there was really a justice system, instead of the multimillion-dollar child welfare system you benefit from, you would all be liable for abuse and neglect."

Jake held his breath. Kelly/Stacy was strangely eloquent. But the weirdest thing of all was that she could have been reading from a speech made by Porter Garrett. Why had she killed him, when he had supported her, believed the same things?

Jake saw the lead cop nod at the men behind him and duck through the front door.

"Steingart, you're leaving us no choice," warned the captain on the megaphone. "Come out now."

Steingart ignored him. "Porter Garrett was no different from any other politician. He was worse. Using us to try to win the election."

Jake tasted bile, hearing her name his friend with such hatred in her voice.

More bullets rained out. One of the cops clasped his arm and fell. The SWAT team rushed into the house.

"Call me a suicide bomber!" yelled Steingart one more time. The words fell into the dust. Silence. Then a massive explosion of firepower. Jake hunkered down flat against the desert sand as the bullets sprayed.

When he thought about it all later, it seemed remarkable that more people hadn't gotten hurt. Especially after he walked in with the captain, once the SWAT team gave the all-clear, and saw that Steingart had been blasted back against a wall, spread-eagled, blood pouring from several bullet holes in her torso. An arm had been partially ripped off and hung uselessly at her side. Her black hair was wild and greasy and clotted with blood and tissue. Dead eyes stared, unseeing, from her face. What was left of her body showed her to be compact and wiry, small and strong.

Jake stared and stared and then turned away, shaking his head in an effort not to react publicly in some grotesque way—vomiting, crying, laughing. In the horror of the scene, the explosive mixture of adrenaline and testosterone, he felt a profound relief.

It wasn't Kelly. Stacy Steingart was someone else.

He acknowledged to himself that he was also feeling something new just as viscerally. Jake had seen his share of death over the course of his career, but he had never felt such an *electrifying satisfaction* about it. *Bloodlust* was the only word for it—this woman's blood in exchange for Porter's. Jake picked his way around blood and tissue on the floor and went outside. Somewhere nearby a dog barked incessantly. Jake lit a cigarette to calm his shaking hands and watched police officers swarming around the scene. He was sure that after a few days of conducting fingerprint, DNA, and tissue analyses, the investigation would incontrovertibly identify Stacy Steingart as Congressman Garrett's killer.

* * *

The security guard at the bank grabbed Kelly as she ran by and forced her to the floor. He twisted her arms behind her back.

"Amazing." He shook his head as he studied her face, which looked nothing like the image he held before him. "Here's your ID." He lifted the document in front of her eyes. "And here's mine." He flashed his badge.

Kelly knew her number was up but remained cool and calm. "Excuse me. Where is the restroom?"

"For you? In jail!" the man crowed. "You have the right to remain silent . . ."

Years ago, her husband had prepared her for this moment. "Freeze!" he had taught her. "Freeze every emotion that could give you away!"

Instantly, Kelly numbed her emotions—the way she used to do during the interminable practice runs. "No matter what they ask you, you say nothing. No emotions, no voice . . . Remember, you are a *first-time* offender, so the law is on your side!"

Kelly didn't resist. She simply closed her eyes and let herself be dragged into the police car.

* * *

Jake flicked his cigarette into the sand and ground it out with his heel. His phone vibrated.

"It's me," said Joyce, her voice odd. "They got your Natalie St. Clair/Kelly Jensen et cetera, et cetera. She's in Long Beach." Jake's stomach tightened. There was a crackling on the line, dead air cut through with static.

"Jake?"

"I'm listening."

"Does that mean anything to you?"

Jake hesitated. "Yes," he admitted.

"She's the girl?"

"Yes."

"Well, there's something strange."

Jake tapped another cigarette out of the pack. He was buzzing, still pumped from the shoot-out and knowing that Porter's killer had paid with her life. "What?"

"She says that you're her lawyer. She says you represent her."

PART TWO

CHAPTER 16

KELLY KEPT HER EYES SHUT TIGHT. SHE FELT HER
wig being pulled off. Someone washed her face clean. She was a toy,
a rubber doll. Her time in custody so far had been no worse than any
other in her large catalogue of dark moments. None of it mattered.
She didn't mind being pushed and pulled. Her senses were shut off.
She felt nothing.

A social worker came to her cell and asked if she had children,
but she refused to talk. Then she was led to a room. She heard a man
asking her to open her eyes. Obediently, she opened her eyes and
stared blankly into midair. The small room she was in had a table and
a few other chairs like the one she was seated on. The two windows
on the far wall were covered with beige, wide-slatted blinds. Acoustic
tile like rotted-out cheese lined the ceiling. A dry-erase board hung
on the brick wall opposite the windows.

"What's a beautiful girl like you doing robbing banks?" the man
asked.

Kelly found a place on the ceiling where a leak had left a coffee-colored stain. She followed its contours with her eyes and said nothing.

"You need the money?" he pressed. "Couldn't get enough 'dates'?"

Kelly bit the inside of her cheek and continued staring at the ceiling stain. She wasn't about to rise to any of his bait.

"By the way, you look great as a blonde," he said.

She remained silent.

"How about some coffee? Cigarette?" The detective leaned against the wall, his arms crossed over his white button-down shirt and bright tie. Kelly could detect the effort he was making to warm his voice. She didn't answer, and still didn't look at him.

"My name's Hal Weaver. Care to introduce yourself?"

Silence.

Weaver sighed. He paced to the door, acted like he was reconsidering, came back, and sat in a chair across the table from her.

"Look, you're obviously part of an interstate check fraud ring. That's a *federal* offense. You can get some very hard time for that."

Kelly didn't move a muscle.

Weaver spread his hands on the table and started drumming his fingers. The gray vinyl–covered pasteboard was battered. His thumb found a triangular gouge and started worrying it.

"Listen, I cleared the room and shut off the tape. This is off the record . . . We can be useful to each other." Kelly heard his smile—the creak of cheekbones, the suction of his lips pulling off his teeth. She pressed her hands, prayer-style, between her knees and sat up straight in her chair. Her head was cocked at an angle and her eyes followed the arc into the air, as though she were a Renaissance cherub peering innocently up toward heaven. The pose or the silence finally got to Weaver.

He put his face a half inch from Kelly's. She felt his angry exhale, smelled stale coffee and grease on his breath. But her mask didn't crack.

"This is your last chance. Don't you have anything to say?"

Calmly, Kelly spoke. "I have the right to remain silent."

Weaver slammed his palms on the table. Kelly didn't flinch. For the first time, she looked him in the eye. He glared at her, then turned away and leaned against the windowsill. She saw his jaw, in profile, grinding violently.

The door opened and another man—small, pale, and thin, wearing a white T-shirt under a black leather sports jacket—sauntered in. He walked around the room, inspecting Kelly from every angle.

"Have we met before?" he asked.

Kelly said nothing.

The small man continued to stare at her.

She looked blankly at the ceiling stain.

"Mind-boggling," the man muttered. He jerked his head at Weaver. "Got something interesting to show you out here."

As the men left the room, Kelly exhaled soundlessly through her mouth. She was determined to give them nothing. Jake Brooks would get her message. The one thing that threatened to crack her was not having a daily report about Kevin and Libby. She had talked to Holly hurriedly after her arrest, and now she just had to believe they were still in the trailer park, lying low.

Kelly was alone in the room for about fifteen minutes. She could hear cars swishing by outside the windows. A faint hum, the pitch of a computer or refrigerator, issued from somewhere out of sight. Some footsteps passed by the door and faded away.

When Weaver and the other man came back into the room, they could barely contain their excitement, the looks on their faces like first-grade boys who had just learned how to make underarm farts.

Weaver spoke first. "I'm going to introduce myself again. I'm Hal Weaver. And you are . . . Natalie St. Clair. Right?"

Kelly started a mantra in her head: *All's well that ends well . . . Stay in control . . . Less is more . . . Silence is golden.*

"Your fingerprints have shown up in some very interesting places," put in the other man.

All's well that ends well . . . Stay in control . . . Less is more . . . Silence is golden.

The men had unraveled quite a bit of her life, and they laid it out before her in their badgering way. She was silent through all of it, even when they placed her at the scene of Porter's murder and tried to imply she'd had something to do with it; even when they asked about her foster parents and running away. When they unspooled her life all the way back to her mother's murder and her father's life sentence, the inside of her cheek bled from biting it. But still she refused to speak.

Finally, the smaller man just looked at Weaver and shook his head. Weaver stomped to the door and shouted into the hall.

"Would someone get that fucking lawyer in here?"

* * *

The Long Beach police headquarters, like every other urban police station, was a human sewer, backed up and oozing people into every available corner and surface. The lobby was a cacophony of shouts, threats, pleas, and cell phone jingles. An orderly line of yuppies reporting minor thefts snaked along a side wall, cautiously eyeing the drug addicts, hookers, and carjackers.

This was Jake's domain, however, and he strode in, nodding to the officers on duty.

Weaver and his partner were hovering like frustrated hawks on either side of Kelly when Jake pushed open the door into the room. All three of them wheeled around, the small man looking surprised, Weaver pissed off. Kelly's face was unexpectedly calm, like a Madonna in a painting, with just a curl of seductive irony around her mouth. Even after nearly a week of thinking about practically nothing or no one *but* Kelly Jensen, Jake was utterly unprepared for the beauty he had first been attracted to during her act at Shrake's.

One hand still on the doorknob, he pounded on the inside of the door with his other hand, as if he had forgotten to knock before entering. "Hello, gentlemen," he said, not looking at the men. He purposely addressed the wall above and behind them. "There I was in my office, waiting for my client to call, when I had a premonition . . . And guess what that premonition was?" He held up his hand, halting a reply from either one of them. "It was that you guys, just like this brick wall, were going to be deaf, dumb, and blind to the law."

Weaver growled. "Enough of your fuckin' games, Brooks. We've got her nailed."

Jake snorted. "What you need is a dose of reality, my friend." He looked over at Kelly. She raised an eyebrow about a millimeter. He smiled at her.

"Gave up the song-and-dance act, eh?"

Kelly responded almost in a monotone. "I pulled a groin muscle."

Her voice was buttery smooth, like caramel sauce. Jake was momentarily caught off guard. The two detectives seemed surprised to hear her speak too.

"A groin muscle?"

Kelly winked at him. "Not my own."

Weaver's patience was running on empty. He whirled on Jake.

"This isn't Monopoly. She's not landing on Chance or Community Service. She is going straight to Jail. There's enough evidence against her to lock her up for a long time."

Jake patted Weaver on the back. "I'm looking forward to hearing more about your crack investigative work at the preliminary hearing."

He turned and offered Kelly his hand to help her out of the chair. "Your arraignment's in forty-five minutes at the courthouse. We can walk from here. You don't have to think about these bozos anymore until the trial."

While relieved to be out of the interrogation room, Kelly was still on high alert. She could smell his adrenaline pumping at the challenge she presented. She had instinctively known Jake Brooks would come to her defense and would never believe her to be Porter's murderer; she'd sensed his trust in Porter's judgment. But she didn't yet know how much she could trust him.

On the walk to the courthouse, Jake pressed Kelly for the answers to three questions: Where were her kids? What was her registered address? Where was she working? If they had to post bail, so be it, but it would be a hell of a lot easier if he could get her released on her own recognizance. Unfortunately, her answers—as terse and non-elaborative as his questions—didn't make OR very feasible. Kids? She couldn't say without putting them in danger. Address? Las Vegas. Job? Unemployed. Jake felt like a racehorse being loaded into the gate by a green jockey. This was pathetic. This was impossible. This was fucking exciting!

Kelly glanced at Jake and saw his nostrils flare. Was he enjoying this? She tried to picture him with Porter. Jake's features were so much sharper, more chiseled than Porter's softer face. Porter trusted Jake, she reminded herself. Could she?

Jake tried again. "You *do* have kids?"

Kelly knew he needed the information. "Two. A boy and a girl."

"Where are they?"

"I told you. I can't say."

"With you? Nearby? Out of state?"

"They're being properly cared for, okay? Child Protective Services would be fine with it."

"With friends? Their father?"

Jake saw Kelly's face shut down. He eased up.

"What are you doing in LA?"

"I had—business here."

Jake squinted. This case was going to be a bitch.

If the police station was a human sewer, the courthouse was the sewage processing plant, a factory for separating, sorting, and organizing the components of the manure. All the characters from the police station were present, but here in the courthouse they were calmer, quieter, and more anxious.

Kelly and Jake waited their turn, watching the accused approach the judge. Some had attorneys with them; many more did not. The scene was familiar to both of them: Kelly from her hours spent in juvenile courts as a foster child and Jake from his many years in front of the bench. They both sized up the judge, a muscular young Asian man with very short, almost shaved hair and with robes that looked a size too small. The prosecuting attorney barely noticed them. When Kelly's name was called, they stood together and Jake followed her to the front of the courtroom.

As he had done with every case before hers, the judge cleared his throat, put on his glasses, and read the charges.

"Case number Five-oh-three-oh-four-dash-eight-nine. Natalie St. Clair, aka Kelly Jensen, you are charged with counterfeiting, identity theft, and conspiracy to defraud. How do you plead?"

"Not guilty, your honor."

"Not guilty," said Jake at the same time. Kelly glanced at him.

The judge looked up and took off his glasses. That he recognized Jake was clear. Whether that was going to help was not.

"Unless either of you objects, I'm going to enter a trial date of six weeks from now." He looked first at Kelly, who nodded. He looked at Jake.

"No objection, your honor."

Kelly sensed a movement to her right and saw the bailiff approach the judge and place the file folder he was carrying in front of him. On went the glasses again, as the judge studied the papers inside. Kelly swiveled around. The small detective who had interrogated her was standing in the back of the courtroom. He grinned at her and touched two fingers to the side of his forehead in salute.

Under her breath she said to Jake, "That detective is here."

"I know," murmured Jake. "I was expecting this."

"Your honor," Jake said loudly. "I'd like to request that my client be released on her own recognizance."

The judge kept reading. After ten seconds that felt like ten minutes, he looked up. Off came the glasses. He tapped the file folder with them.

"On what grounds? I see some convincing arguments here that she's a flight risk."

"Your honor . . ." Jake paused and thought quickly. Her kids were in Nevada. Her last job was in Nevada. Her last address was in Nevada. She *was* a flight risk. "My client has left her job in Nevada and is relocating to Southern California."

"What's she planning to do here?"

"She's in the entertainment industry. Actress. She has letters of interest from agents. I can get you copies . . ."

The judge shook his head. "I'd rather see lottery tickets."

Jake quickly thought through Kelly's story, looking for a way out.

"Your honor, I'd like to request supervised own recognizance," he said. "My supervision."

Kelly turned to him with a look impossible to decipher—part shock, part outrage, part gratitude.

The judge locked eyes with Jake. "You've got your reputation to consider, counselor."

"My point exactly," answered Jake.

It occurred to the judge that at last CNN might stop calling to book Jake Brooks as the ever-ready legal talking head with verbal diarrhea. He glanced crossly at the detective against the back wall with intense dislike. He had met that weasel before, and they hadn't made fast friends. He wasn't going to be bullied in his own courtroom. He looked at Kelly and grimaced.

"Ms. St. Clair, you are released into the supervised recognizance of Mr. Jake Brooks. Trial date is in six weeks. The bailiff will give you the time and courtroom. Next case!"

Kelly kept her mouth shut all the way out of the courtroom. Once they were outside in the fresh air, she took a breath and laid into Jake. "You're my babysitter now?"

Jake grinned and nodded.

"It's better than more jail," he said simply. "And you'd have had to give up a lot more information to post bail."

Kelly went silent and followed Jake to his car. He opened the passenger door for her. A saxophone case was on the backseat, belted in like a child. A substitute for a woman, perhaps? Kelly peered back at Jake.

"Allow me to introduce you to my addiction—my sax," he said, still grinning. He leaned close. "So, just how many of these little capers have you pulled?"

Kelly raised her chin and shook her head.

"Where are you taking me?"

"My office."

Kelly stepped into his car, flashing her legs.

The kind of legs I wouldn't mind climbing over, thought Jake. And then, *Jesus, what are you thinking? Your best friend's girlfriend? Your dead best friend's girlfriend?*

"Hey, Brooks!"

Jake spun around. Standing there were Brewer and Norris, the FBI agents he had alienated the morning of Porter's murder. The ones who were taking credit for bringing Stacy Steingart to justice.

Norris sneered. "Hey, Natalie St. Clair. Why'd you do it? Why'd you murder your boyfriend?"

Brewer couldn't resist needling her too. "Your fingerprints are all over Garrett's room. We know you were there."

Kelly's eyes slid from the FBI agents to Jake, judging the danger. But she didn't have time to figure out an escape before Jake stepped between her and the men.

"Are you losers auditioning for a TV show? You think my client's going to break down here in the parking lot? Let me remind you that you just *shot and killed* the woman you said was Congressman Garrett's killer. So unless you're going to arrest my client and tell the world you just killed the wrong person—on the government's behalf—you can fuck off."

Jake's voice was calm, but his muscles were tensed, like an animal about to spring.

"What about the prints?" pressed Brewer.

"You asshole," muttered Jake. "What *about* the prints? My client could have been in that room at any time, for any reason. She could be a professional gambler, a hooker, or a maid. Maybe she's a drag queen. Or maybe she's just an innocent bystander that you are in the process of harassing." He shut Kelly's door firmly and strode to the driver's door. "See you around," he said, smiling. Then he fired the engine and roared away.

They drove in silence. Kelly leaned against the passenger door, looking out the window. She glanced at Jake. He was an arrogant prick—an intelligent, good-looking, arrogant prick. She remembered how infuriating he'd been the night he'd seen her perform at Shrake's. She guessed they had involuntarily stung each other that first night at the club. Porter had never gotten under her skin like that, never pushed her buttons. He had always been stable and yielding. But there was something more pressing she had to think about now.

"They found Porter's killer?" she whispered.

Jake glanced at her as he steered the car left on a green arrow. "Have you heard any news since yesterday?"

Kelly's breath caught. She shook her head.

"No?" Jake flicked on the radio. It was tuned to an all-news station. They listened to a traffic report and two ads. Then the announcer came on.

> **Updating our lead story at this hour, FBI sources are saying the woman killed when a SWAT team stormed a compound in northern Nevada late yesterday had sent threatening letters to Congressman Porter Garrett. Drafts of six different letters were found during a search of the buildings. The late congressman was found dead in a Las Vegas hotel room last week . . .**

Kelly felt Jake looking for her reaction. She turned to him.

"Is this the truth?"

Jake laughed. "It's on the news. It must be true, right?" He turned serious when he saw her face. "The DNA did it. Porter was found— did you know this?—with some hairs clenched in his fist and skin under his nails. They checked out with the suspect. Stacy Steingart."

Kelly's face froze.

"You know," Jake said, "I think he grabbed those hairs on

purpose. Even in death his first thought was to protect someone and lead the detectives to the killer." Jake looked over at Kelly. "To protect a lover, maybe?" He let his voice trail off.

Kelly shook her head to keep the tears from forming in her eyes.

* * *

Settled a little while later in his office, Jake sat on top of his desk, his feet resting on the arms of his chair. Kelly sat in a nearby chair, below him. She knew he was trying to make her uncomfortable enough to get a rise out of her. When she didn't recoil, he started talking.

"They've set up attorney-client privilege and the confidentiality laws for a reason. You can talk to me."

Kelly smirked. "But I haven't hired you . . . yet."

Jake hopped off his desk and handed her the phone. "Go ahead. Find yourself a better lawyer."

Kelly picked up her Sidekick and pushed some buttons. Jake looked surprised, but listened attentively while she talked.

"Hello, Hol—Yes. Is everything okay there?" Kelly exhaled, and a sheet of tension slid from her body. "No. I'm still going to be a while. Thanks. Don't worry. Thanks for everything. Give them my love. I'm fine, really . . . Thank you. Thanks, Hol. I don't know, another week, maybe two? Oh, thank you. I couldn't do it without you guys . . . I love you too." She hung up.

Jake teased, "An accomplice?"

Kelly smiled at him charmingly. "You could call it that."

She leaned back in the leather chair, suddenly sapped of every bit of energy. She kept her eyes closed. "I've got to go somewhere and sleep a little."

"Where are you planning on going?"

"Hotel?"

"You can't."

Kelly's eyes flew open. "Excuse me, but who died and made you my prison guard?"

There was an awkward pause as they both realized what she had said. Kelly faltered for a moment and opened her mouth to speak. Nothing came out except a sighing sound, something like the *aaahhhh* of someone who's been punched in the stomach.

Jake wanted to fold her up in his arms, but he reached out and cupped her shoulder instead. It was trembling. Her chin dropped to her chest.

"I'm fine," she insisted.

Gently he said, "Actually, the judge made me your temporary guardian. Not your prison guard."

Kelly was silent.

"It's going to be okay," Jake whispered.

"Why do people always say that?" She looked up at him.

"I'm going to help you make it okay."

He said it with such conviction, Kelly almost believed him. "Porter trusted you."

"Yes, he did."

"He trusted me, too."

"Apparently." Jake tried to say it matter-of-factly, without bitterness. He nearly succeeded.

"There aren't many people I can trust."

"I promise I'm not going to let you down."

Like a child surrendering to an adult, Kelly gave in. "Where do I go now?"

"My place. I have a nice guest room. A bath for you. A cup of tea, or something stronger if you like. Then you talk—you tell me everything."

Kelly grimaced. "I think I can handle the nice room, the bath, and the tea."

CHAPTER 17

UNLIKE HIS OFFICE, JAKE'S APARTMENT WAS sterile, like the rooms in a furniture catalogue, probably because he never spent any time there and the housekeeper came twice a week. It was in a high-rise on Ocean Avenue in Santa Monica, overlooking the Pacific. The pier with its Ferris wheel and roller coaster was down the vista to the left. Up to the right was Malibu.

Kelly came out to the living room wrapped in a white terry-cloth robe with FOUR SEASONS BANGKOK stitched in a gold circle over her left breast. Her hair was noticeably darker when wet. She was barefoot, and Jake saw that her toenails were unpainted—unlike most of the pedicured feet that normally traipsed through his apartment on the ends of the long legs of his girlfriends.

"Looks like you get around." Kelly shrugged at the insignia on the robe.

"God only knows how some of these things end up in my closet.

Where's that one from?" Jake leaned forward for a closer look, and Kelly held her hair out of the way.

"Bangkok. Don't remember it at all."

"I'll bet you don't," Kelly said.

"Name your poison," said Jake.

"Mineral water. Followed by a very dry martini."

While Jake fixed the drinks, Kelly put her feet up on the coffee table next to three books. They were stacked, their spines aligned. *Arch*, *Wood*, and *Stone*, read the titles. A green glass bowl of smooth black rocks sat near the stack. Jake handed Kelly her drinks, and she drank the water quickly, in just a few gulps.

After a while she picked up the martini and sipped it silently for a while, watching Jake poke at the fireplace. He seemed like less of an arrogant asshole kneeling there, fumbling with the wood chips and the poker. He had changed out of his suit into jeans and a dark green T-shirt. He looked younger. Kelly tried to picture Porter and Jake hanging out together in law school. The more she tried to picture them as friends in their professional lives, though, the harder it was to imagine. Porter was so vibrant and open, such an optimist and a dreamer. He could talk for hours, literally, about laws he was writing, about history, geopolitics, parenting and love, movies and food. He dealt with everyone openly and generously.

Kelly eyed Jake's toned back muscles beneath his T-shirt. He was so much more direct, so much more intense. He seemed to be constantly analyzing, processing, predicting—his superfine mind noticing and filing everything away for future use. Yet here he was, too hasty to build a long-lasting fire. Kelly watched him until she couldn't stand it a minute more.

"Let me do that." Kelly tightened the belt on her robe as she walked over to arrange the kindling on the fireplace grate. The flame caught instantly, and she crossed the room and climbed back onto the couch. Jake sat across from her diagonally in a club chair and grinned.

"You may be shocked to hear I was never a Boy Scout."

"Porter was."

"Not just a Boy Scout. An Eagle Scout, and didn't we all know it." Jake picked up his shot glass, threw back the tequila, and tapped the glass on the palm of his hand, surprised at the surge of anger he felt. Mad at Porter? Jealous?

Jake had decided not to pussyfoot around with Kelly. There was something unnerving and electrifying in the way she went from vulnerable to seductive to calculating, just by tilting her head. He had been with many sensual women in his life—actresses, models, call girls—but never had he met a woman so attuned to every cadence of conversation, every plane of a room, every molecule of scent. It was as if she already knew all his secrets and predilections, and each of her comments and movements was calibrated with that information in mind. He had to watch his step. But it was pissing him off.

"Is that where you want to start? With Porter?" He tried to keep his voice neutral, and failed.

"Porter and I were in love. That's all there is to it."

"It didn't bother you that he had a wife and kids? It doesn't seem that you had the best intention for his family." He hit hard, waiting for her reaction.

"Best intention for his family," she repeated. Her mind wandered to the first time Porter had brushed his hand against hers, that morning at the Vegas coffee shop as he reached out to pick up Kevin's toy that had fallen at his feet. She could never forget the puzzled look they'd each had in their eyes at the recognition of an unavoidable magnetic force. Their hands touching and his gentle voice had warmed her spine.

"I got it," he'd said. They had both laughed as he joined her and her kids, as naturally as though they belonged together. Somehow she had known that love was inevitable.

"His wife didn't love him, and I made sure I didn't come between him and his kids. I was satisfied with the crumbs. It wasn't ownership. It was about love."

Jake knew that could have been true. He decided to retract. "Did you get a chance to say good-bye?"

Kelly paused and then spoke carefully. "You know, I was with him right before he died. He didn't know it was a final good-bye, but I left town that night after I saw him. I was on my way to Mexico—with the kids. When I heard the news, about his, um, death, I came to LA instead. I had to be at the funeral. It was all too sudden."

Jake looked confused. "You were there? I didn't see—"

Kelly reached out and grabbed his right hand in hers. "We all need friends, Mr. Brooks," she said in a voice tinged with a British accent.

Jake jerked away as though her hands were a hot frying pan.

"That was *you*?" He gaped at her. Throwing on a Marilyn Monroe costume was one thing. Completely embodying an elderly woman at a funeral was something else. Maybe she *was* more dangerous than she appeared. Maybe . . .

Jake became aware of an earthy chime, like a marimba. Kelly was laughing. Her mouth was wide open and she was drawing in breath like a drowning person, laughing without restraint.

"That was really you?" he asked again, unable to keep from smiling.

"I'm a woman of a few unusual talents, Mr. Brooks."

"Obviously."

"Your face . . . that was priceless. You want my whole story? Get me another drink and I'll feed your curiosity."

"I'm your lawyer, you know," Jake said pedantically. "Everything you tell me is privileged."

"Yes, I realize that, counselor. And I'm sure by now you've figured out how deeply I trust attorneys." She laughed some more. Like everything else about her, it was sexy and unique, but tinged with sadness and a tone of danger.

Jake mixed another martini, and Kelly started at the beginning. She told him about finding her mother dead in a pool of blood. How she hated her father for taking her mother away. How, after he was imprisoned, she ended up in foster care. She described the many homes she was passed around to and finally described life at the Gordons'. She skipped the details of the abuse, instead lifting her robe above her knee to show him a couple of scars that told the story for her. She told him about all the times she ran away, sometimes making it for a few days or more on the street before she was brought back. The severe beatings when she was returned.

Kelly paused and looked at Jake. On his face was a mixture of anger and compassion. She smiled.

"You might need another drink for this next part."

Jake shook his head. "I'm okay," he said. "Lay it on me."

"Well, it started like any love story. I was living on the street in Houston. It was ideal for a teenager, actually. Lots of freedom, interesting people to meet, things to learn—like how to get dinner out of a garbage can and how to steal tips from the change jar at Starbucks. Then Prince Charming arrived one day and swept me off my feet. Bought me a steak-and-baked-potato dinner, even went all out and treated me to a milk shake. I went home with him that day, married him on the day I turned sixteen—he wrote eighteen on the marriage license. Oh, and we had the best honeymoon. He raped and sodomized me, then kept it up until I left him. We have two kids. That's about it. You know most of the rest."

Kelly looked at Jake provocatively. He tried to smile, intrigued and saddened by her sarcasm. He decided to get off the subject for a while.

"Tell me about this bank scam. Why were you impersonating an old lady?"

Kelly exhaled. "It seemed like a good idea at the time."

"I really enjoy playing Who's Fooling Who with you, but the truth at this point might be a little more effective."

"The truth?" she repeated, chuckling as if the idea of it was funny.

Jake nodded.

"Okay, I'll back up a little, run through the story once more. I ran away from my husband about two years ago and set myself up in Vegas. Not long after I got there, I met Porter. The last thing I planned on was falling in love with anyone, especially a public figure. Like I told you, on the night Porter was . . . on the night Porter died, I was leaving town again. I had everything packed and ready to go after the show. I had to escape the fishbowl. It was getting too dangerous for both him and me. My plan was to see Porter one last time after I performed, and then leave with the kids in the middle of the night."

"You put on a hell of a show that night."

Kelly smiled. "Some of the customers can be such arrogant voyeurs," she said. "It's as if they think they can strip and penetrate you right on the stage."

Jake grinned, pleased he had made such an impression and that she was smiling about it. He nodded for her to continue.

"I was headed for Mexico."

"Because . . . ?"

"My vulture of a husband had found me. He was coming after me—us—again. I can always sense when he's on my tail."

Jake clenched his jaw. "Your life is filled with vicious animals, voyeurs, human vultures, assholes, rats . . . Go on."

"I was taking the kids to Mexico. I was hoping that this time we could just disappear. I was already in Arizona when I heard that

Porter had been killed. It was such a shock. I had said good-bye, but it wasn't supposed to end like that."

"What do you mean?"

"After the show I went to see Porter at his hotel. Like I said, I had planned it to be our last time together, but he didn't know that."

"You didn't tell him you were running away?"

"It was for his own good. I didn't want him to lose momentum in the last few weeks of the campaign. But I did tell him we needed to stop seeing each other. He was pissed about that. We got into a huge fight, actually. We both said things we didn't mean, words that stay stuck in your gut forever . . . When I found out he'd been killed, I had to go to his funeral. I had to say a proper good-bye."

Jake thought again of Kelly's extraordinary disguise at the funeral. There had been no doubt in his mind that Lydia Haines had been an old woman. She had even . . . Jake suddenly wondered about her coughing fit and her abrupt departure from the gravesite.

"What was the coughing performance at the funeral, then? A little acting authenticity thrown in?" Jake smiled.

Kelly stared at him coolly. "Surprise, surprise. My husband, Mr. Midas Touch, was at the funeral. I had no idea he would be there. I had to get out of there fast, before his gold fingers put a lock on me. You actually helped shield me from him."

Jake's mind raced. Her husband? At Porter's funeral? He thought back to the scene. Who was standing there? With a jolt, Jake saw the picture in his head. Randy Carlen, the hotel mogul. He had been standing between Jake and Suzanne. Kelly had had to pass him as the old lady Lydia Haines, maybe even shake his hand. When Kelly had started coughing, Jake had put an arm around her, inadvertently hiding her from view, and put her in a taxi.

"Randy Carlen is your ex-husband?"

"No," Kelly said levelly. "Todd Gillis is."

CHAPTER 18

JAKE'S MIND WAS SWIMMING. "TODD GILLIS?" HE asked. "The banker?"

Kelly nodded, a regretful smile playing at the corners of her mouth. "He is a master of protecting his image. To the world he is the most elegant, well-spoken, charity-supporting . . ." She trailed off. "All of it is an act. Believe me, if I could change the past, I would choose being homeless. At least the homeless can sometimes sleep at night. Most of them don't live in fear for their children's lives. He got me pregnant while I was still petrified of ending up on the streets and back in foster care."

Kelly sipped the rest of her martini and put the glass on the table. She was playing for time. Porter was the only other person she had told the whole story to, and now he was dead. She regarded Jake carefully before plunging ahead.

"Sexual abuse was just for sport. Fulfilling all his fucked-up fantasies," she began. "He also used me another way. It was actually quite simple."

Kelly explained the whole scam. How, using his access as CEO of the bank, Gillis would scour the records for accounts that were inactive but contained more than $20,000. At the time, most of his banks were in Texas, a state full of women rich enough and cagey enough to hide a couple of grand in a few different banks for a rainy day. Once he found the account he wanted, Gillis would force Kelly to impersonate the holder of the account. In disguise, and always working on a Friday or Saturday, Kelly would deposit forged corporate checks into a number of strangers' accounts and invest in a stock for which Gillis had inside information. Early Monday morning, the stock would rise, and later that day, Kelly, still disguised as the account holder, would withdraw the amount of the corporate check plus the profit wired into the account from the sale of the rising stock, all in cash. The amount in the strangers' accounts remained the same. Sometimes Gillis made Kelly deposit as many as fifteen different corporate checks in a day, amounting to as much as $130,000. But he was always careful to keep the amount of each check under $10,000. Anything more had to be reported to the IRS.

"There were no traces. Mostly, the women I impersonated never knew about the deposits and withdrawals. When the discrepancies in the statements were noticed—two weeks later, if at all—the women claimed, rightly, that they had never bought or sold the stocks. The amount in each case was too insignificant to raise a stink about. They chalked it up to a banking error, and no one looked at the overall scheme."

"Why did you always work on Fridays or Saturdays?"

"The banks never count deposits made on Friday afternoon or Saturday. They always leave the accounting until Monday."

"So Gillis was making money from both sides."

"That's right. It was pretty smart, actually. He was getting the money out of the accounts and—from the bank's end—the thefts were insured by the federal government. And it was virtually fool-proof, since he owned the bank."

"But it all depended on your disguises, on your skill at—"

"Well, I did say I have a few unusual talents."

The truth was that it had been the easiest thing Kelly had ever done—to become someone else. Slipping into another's skin, another's world, became something she looked forward to. Even as she deplored what Gillis forced her to do, a part of her had loved the chance to leave her real self far behind.

"In reality, most people hardly ever visit their bankers anymore, with ATMs, online banking, phone banking, different branches, and a revolving door of clerks and tellers," Kelly continued. "Identities center around names, mothers' maiden names, and Social Security numbers. But there is always the chance that someone makes it a habit to visit their money."

"Did you tell Porter all this?"

Kelly gave Jake a look that said, *Why would I tell you something I didn't tell him?* Jake's irritation rose.

"I mean, what was Porter's take on it?"

"He wanted to find a way of bringing Todd to justice, of course. You know how much he believed in the ultimate good of the justice system. He told me I'd come out fine in a trial. I had clearly been manipulated from a young age. Todd had used me like Patty Hearst had been used. I wanted to believe what Porter was saying, but I knew his undying belief in the justice system—I mean, it's beautiful idealism, but it's also a bit of a Pollyanna syndrome. I knew Todd too well—I *know* him too well. He'd pay off witnesses for the prosecution and end up looking like Gandhi. Todd knows how to use the law in his favor, how to twist and turn facts. And after all, I was a runaway, a 'problem child,' which would fit the portrait of a criminal. So I convinced Porter to drop it. Which only made him more and more fixated on finding ways to protect me."

"Like?"

"He wanted to set up bank accounts for me, find ways of supporting me financially. But I know I'll only really be safe when Todd decides that I'm not worth the trouble."

Jake was reeling with this new image of Gillis, but he wasn't really surprised. He'd seen too much of the brutality of humans to be surprised by anything. He stared at Kelly. She seemed to have softened with the drinks. Or maybe it was the result of being able to open up to another person. She gazed ruminatively into the fire.

"Ever since I can remember, I've always prayed for freedom. Personal. Emotional. The kind of freedom that allows you to go to sleep at night without waking up in a cold sweat. In my mind I always heard a voice saying, 'Be careful what you wish for.' But I always wished anyway. Every fountain with a coin in it, every evening star, even blowing on dandelions. But the voice was right. Instead of freedom, when I married Todd I fell into a prison that made my life with the Gordons look like a safe haven."

"So why didn't you run away sooner? On your own, before you had children—or even with your kids?"

Kelly snorted. "At first I was underage, remember, and could have been returned to a new foster home, if not the Gordons. Eventually I did leave him. But I had to wait until my son and daughter were independently mobile. I couldn't be weighed down by strollers and diapers. I had to move fast in a world where everybody's owned by the warden."

"Somewhere in that story is battered woman syndrome."

"Perhaps, but the law is used at will by people with money and power. It's like Clinton said about his act of indulgence: I did it just because I could. People like Todd Gillis do it because they can. And that's the worst crime of all." Kelly paused, lost in thought for a moment, before continuing.

"No, that's not the worst crime of all. The worst crime of all is when you amass so much wealth and power that everyone around you has to abide by your will. And hearing 'no' becomes a huge offense. An offense that warrants retaliation through unthinkable actions, the kind of things that a man like Todd, this kind of husband, justifies in his own mind."

"You're talking about the Bill Gates level of wealth?"

"Well, yes, but this is not only about the top one percent. It's about every woman whose survival depends on her husband's will, especially when she has children, like me."

"Aren't you just justifying your actions?"

"No. It's your family law system that got me here. Think about it. Imagine being married to someone as ruthless as but much smarter than O. J. Simpson, more in control. Would you be willing to leave him with your children fifty percent of the time? Isn't that how Nicole got murdered? By having to remain connected to him because of their children? That's why so many women have to go outside the law. They do it every day. From the richest to the poorest."

"I'm glad you have such a high regard for men."

"Well, the only man I totally trusted—until Porter—murdered my mother."

"Welcome to the mind-set of a hooker."

"Is that your best defense? Being glib?"

"Well, prostitutes are the extreme personification of male loathing. Is that better?"

"This is not about loathing or about some general theory about women, about mothers. This is about the reality of *this* mother protecting her children."

"So how did Porter fit into that scenario? Or should I say 'fit into your arms'?"

"You, better than anyone, should know that Porter is an exception to the rule. That's why you supported him as a leader, right?" Kelly's eyes filled with tears. "He was a one-off."

Jake looked away. He had to hide his emotion from Kelly. But it was what he wanted to hear. She had really loved Porter. They sat in silence. No woman had ever spoken to him like that, with such depth of honest thought and emotion. She had an understanding of life that, in his experience, most people didn't have. The degree of superficiality in his own thought processes became all too apparent.

Jake broke the silence. "You're right. Crime is born in abuse, and abuse is born in apathy."

"And apathy is born in ego and selfishness. That's who Todd Gillis is, a narcissist."

"Okay, then. Put his mistreatment of you to the side for a moment. Gillis uses a dependent society outcast—no offense—"

"None taken. And I think he had others, too. I don't think I was the only one."

"Okay, dependent society *outcasts* to rip off his own banks. He keeps the money, gets paid back by the government, and buys more branches. It's so transparent, how come nobody squeals? How's that possible?"

"Nobody below him squeals because they're terrified of him. In the name of loyalty, he makes sure he has something on every one of them. Nobody above him squeals because they're all making money off him. Plus, he's one of the top donors to both political parties. He's got access to lawmakers and the White House. Real power.

"He's backed the candidates in the last four presidential campaigns. Hardly ever in big fund-raising events—always in a one-on-one meeting, so it's never publicized. Plus, every one of his employees writes a check for the maximum $2,000 donation."

"What does Gillis want from you now?"

Kelly started to answer, then laughed. "I don't know. I really don't understand why he bothers to haunt me. I know he couldn't care less about me or the kids. It could just be his need to win, or it could be more. I honestly don't know." But deep down, Kelly did know: Gillis wanted her, plain and simple. He wanted to own her, to dominate her. And Gillis always got what he wanted. He never allowed himself to lose.

"Did you tell the cops about him?"

Kelly shook her head. "Of course not. I remained silent." She grinned.

Jake grinned back. "What about Joan Davis?"

"Like I've been saying, when you own the money, you can make up the rules. Believe it or not, Joan Davis is one of the most common names in America. In every American Capital bank there is a Joan Davis account, a dummy account Gillis set up.

"When an in-transit or nonexistent cash is recorded in more than one Joan Davis account, the bank pays on an un-funded deposit. For example, a check is deposited into an account. Before the cash is collected by the bank, a check is written against the same account and deposited into another Joan Davis account, or cashed. The increased use of wire transfers allows this type of scheme to be perpetuated very quickly.

"Another advantage is his ability to manufacture check makers—machines that indent and authenticate checks to route money into accounts. I stole one when I left him. I knew he'd never shut those Joan Davis accounts down. He needs them too much, and he'd know it was like leaving an open trap for me to fall into. That's why

I had to work fast the day I decided to access them." Kelly took a breath.

"But he caught up with me. Which is when I decided to introduce myself to you."

Jake did a double take. "You got arrested on purpose?"

Kelly smiled in her Mona Lisa way. "Did it get your attention? Let's just say it seemed quicker than going through your secretary."

Jake could only shake his head. Everywhere he turned, Kelly was a step ahead of him. He wasn't used to it.

"I have an idea," he started. "The FBI has Porter's murder wrapped up. But even after they officially exonerate you, they're going to be looking to nail you for the bank heists you pulled. But they have been known to look the other way if a person can help reel in a bigger fish."

Kelly shook her head vigorously. "No government agency would ever lean on him. He's in thick with the White House, governors, senators . . . all the money grabbers that lead our country."

"No, no, hear me out," Jake said. "The new fund-raising reform laws make him less significant. The feds could spin it any way they want."

"No way. Todd has access to all the bank's employee-donors. He makes it up to them in bonuses. He's like a union—what he says goes. Todd Gillis is the smartest man I've ever met. Trust me, he's armed with thousands of employees who can write checks."

The smartest man she's ever met? Jake was irritated to find himself stung. *What about Porter? What about* me?

As though she had read his mind, Kelly corrected herself. "Perhaps 'smartest' is the wrong word. 'Cleverest' or 'most conniving' is more accurate." Kelly paused. "We've got to come up with something else."

"What's his motive? What's the conflict? And what's his plan?"

Jake drew a line across the top of a legal pad and looked at Kelly. "Let's start with three columns: What do we know? What does Gillis know about your situation? And what is stacked up against you at the moment?"

"You mean out here on my own recognizance? Or should I say, yours?"

"You've positioned it well, haven't you?" Jake smiled knowingly. He tossed his legal pad on the table, threw the pen on top of it. "I think we've done enough for one night. Do you like the blues?"

Kelly frowned. "Are you asking me out?"

"Do you ever give a guy a break?"

Kelly glared.

"Of course I'm not asking you out," said Jake. "You're a client. I'm just talking a little R&R."

"I hope you don't mean risk and retribution."

Jake smiled. *This woman's mind . . .*

"A little risqué music, maybe."

Kelly blew some air out through her mouth. "I don't know—"

"Come on."

"Todd could have someone out there watching us . . . Something weird happened to my car right after I left Vegas."

Jake waited for her to continue.

"Someone moved it while we were eating in a diner. Left a note on the front seat with a smiley face on it. Just the type of thing Todd would do. Or have someone do for him."

"But nothing's happened since?"

"He's playing cat and mouse. Like I said, someone was on my tail just before the Long Beach bank job."

Jake thought for a moment. "I have an idea."

* * *

An hour later, Jake drove alone out of his building. He circled a few blocks, then pulled behind a gas station. A man in an overcoat and baseball cap got into the passenger's seat. Jake peeled off and headed toward the freeway.

"See, that worked," he said, excited by the deception. Kelly smiled indulgently and pulled the cap down over her eyes. They drove silently over the Sepulveda Pass. Ventura Boulevard, a disconcerting combination of suburban chain stores and hip boutiques, took them to Studio City. Jake pulled into a gravel parking lot next to what looked like a shack. The skinny black guy at the door jerked his chin up at Jake. Jake gave him a ten-dollar bill and held the door open for Kelly.

A blast of music rushed over her as she stepped inside the crumbling club. A man was moaning his way through "Welfare Woman" in a gravelly voice that had seen more pain than Kelly had. She was surprised to see that the singer was white, wearing black Ray-Bans.

"Bryan Lee," murmured Jake. "From New Orleans. Blind."

Kelly nodded, taking off the cap, and followed Jake to a corner table by the stage. From the waiter's body language, she figured it was Jake's regular table. She was intrigued but didn't want to show it. A couple of people waved as Jake passed. Before they'd even sat down, a waiter brought a bottle of Chianti and poured it. Kelly watched the waiters weaving around the tightly packed tables, slapping down huge, stuffed baked potatoes in time with the music. Before long, two plates descended on their table, each potato nearly the size of a loaf of bread. Steam curled up from the fluffy, mashed insides, glistening with cheese and vegetables.

"Is that a prop?" Kelly peered. "Grown and bred for Holly-weird?"

"Eat it. You need it."

They ate and drank and listened to the music. Jake stole a couple of looks at Kelly. Even wearing almost no makeup, and with her hair in a ponytail, she pulled every eye in the place. She moved like a cat: nonchalant yet purposeful, disdainful yet aware of others' eyes. But at this place, no one looked for long. It was one of the reasons Jake loved it.

When the song ended, one of the musicians jumped off the stage and shuffled over to Jake. He handed him a saxophone, inviting him onstage. Jake feigned resistance, then followed the man up toward the band. When he closed his eyes and started playing, his music was enticing and emotional, his fingers touching the instrument with the precision of a surgeon and the sensitivity of a lover.

As Jake drowned deeper and deeper into the music, Kelly felt herself becoming numb. She gulped her wine.

The crowd clapped and whistled.

"Ladies and gentlemen, let's hear it for the down and dirty sound of Jake Brooks!"

After the set, Jake came back to the table. He was flying.

"Where'd you learn to play like that?" Kelly asked politely.

Jake started his humble routine. "Picked it up, here and there. Lessons since I was six. Minor in music. Hours of playing-to-stave-off-loneliness masquerading as practice."

"You're lucky you have a place to do it."

Jake stared demurely into his wineglass but caught the tone in Kelly's voice. Was she sober? Her eyes had moved out of the solar system; her face looked dead.

"Let's get out of here." Jake took Kelly's hand and led her out of the smoke.

They drove up the hill at Griffith Park, barely uttering a word. Jake pulled over and they sat in the car, the glowing spider's web of the lights of Los Angeles spread out below them.

"You know, the DA is nothing more than a politician. The cops are just snooping coyotes in heat. We'll find a way out."

Kelly snorted. "Nice people you play with."

"The accused are entitled to a competent defense. I defend them with every skill I have—charming the jury, playing the media. I'm a performing media litigator."

"So you publicly manipulate loopholes in the law?"

"If that's the way you want to look at it. Another way to see it is this: The shades of gray are infinite. Some people are most comfortable with black or white. The law is really much more suited to gray. That's where I belong, in the gray zone. I actually like to settle cases behind closed doors or outside the courtroom whenever possible. There's more truth there, really, than in the black and white."

Kelly watched his face in the moonlight. The side of his nose bore a small scar she hadn't noticed earlier. He looked like a cowboy, or someone else who'd seen a lot—an old soul. There was no question: Women must find him magnetic.

"I have a feeling Todd had something to do with Porter's death."

His eyes lingered on her throat. "Then help me get him."

"You can help with the law. But only I can get Gillis."

Jake squeezed his teeth together. She was maddening. Normally he would start badgering at this point, pouring on the logic and the drama. But he knew it wouldn't work with her.

"Okay, Kelly—or Natalie—or whoever you are." He saw her eyes flick minutely. "I'll help you as much as you'll let me."

"Fine. That'll work."

Jake noted that she didn't thank him. They drove home without speaking, trying to talk themselves out of feeling a new intimacy in their silence.

CHAPTER 19

FRANK PULLED HIS JEEP ONTO THE GRAVEL
outside his small ranch house. Exhausted from a busy night tending
bar, he approached the front door sluggishly, fishing for his keys, feeling each one with his fingers before selecting the right one.

He started to put it into the lock when he realized the outdoor
light was on. Was Holly back with the kids? Nah—when she'd taken
Kelly's kids in the RV north, she said they'd be gone for a while. You
could disappear just about completely in the anonymous trailer parks
of the Nevada desert. Still, Frank felt a twinge of hope: Maybe things
had worked out for Kelly. Maybe Holly had come back. Even after
just one night, he missed her. All their years together, and she still
turned him on like no other woman ever could. He loved his wife
and desired her at the same time. He knew that this was rare, that it
made him a lucky man.

He sensed more than heard the crunch of gravel behind him.
Whipping around, he saw, illuminated by the porch light, the huge

form of a man. One of the man's hands was hidden in his jacket. Frank knew better than to move.

"Mr. Gillis is waiting for you inside."

Frank stood still while the bodyguard pushed open the front door and motioned him in. He forced down the rage and fear that surged simultaneously in his stomach.

Gillis was just as Frank had pictured him, just as Kelly had described. Manicured, handsome, as alert and strong and dangerous as a mountain lion. He was sitting on Frank and Holly's comfortable old couch, arms outstretched across the back of it, one ankle draped over his knee. He held up a syringe.

"Where are my kids, Frank?" he asked, his voice completely relaxed.

Frank remained silent, judging his options.

Gillis jiggled the syringe. "Poor kid. Maybe someday they'll come up with better ways of getting the insulin. Kelly"—he said the name with a sneer—"tries so hard. But it can't be easy to be a working mom with a diabetic kid."

Gillis tossed the syringe on the coffee table. "Still, you'd think she could get her on a pump." He leveled his cold eyes at Frank. "You going to tell me where they are?"

Frank was actively forcing back his desire to tackle Gillis and pummel him. Tending bar, he had met thousands of people. The toughest and loudest were disarmed by his silent glare, by the suggestion of menace rather than the practice of it. But Gillis was completely different. It was as though he was beyond fear. Frank had seen that only once—in a man high on PCP who had sailed over the bar in a fit of rage and smashed him against the mirrored backsplash. It had taken the help of two bouncers to subdue the man, whose wild eyes never did succumb to force, even when, battered and bloodied, he was loaded into a cop car.

Gillis's eyes were clear, and he was obviously sober. Frank ran the options through his brain. Lie? Tell Gillis that Holly took the kids to California? Stay silent? How much did Gillis already know? No wonder Kelly always looked like a hunted animal. That's exactly what she was.

Gillis was watching Frank's face. Suddenly he started chuckling. He shook his head as though admonishing a child.

"Decisions, decisions," he smirked. "Well, I'll tell you what I'm going to do. I'm not going to kill the messenger. You, that is. You just tell Holly to take good care of my kids." He stood up abruptly and growled the next words right in Frank's face. "And tell Kelly that I'll slap her with kidnapping charges if she even breathes the wrong way. I can put her behind bars in less than a day."

Gillis turned on his heel and took two steps toward the door, then seemed to change his mind. He flicked his fingers, and before Frank knew what hit him, he'd slumped to the ground, too groggy to resist when the bodyguard who stood behind him took him by the neck and dragged him to the Mercedes at the curb.

CHAPTER 20

SOMEONE WAS POUNDING ON THE DOOR.

Where am I? What time is it? Kelly scrambled out of bed. She glanced around the black room for a clock. Four thirty. Jake's apartment.

"Kelly? Kelly?" Jake hammered again on the door.

"What?" Kelly blinked as she opened the guest room door and looked into the lit hallway.

"Everything's okay, but—"

"Oh, God, what's happened?"

"Everything's—"

"Don't . . . just tell me."

Jake stood in the hall a little way back from the doorway, like a kid selling magazine subscriptions. "They roughed up your friend Frank. He didn't tell them anything. But they had his cell phone and forced him to call Holly. They found the RV at a trailer park north of Vegas."

"Oh, God . . ."

Jake held up a hand. "It's alright. Two of them broke in, scared the shit out of Holly. They had Libby in the car when my guys got there."

"Your guys?"

"I posted a couple of retired cops out there."

"How did you even—"

"I traced your call to Holly . . . At my office yesterday. I called the phone company."

"Are Kevin and Libby—"

"They're fine. We've moved them to a safer place, the home of a friend of mine—"

"Where?"

"Remember the Platinum Widow?"

Kelly sighed a tiny sigh of relief. "The bombshell that had her husband killed."

"No one will look for them there. She's got a huge compound in Lake Tahoe. The place is so wired, a butterfly couldn't enter without getting someone's attention. Really. They're safe. I promise."

Kelly whirled back toward the bedroom. "They must be terrified. I've got to get there." She grabbed her duffel bag, which was luckily left intact when Jake's guys retrieved it and the Rent-A-Wreck she'd left behind. She made several passes around the room, looking for things to put in it. She turned to Jake, her face streaked with anxiety.

"What do I do?"

Her helplessness punched him in the stomach.

"Give them a couple of hours. It's still the middle of the night. You can call them in the morning. You can't go there. It could be seen as evidence of flight. We can't bring them here—too dangerous. I promise, they are completely safe. And as soon as we can get you all back together, we will."

She closed her eyes, pained. "I need a cup of coffee." She strode toward the doorway but, before she could cross it, fell into Jake's arms instead. He was ready for her.

Pick her up, put her on the bed, lie next to her, and hold her in your arms. Jake tried to get his body to follow his heart, but it wouldn't. Instead, he tightened his arms around Kelly and stood there awkwardly until her trembling subsided.

As quickly as it had come up, it was over. She pushed him away. "Thanks," she said curtly.

He followed her into his blue-and-white kitchen, where she started opening and closing doors.

"You ever cook in here?" she said abruptly.

"Does microwaving count?"

"Coffee?"

"Look in there."

Kelly opened a cabinet and pulled out a grinder and filters. She found beans in a jar on the counter. Jake was watching her, mindlessly chatting as his eyes took in the way her body moved around the kitchen.

"I defended this kid once," he said, sitting down. "He was only eighteen. No priors, up for grand theft. The DA was saying that they got him dead bang. But I wasn't about to surrender him to the Nazis. By the time I was through with the psychobabble, the jury was ready to send the DA up for life for being so abusive to this poor, misunderstood child. So, what does the kid do when the trial is over? He walks right out to the parking lot and steals the judge's car!"

Kelly laughed. It sounded like a puppy yip. "I hope these eggs are fresh," she said, cracking one into a bowl.

As Jake talked, Kelly made cheese omelets. She found hash browns in the freezer and thawed them. She assigned Jake to wash berries and cut some fruit. It helped to have a project. They maneuvered politely around each other—and around the five-hundred-pound gorilla in the room, the undeniable strings that had begun to attach them.

Kelly served the food at the kitchen table, with paper napkins. They chewed silently. Finally, she lowered her fork.

"Why did you choose crime as your life's work?"

Jake swallowed. "Why did you?"

Kelly speared a blueberry on each tine of her fork. "Let me put it this way: It was a means to an *end*. You?" She curled her lips around the four blueberries.

Jake watched them disappear into her mouth, thinking, *She could be the female version of me.* "I've thought about that a lot," he said, "especially lately, with everything that's happened." They paused to let their mutual guilt and grief over Porter register. Jake drew a series of parallel lines on his place mat with his knife. Then he tapped the point on his thumb and responded, "I'm a storyteller. The criminal is my antihero, and the jury is my audience. That's what I've come up with after twenty years."

Kelly looked away. *What a showman*, she thought. It must be intoxicating to outsmart the prosecution. A lawyer with a conscience who isn't afraid to look under rocks to discover someone's real motivation.

She thought of Gillis and his lawyers, who used to make fun of the justice system—especially the judges who went by the book and hardly ever used their own "judgment" to set precedent in the law. Gillis called them all whores: "Anyone who is dependent on a public election is a whore, whether it's a judge or a politician. By virtue of depending on contributions, they are bound to sell out." Her own opinion of lawyers had been formed at a young age, bolstered by year after year of the justice system failing her, not believing what she said simply because she was a child. Was it possible Jake was an exception?

She looked up at him. "But it's not a story. You're dealing with people's lives."

"I don't get attached. Believe me, my clients don't want to be my pals either. Once the case is over, even when the outcome is good, the client never looks back. I'm a reminder of bad times."

"So you do what you've got to do."

"Basically."

"Why me, then?"

Jake put the knife down. "I have a hunch that you can help me. As you put it, you're a means to an end."

A means to an end? Kelly drained her coffee. It was the last sip—gritty and cold. She stared at him over the lip of her cup.

"I need to know the truth about Porter's murder," said Jake. "You're the only one who can help me there."

Kelly eyed him suspiciously.

Jake felt his heart say, *Take her hand and tell her it really will be okay.* Instead, he leaned back and crossed his arms. His voice came out sterner than he intended. "When I cross legal paths with a suspect, I always say, 'If you are going to run, now is the time. Otherwise, I'll hold your hand through hell—and it *will* be hell.'"

"Jake." Kelly's voice broke, and she sighed impatiently before starting again. "I can't go to jail. My kids . . . I'm all they've got."

"Come on, Kelly, you've known the risks all along—"

"Yes, but there was no other choice, with Gillis out there. I need him behind bars. This case, handled well, will make him the target. Once the floodgates open, lots of people may talk, even if he put the fear of death in them . . . Tell me if I'm going to end up doing time. If there's even a remote chance . . . I'll take my kids and run."

Jake knew what it was like to be cornered. But he also knew when to press his advantage. "Last night you said you were going to do this your way. Now are you ready to do it my way?"

Kelly's eyes bored into his. She had no room to negotiate anymore. She wadded up her napkin and nodded. At once she felt a rush of relief—and dread.

"Great," Jake blurted out, relieved. "We'll go see Law Boy, and sometime later that monkey with the badge who calls himself an FBI agent. We'll make a deal."

He covered her hand with his. They stayed that way for a few heartbeats. Then, without looking at him, Kelly got up to do the dishes and slid her hand away from his grasp.

CHAPTER 21

DRESSED IN A GRAY-BLACK BUSINESS SUIT WITH her hair pulled back, Kelly could easily have been mistaken for a young attorney. She walked side by side with Jake down the long hall on an upper floor of the federal building in West Los Angeles. Out of habit, she took in all the faces of the people they passed. Most of them held the resigned fury she'd seen in so many government workers.

Jake stopped in front of a door. A brass plate read BRYAN NORMAN, U.S. ATTORNEY.

"Aka Law Boy," he whispered, and pushed the door open.

On the drive over, he had briefed Kelly on the man she was about to meet. What struck her most about his revelations was that the U.S. attorneys' lives revolved around climbing the ladder of position and power. "They're all guilty of the same crime," he said disdainfully, "the crime of ambition. They'd put their own mothers on trial and behind bars in order to get ahead."

And yet Jake put away his disgust and exuded only charm as he greeted Norman's receptionist. "Maggie. We meet again."

"Always a pleasure, Mr. Brooks."

Kelly skipped her eyes over the young woman, who would have been ridiculously easy to impersonate. Standard brown hair, blonde highlights. Scoop-neck, tight white shirt, full breasts. Black suit jacket, short black suit skirt. No accessories, no color, no patterns. Very LA. She glared up at Kelly like a rival.

"Is he ready for us?" inquired Jake.

Maggie leaned forward, her breasts pressing against her blouse, and whispered, "He's been fussing around in there waiting for you. I've got to say, he doesn't seem very happy."

"He's gonna be even more unhappy after we leave," said Jake as if imparting a big secret. He winked at her, and Kelly was amused to see the receptionist's chest rise in response.

Maggie lifted the phone to buzz Norman, but before she had a chance to announce them, he barked, "Send them in!"

Jake followed Kelly into a large, beautifully furnished office. Japanese art was displayed on the walls, including an antique kimono encased in Plexiglas.

In contrast to his elegant office, Bryan Norman was Mr. Average. Mousy hair, thin lips, smallish eyes of a nondescript color. Average height, average weight. The kind of guy no one had ever noticed—in high school, elementary school, or even kindergarten.

Kelly noticed one other thing: This "Law Boy" did not disguise his loathing for Jake, who plopped into a chair across from the desk.

"After the last time I saw you in court, I didn't think you'd be so eager to take me on again, Norm."

"I'm a glutton for punishment, Brooks." Norman looked disappointed at failing to find an abbreviated form of Jake's last name to throw back at him. "Y'see, the downside of being a U.S. attorney is having to abide by the law—something you could stand to get reacquainted with."

Jake looked over at Kelly and explained in a loud aside, "Some attorneys are so anal they wipe their asses with cotton balls."

Kelly was surprised at Jake's attempt to offend Norman. She looked over at the man. *How pissed is he?* she wondered. Two white dots had appeared on his jawbones.

"Let's get down to the dirty business at hand, shall we?" he said.

Kelly felt the federal prosecutor sizing her up. She did not react. She simply listened to him as he continued.

"We've got witnesses, a security video, your disguise. Hell, we've got *you*." He hesitated for emphasis. "I see no reason to make any deals, but you *are* gonna give me some information."

Jake burst out laughing. Then he spat out, "Funny. I understood communication to be the *exchange* of information."

Norman ignored Jake and turned on Kelly.

"Either I get cooperation or the next time you see your kids, they'll be in their twenties."

Kelly's eyes widened in fear. Jake caught it and jumped in for the save, slapping his palm to his ear as if to clear it.

"Did I just hear the U.S. attorney attempt to blackmail my client?" Jake pulled a mini tape recorder from his pocket, pushed REWIND, and played Norman's words back to him.

Norman growled. "Give me a break with the parlor tricks. That's inadmissible and irrelevant, and you know it."

Jake rolled his eyes and put the small machine on Norman's desk.

"Really? So what, in your opinion, *is* relevant here? We're talking first offense with probability of probation at best, and this BS you're throwing at her? It's pure fabrication. For the purpose of manipulation."

Norman pulled his lips together like a llama getting ready to spit. His lower jaw moved back and forth. "I'm not buying this 'no priors' crap, excuse my French."

Jake feigned exasperation. "The jury will. Lemme see . . . a young mother, two small children, helpless. You tell me how they're gonna deliberate."

Norman's façade cracked. He knew Jake could be right. But still he made an attempt to brush it off. "Take a hike, Brooks."

Jake clapped a hand on his chest as though he'd been stabbed. "You don't mean that, Norm. And you know why you don't mean that? Because I'm gonna save your butt."

Kelly almost chuckled. She could practically smell the testosterone. The childishness of their exchange would have been amusing if it wasn't her life, and her kids, they were sparring with.

The men stared at each other, estimating the weakness in their respective positions. Norman took just a little too long to respond, a subtle acknowledgment of his marginal disadvantage.

Jake seized the moment. "She gives you the MO—how he works, where he works, et cetera—and she walks."

He'd pushed Norman just a bit too far. The prosecutor stood. "You're dreaming, Brooks. We're going all the way with this one. Get out of here." He flung his hands girlishly at the door.

Jake knew the sound of an empty threat. He leaned languidly over to Kelly. "The acoustics must be bad in here."

I hope to God you know what you're doing, thought Kelly.

"Let me crank up the volume . . ." Jake raised his voice. "She's a FIRST-time offender. This is the FIRST and ONLY offense that you've got on her as an adult. Furthermore, she's just a PAWN, and I'm offering you a KEY to INFORMATION HEAVEN, which together with even a tiny bit of gray matter, results in a major BUST."

Norman leaned forward on his desk to avoid the indignity of

sitting down right away. "Yeah, yeah, but a conviction in hand would be good for me right now," he said, attempting to effect a blasé expression to match his voice.

Jake slammed his open palm on Norman's desk, appearing to be at the end of his patience. "Here I am, trying to give you the real criminal and save the taxpayers millions of reimbursement dollars, and all you do is threaten my client, who has already been victimized and used as a pawn in a major banking fraud. Give me a break. I can forgive almost anything but stupidity."

Norman's face was as expressive as a cow's.

Jake abruptly stood up and took Kelly's arm.

"Where do you think you're going?"

Jake responded over his shoulder. "To see your boss. I hear he's got some brain cells left in his head."

They were almost at the door when Norman growled, "Get your butts back in here. I want details, names . . ."

Kelly turned. She looked directly into Norman's eyes. She had the plan. It would depend on so much going her way, but she had it.

"It's Todd Gillis," she said softly.

"Horseshit!" Norman yelled back. "Wait, what did you say?"

Son of a bitch, fuck . . . What the hell is she doing? thought Jake. She's throwing out the carrot in full Technicolor. He had told her that in the gray zone you don't reveal anything. It's all about knowing when to hold them, when to fold them, and when to play your ace. He'd thought she understood: Think of something they'll want to cover up. Threaten them with the media—that's always effective. *Was she even listening to me?* he thought.

Aloud, he said, "My friends down at the *Times* might be very interested to know that the people's representative is refusing to save their money. My client doesn't need to risk her kids' lives by snitching for you. In fact, she doesn't have to help you with any information.

She's offering to be on your team and to cooperate. I have no doubt that the judge is going to look very favorably at her actions."

Norman paused just long enough that Jake thought he'd overshot again. He looked at Kelly. "Gillis is the fish?"

Kelly looked deferentially down at her hands and nodded. Norman's brown eyes blinked and he sat down. "Okay. If you're saying you can deliver Gillis, you've got a deal. But you'd better fucking give him to me on a silver platter."

* * *

As they left the federal building, Jake felt as though he was invisible. Kelly moved without looking back. Her steps were light and lazy. She didn't say a single word.

What the fuck's with her? Jake asked himself. She was shutting him out.

Kelly stepped into his car without thanking him for holding the door open. She was staring at something in midair. Her eyes never moved when he slammed the car into gear and drove off.

Jake laid into her for going against his plan, but crowed that her change of tactic had worked.

Kelly said nothing.

When they reached his office, she still wasn't talking. When Jake finally asked her what was going on, she just shook her head and asked for the key to the restroom reserved for his clients.

Jake waited in his office, excited to get started. He wanted to nail Gillis, too, and now he knew they could do it.

Fifteen minutes went by. Finally, he asked Joyce to check the restroom. Kelly wasn't there. She had disappeared without a trace.

CHAPTER 22

THE NEXT DAY, THROUGH THE OPEN BLINDS IN
his office, Jake stared at the office workers streaming over the pedestrian bridge to the Century City mall. Kelly had been missing for almost twenty-four hours. *Where is she?* He'd called Jeanette Pantelli, but Kelly hadn't arrived to check on her kids. Or at least, no one who fit the description of Kelly Jensen/Kelly Gillis/Natalie St. Clair had been in the vicinity. God only knew what Kelly could disguise herself as if she really wanted to sneak up to Tahoe, undetected, to see them. She was like water: She could take any form that suited her. And, like water, she was soft and silent, yet deadly if need be.

Jake was furious—with her, with himself. Once more the events of yesterday, after he'd discovered Kelly was missing, played out in his mind. He felt his pulse quickening now, just as it had when he'd raced to his apartment to see if she'd gone there. He had entered the guest room without knocking. It didn't matter; she wasn't there. She had left her duffel bag in the closet. Jake didn't even hesitate. He dove into the bag as if it contained the secrets of the universe.

He pulled out a pile of scarves that smelled like her—not of perfume, but of fresh, crisp air, like it came from near the sea or a mountain peak. A couple of hats. Three pairs of sunglasses in different styles. Assorted vials and compacts and tubes in a small makeup bag, along with Q-tips in a plastic pouch and a substance the texture and color of Silly Putty. A Ziploc held Band-Aids, tampons, dental floss, mouthwash, adhesive tape, an instant cold pack, a roll of quarters, and a Power Bar.

Jake ran his hand around the bottom of the bag and pulled out a bottle. Tums, half empty. On the bag's exterior, one side pocket was stuffed with used Kleenex smeared with beige makeup and red lipstick. The other pocket held a cache of fresh packets of Kleenex. That was all.

Jake sat down on the bed and turned the duffel upside down, shaking it hard. He hefted it with two hands. Something didn't seem right. He felt all the way around the inside again. Nothing. No lumps, no bulges. He felt all the seams, tapped on the hard bottom. Nothing. Jake looked up guiltily, expecting Kelly to walk in, but his apartment was silent.

The cops would have X-rayed her bag when she was arrested, so Jake wasn't sure what he was looking for. He was about to give up when a white thread on the bottom corner caught his eye. He pulled it, and the bottom of the duffel opened. The thick cardboard base slid out easily, and he tossed it aside. Jake slipped his hand all the way around the thin space, feeling carefully in the corners. Nothing. With a frustrated shout, he hurled the bag to the floor. It landed half on top of the cardboard—and that's when he saw it. The layers of cardboard were just slightly separated. They came apart easily in his fingers, and out fluttered a photograph.

Jake stared at it, curious. He spotted Kelly immediately. She was young, wearing a fake-looking smile. On either side of her were the Gordons, standing a little too close, pressing in on Kelly as if they thought she would fly away. The picture was a poignant reminder of Kelly's tragic past. Jake wondered why she kept it with her. He glanced at the rest of the picture. Three other children stood on the other sides of the Gordons, presumably their other foster children.

Jake stared, frozen in disbelief. He looked harder, not able to comprehend what he was seeing. Could it be true? The other children were two boys and a girl. All three looked underfed and unhappy. But the girl looked out with a particular malevolence, and Jake found himself staring into the eyes of Stacy Steingart.

He exploded with rage, punching the wall. Kelly knew Stacy Steingart—Porter's killer? They had been foster kids at the Gordons' at the same time? He had been too quick to believe Kelly was innocent. He had fallen for her sob stories the same way Porter had. But the difference was, he had no excuse. Porter was the idealist, not him.

Not quite sure what he was doing, Jake carried the photo to the living room. His thinking up to this point had been smudged—he was aware of that now. Logic and strategy had been going up against compassion and attraction. He knew that the only sane thing to do at this moment was to take the photograph and everything he knew to the FBI and to Law Boy. He would let them take over, find Kelly, and do with her as they wanted.

Yet he stood in the living room deliberating. And as he opened *The Sibley Guide to Birds* and slipped the picture between pages eighty-nine and ninety, one thing was as clear as vodka: He was concealing evidence. He had just crossed the line from defense attorney to accessory.

Jake had spent the rest of the day and most of a restless night trying to track Kelly down. He was in too deep now. And to top it off, she'd been entrusted to his recognizance—her disappearance could mean the end of his career. The minute she disappeared, he should've had the cops, the sheriffs, the SWAT teams after her. After all, she was a potential accessory to murder.

Joyce's voice pulled Jake back to the reality of his office. "Still no answer," she said from the doorway. "I've been trying every fifteen minutes."

Jake let the blinds clatter against the window. "I don't fucking believe it," he muttered.

Perching on the edge of his sofa and lighting a cigarette, Joyce watched Jake lift a portable ironing board from behind the door and carefully balance it on two stacks of law books. Then he took off his shirt and stuffed it into a laundry bag labeled DIRTY.

Hanging next to this laundry bag was another, marked CLEAN. Jake pulled out a shirt and fussily fitted the yoke over the end of the ironing board. Ever since college, Jake had done his own shirts. "Keep your dirty laundry to yourself"—it was a priority in protecting his privacy.

Joyce took a long drag off her cigarette and rested her feet on a stack of legal papers. For as long as she had worked for Jake, she'd enjoyed this ironing routine. It had become a signal that he wanted her input. Today, however, her enjoyment was marred by his evident distress over this Kelly woman.

Joyce exhaled a plume of smoke from the corner of her mouth. "Look at the positive side: First loss is best loss. That girl was a disaster ready to happen. Now maybe she's not your problem anymore." She had taken an instant dislike to Kelly and now had trouble disguising the pleasure in her voice.

"She intrigued me," Jake said simply. He slipped the shirt off the board and started on the collar. He said nothing, in violation of their usual discussion rules. He was supposed to start thinking aloud, and Joyce would insert sage comments and advice. Joyce smoked silently, a little peeved. When she'd finished her cigarette and Jake still hadn't spoken another word, she started to move toward the door.

"Well, you sure know how to pick them," she said.

Jake looked up, iron in hand, and grinned. It was a hollow expression.

Joyce exhaled loudly. "You want me to keep trying?"

"Yes, every ten minutes." Jake finished up the second sleeve and flipped the shirt to the back. "Thanks."

He knew he had pissed off Joyce, but he couldn't confide in her. He wasn't even sure he could explain it to himself. Why was he continuing to protect Kelly? And risking his own career? To make up for the way the system had abused her and robbed her of her childhood? Why? Could he give her back her childhood or repay her somehow for what the justice system had stolen?

What justice? A child was torn away from her dead mother's arms and thrown into a world of betrayals and abuse. The prisons were filled with Kellys—kids born into a world of little or no choice. Talked to mostly by cynics, among them Jake himself, these kids touched futility in every pathway of life and every encounter. But cynics made poor friends, as his ex-girlfriends would testify.

Jake felt a gnawing in the pit of his stomach—a sensation that had become so familiar to him since Kelly had entered his life. He tasted bile. Why was he choosing to walk her rocky road? Did it all come down to exploring his dark side? Was it that holding her hand through hell—what a clever wordsmith he was—would make her lean on him to the point of total dependency . . . maybe even make her love him? Or was it just his desire to become Jake the Explorer? Was capturing the intangible so exciting, or was it a mere obsession?

Jake was finishing the fourth shirt when Joyce burst into his office. He looked up eagerly. "Did you find her?"

Joyce shook her head, her lips pressed closed severely. "Your private line. It's Todd Gillis."

CHAPTER 23

"I'VE INVITED YOU HERE . . ." GILLIS HESITATED, AS if selecting the wrong words would be the verbal equivalent of clipping the wrong wire to defuse a bomb. He steepled his fingers in front of his lips and glanced down at his desk. "I asked you here because I have information that I'd rather not spill to the cops or the feds."

Although keyed up, Jake said nothing. He resisted leaning forward. After years in his profession, he'd learned just to let people talk. Everyone, except for a skillful few, revealed more during a simple period of his silence than they would under harsh lights or meticulous questioning. He could see Gillis trying to gauge any reactive signals from Jake, any emotional buttons he could push. Jake had been down this road more often than Gillis knew. The intelligence level of his opponents changed, but never the intent. Sociopaths were sociopaths.

Gillis's LA office was dark and stern, even though one entire wall was glass and high enough above the surrounding buildings to let in the sun. Mahogany paneling dimmed two other walls. The fourth contained floor-to-ceiling bookcases filled with books so non-descript they could have been multiple sets of encyclopedias. Centered between the bookshelves was a fireplace, unlit. Gillis's enormous, dark, ornately carved wooden desk was positioned on a raised platform, and Gillis sat behind it with his back to the wall of windows so that he was perpetually backlit and visitors were blinded. It was an affectation designed to intimidate, like the Louis XVI antiques in the reception area and the Renoirs and Monets in the lobby. Jake wasn't falling for any of it.

Gillis creaked forward in his high-backed antique leather chair. "I don't quite know how to say this . . . I guess I'm a little embarrassed." He rubbed his jaw roughly. "The truth is, Porter Garrett's mistress, Kelly Jensen, is my wife."

Jake squinted. Gillis was trying to feel out what he knew, of course. Jake rearranged himself in the low-slung leather guest chair and molded his face into a mask of boredom.

"Really."

Gillis's smile was warm, almost sheepish. "But you've known that for a while. Even before you risked your career and said you'd supervise her recognizance. I have friends at the courthouse. And I'm a friend of Shrake's, you see. He mentioned you'd shown some interest in Kelly."

Jake scowled. "That asshole suffers from a severe case of verbal diarrhea. Who wouldn't be interested in a beautiful, talented singer?"

Gillis fiddled with a paperweight, a cube of shiny, bronze-colored metal, and smiled. "Take it easy. Shrake knew Kelly and I have a past. He was doing what comes naturally to people like him. Gossiping. You see, it was Kelly who left *me* . . ." Gillis paused and looked toward the dark fireplace. Jake watched him swallow a couple of times, his Adam's apple straight in its track. He was surprised to see Gillis allowing himself this vulnerability and was intrigued that the man was capable of it. If that's what it was. Could this ice man have a melting point named Kelly Jensen? Or was he that good an actor?

"Almost two years ago," Gillis continued. "She left *me*. I know she was young when we got married, but I gave her everything she ever dreamed of, everything she wanted. You ever been married, Brooks?"

Jake shook his head. He was surprised to see softness in someone so hard, but at the same time, he didn't trust Gillis's "I am human" epiphany.

"Well, I loved that girl. *Love* her. She took my kids, too. No note. No forwarding address. I wake up one morning and she's gone, vanished."

"Look—"

Gillis held up his hand. "It's alright. The thing is, I searched everywhere for her—wouldn't you? A shrink would say I was addicted to my own wife. Maybe even obsessed. That may be true, but I also didn't want the police involved. A man in my position—the press would have had a field day. I also . . . If another man . . ." Gillis paused again, spinning the paperweight by quarter turns.

"I also didn't want her to get in trouble. There are other things she did—things I could have come after her for."

Jake leaned back and crossed his arms over his chest. He had to mask his growing anxiety about Kelly—her safety, her trustworthiness.

"It's alright, Brooks," said Gillis. "I know a lot of what you know already. But think about it. Taking our kids across state lines without my consent? Kidnapping? Also, she . . ." Gillis jerked to his feet.

"Let's take this outside. I need some air, and I have some things I want to tell you, more privately."

Jake hesitated. What was Gillis worried about? He allowed himself to reveal a touch of sarcasm. "I'm all ears."

Preceding Gillis out the door, Jake glanced at a photograph in a black frame on the wall. He moved closer, hearing Gillis make an impatient sound behind him. A school-age boy was standing next to a man who wore clothing in the style of the late 1960s. The boy's face was open and shining, and he was smiling up at the man. The man's face was cloudy, distracted, looking over the boy's head to the left of the picture. The boy's hand was outstretched to the man, as if inviting him to hold it, but the man's arm remained stiffly by his side.

"Someone you know?" Jake asked.

Gillis muttered impatiently, "My father." He took Jake's elbow firmly and steered him to the door. "We're going this way."

They emerged from a staircase onto the roof of the building. Leaning against a railing, Jake pulled out a cigarette, promising himself again to quit, once this was over. He offered the box to Gillis, who shook his head and looked out over Los Angeles while Jake lit up. The sky was pure ozone—scoured of clouds. The breeze was so strong, they almost had to shout.

"Here's the thing," said Gillis. "I know you've been doing a little freelancing. About Kelly."

Jake exhaled. The wind grabbed the smoke and shredded it over his ear as he processed what Gillis was saying. Gillis knew that Jake was withholding information about Kelly. Because Shrake had blabbed to Gillis about the night Jake came by the club to investigate Kelly, Gillis knew how long Jake had kept the relationship a secret, and he could pinpoint the time for the authorities. Any charges against Jake would be complicated by Jake's testy dealings with the FBI and the U.S attorney. He tried to take a steady breath. Gillis might be contemplating blackmail.

Gillis looked at Jake the way a cat looks at a wounded mouse—as if it wants to play with its prey for a while.

"She was a runaway when I met her," he began. "Scrawny. Scrappy kid. Beat-up. She was in an abusive foster family that was pretty rough on her. This was in Houston. Somehow, she managed to survive. When I met her, she was using her looks for survival, if you know what I mean."

"Prostitution?"

Gillis shook his head. "She always denied turning tricks, but you know, it's pretty rough out there. I don't know what label she wore before I met her—cow, whore, thief. Thing is, I found her, married her, gave her a new life. Saved her from the hellhole she was living in. At least, that's how I thought of it. But you can't take the streets out of a person who's living that life.

"I learned the hard way that she was conning me, too, using my position at the bank to her advantage. I don't know why she bothered. I gave her everything she needed. But she figured out a way to hit my banks."

Jake snorted, trying to cover his agitation. "Someone as smart as her? Why *would* she bother? Any divorce lawyer would have carved you up nicely, leaving her a healthy chunk of the fat."

Gillis looked away. "I don't know how to say this without sounding contrived."

"Try me." Jake sucked on his cigarette.

Gillis's mouth looked as if he had swallowed a wasp, but he managed to bend it into a negligent smirk. "It's like they always say: A whore is a whore—it's all just a matter of price. Don't get me wrong. She'd been fighting for survival her whole life. You know, her mom was murdered when Kelly was six. Her dad got life for it and died in prison, after getting stabbed in a prison brawl."

Jake flicked his cigarette butt with his thumbnail. *Good, you finally told me something I didn't know*, he thought. He wondered if Kelly ever knew the who and the why about her father's death. He kept asking questions.

"How was she hitting your banks?"

"Disguised as other people. Passing bogus payroll checks." Gillis's tie flapped over his shoulder like a pennant. "Kelly can fool anyone. She's incredible. Disappears into other people. Once, when she was thirteen, she ran away. Got a job at a Dairy Queen. She was handing burgers to the cops who were looking for her, and they didn't even notice. Took them three weeks to find her.

"Took me a lot longer than that to find her when she left me—nearly two years. I only caught up with her a few weeks ago. She was under my nose the whole time. I had an army of detectives on her tail. That's how I found out about her and Garrett. I know she was there the night he was killed."

Gillis smoothed a hand over his hair. It flapped right back up again. "But I'm not going to turn my wife, the mother of my children, over to the feds. All I'm saying is—" Gillis broke off and rubbed his lower lip with the knuckle of his forefinger. "She can be a force to reckon with—crafty, cold, and calculating."

Jake tossed the butt to the ground and scuffed it out with his foot. In the bright light, Gillis looked old for his years, a little worn. His jaw, so square indoors in the murky light, was in the slow process of softening. His white collar was tailored snugly around his tan neck, but the skin was a little looser than it seemed at first glance. The pores on his nose were enlarged, and one red capillary feathered across his nostril. His teeth had been whitened, but Jake could see flashes of gold in the back of his mouth when he spoke.

Gillis exhaled audibly, almost a growl. "I'll say it straight. I've got something that could put Kelly behind bars for the rest of her life. I know she's hoping to get the FBI to dig through my banks. I'm just doing you the courtesy of letting you know in advance that whatever she—and you—work out with them, I can hit hard."

"What've you got?"

"Something that could be viewed as conclusive."

Jake snorted. "Like what?"

"Like a murder weapon."

Jake paused to consider. "Then I'd say you have a case but no criminal."

"You haven't seen my evidence."

Jake shrugged, drawing the motion out as he thought. Then he took a gamble and said, as offhandedly as he could, "You know, I used to hate my father too." It had the instant effect he had suspected it would. Gillis's face contorted with rage.

"What are you talking about?"

"That morose picture in your office. I only forgave my dad right before he died. Is yours still alive?"

With effort, Gillis pulled himself straight. "That's not what we're talking about. I don't hate my dad."

Jake just stared at him.

Gillis's lips tightened. "Yes, he made me feel insignificant, because he wanted to be invisible, unnoticed. He called it humility," he stuttered. Then, composing himself, he delivered his coup de grâce: "You're not hearing me. I won't hesitate to crush both you and Kelly."

Jake called his bluff. "If you have what you say."

Gillis transformed suddenly into a four-year-old child. "You don't believe me?"

Jake simply stared.

"You don't believe me?" Gillis shouted again.

Jake regarded the changed man before him. Perhaps he'd just found a very useful chink in Gillis's armor.

The wind picked up, and Jake had to strain to hear Gillis whisper his steely threat: "She may be a lot of things, but she's still my wife!"

Jake's inner alarm screeched inside his gray matter. This man was a deadly hunter. Jake knew that Gillis would never rest until his prey was in his captivity. So the expert defense attorney chose his next words carefully.

"You've hinted a lot, Gillis, but I deal with realities. With things I can touch and see. When you're ready, call me. Until then . . . Well, I'm glad we've had a chance to talk."

Jake left quickly, leaving Gillis alone on the roof. But his brain was clanging with alarms. Would Gillis really blackmail him? What did he have on Kelly? Blood? Hair? A shoe print? Could the feds put together a case on Gillis—at least enough to stall him—before Gillis fought back with what he had?

Back in his Mercedes, Jake called Joyce. Upon hearing there was still no word from Kelly, his rage returned. He was risking every-thing—his career, his reputation, his life—for her. Why was he wast-ing time sparring with Gillis on her behalf? He gripped the steer-ing wheel to keep the anger from boiling over. He made a deal with himself: Kelly had to contact him by tomorrow morning, or he was cutting her loose.

But he hadn't gone two blocks before Joyce called him back. "Gillis wants to see you again," she said. "Right now."

* * *

On the outside, Nate 'n Al was like every other restaurant in Bev-erly Hills. Inside, the décor and ambience screamed Los Angeles of another era. Brown leatherette booths hunkered along the walls and in the center section, around dark laminated wood-grain tables. A counter holding cakes and pastries under plastic domes ran in front of a row of swivel stools. A gaggle of Jewish broads, imported straight from the Bronx, ruled the restaurant, each one down-to-earth, witty, and a know-it-all. Their ringleader was Hot Trudie, everyone's mama and grandma, a full-breasted redhead whose specialty was tables with kids, Beverly Hills locals, or Hollywood's seasoned celebrities.

Arriving first, Jake claimed a seat facing the door. Hot Trudie brought him a cream soda and a lean brisket sandwich, but failed—unusual for her—to engage him in conversation. When Gillis entered Jake clenched his fists under the table. He wouldn't let Gillis see how angry he was.

The men didn't greet each other. Gillis slid in opposite Jake and swung his handsome head to summon Trudie. He ordered black coffee, then leaned back with his arms spread out, Jesus-on-the-cross-style, on the top of the bench and smiled at Jake.

"Feels like a slap in the face when she disappears, doesn't it?"

Jake lifted his soda bottle and tipped it toward the glass, but it was already empty. He had to shake it to get one reluctant drop to slip off its mouth.

"I'm just her lawyer. Must be worse for an abandoned husband."

"Oh, you're there too. I can see that haze she's left all over your face," retorted Gillis as Trudie put down the coffee cup. Gillis ignored her. "You'll never get used to it," he said. "I'll tell you that."

"Is this what you dragged me in here to talk about? I hate to tell you, but the only depleting commodity I have is my time, and I'm not about to waste much more of it." He took a bite of sandwich and immediately wished he hadn't. The meat was unappetizing, and the sauerkraut turned acidic in his mouth.

Gillis watched him chew. After Jake swallowed, he nonchalantly took another bite, showing the other man that he had an appetite. He took two more bites before Gillis spoke.

"Are you ready to discuss evidence?"

Jake feigned apathy. "Any evidence that you might have in your possession would already be dismissible because of potential contamination."

Gillis smiled. "I think even you'd be impressed by what I've got. Although you might have viewed it differently if you'd seen it before you fell for her."

Jake forced the meat down his throat and willed it to stay down. He took a long swallow of ice water and signaled Trudie for another cream soda. "Your hinting around is getting boring."

"I have it right here." Gillis passed a briefcase to Jake under the table. Jake contemplated shoving it back at him, yet he kept it on the seat next to him and lifted the lid. Inside a zippered plastic bag was something covered in rust-brown powder: a knife, short and serrated like a steak knife, its blade no longer shiny, its handle smeared.

"You've gotta be shittin' me," growled Jake.

"I tried to warn you about Kelly. She's capable of anything."

Jake could not believe he was sitting in Nate 'n Al with a half-eaten brisket sandwich on his plate, looking at the murder weapon that had killed his best friend.

"Concealing a murder weapon puts you in the hot seat."

"Friends in the Las Vegas PD gave it to me. They can help me spin it in any direction I want." Gillis waved his hand airily. "Besides, murder weapons go missing all the time. You, of all people, should know that."

Jake flipped the lid down on the briefcase. Kelly's words ran through his head: *He's the smartest man I know.* What did Kelly know about this? Jake cleared his throat. "This could be anything. Blood from a pig, a prostitute, a little old lady."

"If that's how you want to describe your best friend, or should I say 'deceased best friend,' that's your business," Gillis said sarcastically.

Jake literally bit his tongue to keep it under control. "And the rest of it—"

"It'll check out. Believe me. His blood. Her prints."

Jake, his mind frying, looked at Gillis, minutely shaking his head.

Gillis spoke quickly. "You get her back to me, or I'm going to turn this in."

Jake opened his mouth to speak, but Gillis cut him off.

"You're thinking, 'What good does that do him?' I'll tell you. It guarantees that *I* get her, Brooks. Not you. Not Garrett."

"The feds shot Stacy Steingart. They aren't about to reopen the investigation—"

"Let's play a 'what if' game for a minute . . . What if Stacy and Kelly grew up in the same foster home? What if they fought their way to freedom by sucking and fucking and ultimately selling each other out to the nearest bidder . . . yet living in the same hellhole, leaning on their pathetic sisterhood for dear life . . . What if they've both hated men to such a degree that killing Porter was a joint act of revenge?"

Jake's eyes tightened just enough for Gillis to notice. He smiled broadly, like a hunter before the kill.

"Believe what you want." Gillis reached across the space beneath the table and took back the briefcase. "At any time I decide, a judge is going to see a bloody knife with DNA that matches your best friend and prints that match your client." Gillis stood up as Trudie was sashaying by, placing Jake's cream soda in front of him. He grabbed her elbow, stuffed a twenty-dollar bill in her palm, and patted her behind. Trudie whipped out the money, saw it was a twenty, and winked at Gillis as she slid it down her bra.

"Anytime you want a kinda home-cooked meal, you come and get it right here. Trudie'll look after ya," she purred.

Jake watched Gillis leave, his body frozen by shock but his mind flying through the possibilities. How would he get himself out of this? And Kelly?

Gillis wanted to play "what if." But all Jake could think of was everything that could possibly go wrong. What if . . . Murphy's Law hit them in the face?

CHAPTER 24

EVEN FROM THE SKY, AS THE PLANE WAS LANDING in Houston, Jake could sense the humidity he was about to face, the kind of moist heat that penetrated your body and your brain, demanding that you be still and blanketing you with weariness.

When Jake reached the rental car he'd reserved, the first order of business was to turn on the AC full blast. Only when he had cooled down somewhat did he dial his phone and put it to his ear.

"It's been what?" he shouted as he turned the key in the ignition. "By whom?"

The file clerk at the Child Protective Services office drawled in a bored voice, "The file was pulled by the Federal Bureau of Investigation."

Fuck. Jake snapped his phone shut and started driving. Since Gillis took off from the restaurant, Jake had been working every angle he could think of, investigating every connection between Kelly and Stacy Steingart. He had hired private investigators to do the research and activated his contacts in Nevada and Texas. The FBI had beat him to it, though, and now they had Steingart's file from her time as a foster child.

Jake put his hand out to keep a stack of folders and manila envelopes on the passenger seat from sliding to the floor. At least Joyce had been able to provide him with public record documents about Gary Gordon. They detailed an extraordinary revelation: The foster father had been investigated on suspicion of having raped one of the foster daughters in his care. Since she was a minor, the pregnant victim was unnamed, but the time frame matched the years that Kelly had lived at the Gordon house.

No longer trusting Kelly, Jake nonetheless felt a stab of compassion for the horrible life she had endured. He didn't know whether Kelly or perhaps Stacy was the victim; while he didn't wish that brutalization on anyone, he prayed it hadn't been Kelly. According to the documents, it had been concluded, thanks to DNA evidence, that Gordon had been unjustly accused. Gary Gordon had been exonerated.

Stacy Steingart's Child Protective Services file could've helped Jake tie up some loose ends, but that was impossible now that the feds had it. Was there another way of getting the information he needed? It was a long shot. Still, Jake sped up the car, determined to get to his alternative source before anyone else did.

He found the Gordons' street and cruised down it, knowing his nondescript rental car would attract no attention in this neighborhood. He parked in front of the house across the road and waited. The minivan was in the driveway. Gary Gordon was probably at home. Jake wondered how often Cheryl left the house. He needed to get her alone.

After about forty-five minutes, Jake saw movement at the front door. Cheryl Gordon waddled out, a purple shirt billowing over her black Bermuda shorts. Her head jerked around nervously, as though she sensed she was being watched.

Jake was surprised to see her get into the minivan alone. She backed quickly out of the driveway and drove fast down the street, so fast that Jake struggled to keep up with her. She pulled onto a main boulevard and he fell back, letting her weave ahead so she wouldn't suspect she was being followed. She parked at a shopping mall full of the same chain stores as every other mall in America. Looking around furtively again as she climbed out, she closed the car door and headed inside. Jake trailed her at a safe distance.

Inside, the mall was cavernous and chilly. Air-conditioning poured out of unseen vents. Shoppers strolled, bored, along the tiled walkways. Cheryl Gordon walked purposely through the crowds, a woman on a mission.

When she reached her destination, Jake understood why she had seemed so secretive. He wondered whether Gary Gordon knew about his wife's evening visits to this place in the mall. He doubted it.

Cheryl Gordon pushed open the door to Souplantation, took a tray, and began filling it. Piles of salad, pasta, soup, pizza. Jake found a bench and watched her through the window. She returned to the pasta bar three times, each time with a plate as full as the last. She returned multiple times to the dessert bar, too, filling her tray with Jell-O, pudding, ice cream with toppings. She ate everything. Jake would have felt sorry for her if her crimes against Kelly hadn't been so heinous. Her addiction was clear—her emptiness on display for all to see. She'd had a shitty life, too, and she lacked the spiritual or mental reserve to fight back: against Gary, against a system she must have known was destroying children, against her own huge body.

Cheryl Gordon sat, still, at the table for close to ten minutes after she finished eating. She almost seemed to be considering going back for more, but then she stood up. Jake watched her place her napkin on her plate and head toward the back of the restaurant. Most likely she was heading to the restroom. Jake knew he had to act fast. She was probably running out of time, trying to rush back before Gary noticed she was gone.

Jake strode through the doors and followed his mark through the back door that led to the restrooms. The door to the women's room was just swinging shut. He pushed through it, checked the room quickly for other women, and was relieved to see he was alone with Cheryl Gordon. He locked the door and turned around.

Cheryl Gordon had gone white. Her mouth hung slack; her arms flailed uselessly by her sides. Her eyes darted around the room but held a resignation, as though she knew she was trapped.

"Do you remember me?" growled Jake in a low voice.

The woman nodded, unable to speak.

"Do you remember this picture?" Jake held the picture he had found in Kelly's duffel bag in front of Mrs. Gordon's face. The woman's eyes moved over the image of her younger self standing on one side of a teenaged Kelly, Gary Gordon on the other side, and Stacy Steingart standing sullenly off to the side. Mrs. Gordon shook her head, her mouth trembling. Jake grabbed the front of her shirt at the collar and leaned in.

"Who is that standing between you and your husband?"

"N-N-Natalie St. Clair." Her voice was a whisper.

Jake got in closer. "And who is that?" He pointed at Steingart.

"S-s-s-sta—"

"I can't hear you," Jake snarled.

"Stacy Steingart."

"Why are these two together?"

Cheryl Gordon shook her head.

"What was going on between them?"

"Nothing."

Jake twisted the fat woman's collar. Her eyes looked panicky.

"Nothing, I swear," she gasped. "They were just living in the house at the same time."

"What do you know about Steingart?"

"Nothing. I don't know what you mean—"

"You know she killed a congressman?"

Mrs. Gordon's face was expressionless.

"Listen, you piece of shit. The FBI is coming after you soon, but I know more about this situation already than they do. You tell me what you know, and there might be a sliver of a chance you can save your sorry ass."

"We didn't do anything to Natalie—"

"I'm not talking about Natalie. I'm talking about Stacy. I know you did something to her."

"Nothing . . . happened. Gary . . . didn't." Cheryl Gordon's legs were buckling. Jake loosened his grip and followed a hunch.

"Why did you let him rape her?"

Mrs. Gordon's face turned into a mask of panic. "That didn't— he didn't. Even the court said he was innocent. There was DNA—"

Jake kept his voice steady. "Then who did it?"

She shook her head, her mouth a tiny white line above the quivering rolls of her neck, and closed her eyes.

Jake whispered, "Tell you what I'm going to do. I'm going to drag you out of here and drive you back to that bag-of-shit husband of yours and tell him what you do at the mall. That you sneak out of the house and spend his money porking down all this food. Then I'll tell him you told me everything about him—the abuse, the rape, everything. Then I'll tell him you called the FBI and that's why they're going to come knocking on your door tomorrow. You'll be lucky if you live through the beating he gives you, and you know I'm right."

Cheryl Gordon slid to her knees, whimpering.

Suddenly there was a knock on the bathroom door. A woman's voice shouted, "Hey, you about done in there?"

Jake shot a fierce look at Mrs. Gordon. "Tell her you're going to be a while," he growled.

"I'm—I'm going to be a while."

"Well, hurry up. There's other people waiting."

"She said she'd be a while," bellowed Jake. He heard a gasp and the sound of retreating footsteps. *Shit.* Now he really had to work fast.

"The truth. Now. What did you do to Stacy Steingart?"

Cheryl Gordon squirmed. She stammered, "There was this guy. He paid us a lot of money."

"He paid you a lot of money for what?"

"For Stacy. He paid us a lot of money so he could . . . be with her."

"'Be' with her? What do you mean? Fuck her? In your house?"

Mrs. Gordon groaned. "I don't know what he did with her. She went off in his car."

"You sold her off for sex?" Jake could feel his blood rushing to his fists, and he fought to control himself.

"Not for sex. For the weekends."

"Week*ends?* You did this more than once?"

"Weekends. When he wanted her. He brought her back Sunday nights. He paid us a lot of money."

As if that made it okay. In disbelief, Jake heard himself asking, "What about Natalie? Did you do that to her, too?"

"No, never to her . . . He didn't want her. He always sent a muscle man for Stacy. Natalie tried to stop him once. She stood there in front of Stacy's door. The man pushed her aside. Pulled Stacy out of bed and took her. Natalie went after him, kicking him, hitting his back. He shoved her aside and told me to grab her."

Jake felt a stab of relief. "How many other girls did you fuck up like that?"

"No others. Just Stacy. She was the only one the guy wanted."

"Who was he?"

"I don't remember his name."

Jake struggled to keep himself from hitting her. "I don't believe you."

"He never told us his name."

Furious, Jake let go of Cheryl Gordon's shirt and she sprawled to the floor.

A sudden pounding filled the room.

"This is the manager," bellowed a man's voice from the other side of the door. "Open up."

"Give us a minute," said Jake, his voice unnaturally calm, filled with a sudden realization of an impossible possibility. "My wife and I are working something out. I'm sorry for the disturbance. We need one minute."

The manager hesitated, as if he didn't know what to say. "Okay, one minute."

Jake leaned down to Cheryl Gordon, hissing in her ear.

"Who's the guy?"

"He told us not to tell. He paid us not to . . ." She looked at Jake with her piggy eyes, then squeezed them shut.

Jake put his lips to her ear. "Who are you more afraid of—that guy or your husband?"

He felt her slump and knew he had her.

"Like I said before, he told us his name was Michael Young."

Jake was thrown for a loop. *Kelly's long-lost uncle?*

Mrs. Gordon went on. "But . . . but . . . I saw him in a magazine, once. And his name was actually . . . Gillis. Todd Gillis, the bank guy. He has a ton of money."

A wave of dread washed through Jake. He helped Cheryl Gordon to her feet and handed her some tissues. He unlocked the door and pushed her out ahead of him. A scrawny man in a polo shirt with SOUPLANTATION stitched over the breast stood in front of them, keys in hand. An angry-looking woman with bleached hair stood next to him.

"It's about time," she muttered.

Jake barely looked at the manager as he walked by. "It's a family matter. I'm sorry, sir. It won't happen again. We're just leaving now."

The manager still looked uncertain, torn between Cheryl Gordon's obvious distress and Jake's tailored suit and confident demeanor. "Ma'am, you want me to call security?" he yelled after them, but Jake and Mrs. Gordon kept walking. Jake kept his arm on her all the way to the minivan. Then he walked away to his rental car, leaving her to face her husband and her conscience on her own.

CHAPTER 25

WHEN JAKE GOT BACK TO HIS APARTMENT THAT night, it was cold and still, but enough ambient light shone through his uncurtained windows for him to see his way to the kitchen without turning on any lamps. He pulled a beer out of the refrigerator door, changed his mind, and grabbed a Red Bull instead. Popping the top, he wandered back to his dark living room.

He took a long sip and sighed. The pieces were starting to stack up, but he still couldn't see how they all fit together. When he'd checked in at the Houston airport, a concierge had handed him an envelope. It contained a fax from Joyce with a message scrawled across the top: *You can thank me in the morning.* Leafing through the papers, Jake had smiled. It was a copy of Steingart's Child Protective Services file. Joyce had worked her magic.

The confidential file filled in a little more background on what he already knew about Steingart and her horrible abuse at the hands of the Gordons—and Gillis. At sixteen, Steingart became pregnant.

Child Protective Services investigated, on the suspicion that Gordon had raped her. After DNA testing determined that Gordon was not the father, he was exonerated and Steingart had an abortion. The Gordons' story was that she had run away and gotten raped on the street. Jake knew now that this was a lie: Gillis had been taking her on weekends, using her as what could only be called a sex slave. Either Gillis had gotten her pregnant or he had sold her to yet another man who had. Whatever the case, the young Stacy Steingart had confirmed the story that she had run away and been raped on the street.

Jake felt an uncomfortable stab of pity for the woman who had killed his friend. What she had done was unforgivable, but as usual he was readily able to see the reasons why she had become what she was.

The file said that after the investigation of Gordon, Steingart was removed from the house and put in a lockup unit in a residential group home. She remained completely mute during her time there, refusing to talk to anyone about anything, even about her basic daily needs such as food and sleep. There she remained for two years until receiving her emancipation at age eighteen. A line of text noted that the first person she saw after leaving the group home was a psychologist who had tried to reach out to her earlier, when she was still with the Gordons. The notes from that meeting remained confidential. After that visit, Steingart had joined the Marines.

Jake sighed again. It was such a sad, familiar story. He shook his head. Where did Kelly fit into all this? The likelihood was that she had met Gillis through the Gordons. But what about her story about meeting him on the street? Were she and Gillis somehow in this together? It seemed improbable, but Jake didn't know what to believe anymore.

He reached for a cigarette—and in the spurt of the lighter, he saw her.

Kelly sat in his leather club chair, legs crossed, honey-blonde hair fanning over her shoulders. She was barefoot, wearing just a man's T-shirt. *His* T-shirt. His *recently used* T-shirt, on closer inspection. The ultimate seductress—dressed in his own sweat.

Jake moved the lighter to the tip of the cigarette, not uttering a sound. Putting his feet on the coffee table, he exhaled smoke through his mouth. He could hear his heart beating in his ears and wondered whether she could too.

Kelly's voice, when it came, was not buttery and melodic as usual. It had been stretched and pounded and mixed with sand. "I'm sorry."

Jake sucked on his Red Bull. "I met with Gillis."

Kelly looked shocked.

"He said he's got the knife that killed Porter, and your fingerprints are on it."

Kelly looked startled and sounded scared. "He did?"

"Mmm-hmm. He has it in a Ziploc bag, like a cheese sandwich. I saw it."

"He's going to use it. Against me."

"I believe you're right." Jake didn't even try to keep the edge out of his voice.

"But how could he—"

"It's easy to plant evidence if you want. Plunge it right into the investigation."

The heater clicked on, and a gust of warm air whooshed out of the ceiling vent. Even in the dark, Jake saw Kelly jump.

She shivered in the thin shirt. "I didn't kill Porter."

Jake's eyes were hard as he scanned her face, searching for the familiar expression that he had learned to recognize in the faces of the guilty. It wasn't there. He was looking at a wounded animal caught in a hunter's net.

Kelly was silent for the rest of the heater's cycle. It shut itself off with a soft *click-thud*.

Jake ground his cigarette into an ashtray. "You left," he said simply. "Without a word—"

"I was on my way to see my kids, but I realized it could ruin everything." She paused. "I do the disappearing act when I need to think . . . I came back . . . is that okay?"

Jake must have moved first, because he reached her while she was still in the chair. Kelly was ready for him, though, so their movements seemed simultaneous. His lips found her mouth, her tongue, her throat, her shoulder, her breasts. Together they melted to the floor, part ocean, part chocolate. Their clothes tore off easily, without words. They devoured each other. And when Jake finally entered her, it was like he was fucking every woman in the world at once, but for the first time—like losing his virginity with Aphrodite. Not a shred of gray matter left in his head. He couldn't bring Porter back, but maybe together they could turn the page and start living in the now. Although he knew neither he nor Kelly was the kind of person who was capable of fully trusting anyone, he was hooked.

For Kelly, it was all part of the seduction. Their union was a coffin slamming shut. Porter had been in every corner of her mind, but now he was the past. She was on the grass side of the grave, not the dirt side, and she had found another man among the millions, a man who was capable of loving her in spite of her mottled and illegal past, or maybe—and this was something Porter never could have done—*because* he understood and embraced her past.

* * *

The first light of morning found Jake and Kelly huddled together on the couch, relieved and yet frightened.

Kelly murmured, "Who are they going to believe? A bank president or a bank robber?" As Jake rubbed her shoulder, she continued, "This is what I meant when I said he's dangerous. We can't trust the cops or the U.S. attorney. He intends to incriminate me. I've got to do this in my own way."

Jake didn't answer, just kept his arm around her shoulder. After a few moments, he moved his mouth close to her ear and whispered, "Why didn't you tell me you knew Stacy Steingart?"

Kelly pulled back in surprise. "What are you talking about?"

Jake stood up and walked over to his jacket, which lay among the other clothes strewn on the floor. He showed Kelly the picture.

"Where did you get that?" she asked angrily.

Jake just raised his eyebrows.

Kelly threw up her hands in defeat and turned away. "I didn't want you to think I had anything to do with the murder. I should have told you."

"What do you know about her?"

"She didn't talk much. She was distant and sort of mean. We all avoided her. Even the Gordons kept at a distance and didn't touch her."

Jake came back to the couch, handing Kelly the T-shirt she'd been wearing and a blanket from the back of a chair. He pulled on his jeans and then helped wrap her in the blanket, like you would a child.

"I have to tell you something," he said gently. She looked at him, her green eyes reflecting a combination of trust, apprehension, and questions and evasions of her own.

"I've just come from seeing Cheryl Gordon." Kelly started, but Jake held up his hands. "Hear me out. I found some information in public files about the Gordons and Steingart, and then I got the classified files that confirmed it. Were you aware that Stacy was raped when she was sixteen? And there was a suspicion that Gary Gordon had done it?"

"You saw Cheryl Gordon?" Kelly said slowly, then nodded. "It was an awful time at the house. Worse than usual."

Jake grimaced. "I had to see her. A hunch. I forced her to give me more details. I don't know how to say this." Gently, he brushed some hair out of her eyes. "They, the Gordons, were taking money from someone who was paying to keep Stacy over the weekends. Basically, they turned her into a sex slave."

Jake watched a cloud slide over Kelly's face. He pressed on. "I pushed Cheryl Gordon to the wall, and she admitted that the man who paid them to take Stacy was Gillis."

Kelly looked confused. "Cheryl Gordon . . . she knew Gillis?"

They sat in silence for a moment as Jake watched the awful realization arise in Kelly's eyes. When she finally spoke, it was as if she was detached and alone. "Meeting me in the alley was premeditated."

Jake nodded, his hand gently reaching out for hers.

"He . . . he must've known all about me. He must have seen me at the Gordons'. He knew who I was."

Jake tried to take Kelly in his arms, but she pushed him away. She opened her mouth but no sound came out.

"Kelly," pleaded Jake. "I'm here. I will do everything I can to . . ."

Kelly wasn't listening. She seemed to have drawn a curtain around herself. "He'd been watching me ever since I was at the Gordons'." Kelly looked at Jake with an expression of pure disbelief.

Jake could only nod his head. "I'm so sor—"

Their conversation was violently interrupted by forceful pounding on the front door.

CHAPTER 26

"FBI!" BELLOWED A LOUD VOICE. "WE KNOW NATALIE St. Clair is in there. Come out immediately with your hands up! Your coconspirator Stacy Steingart is dead! Don't try anything foolish!" Jake grabbed Kelly's arm and pulled her down the hallway toward the bedrooms. Stopping in the guest room, he grabbed a pair of her jeans and threw them at her.

"Put these on," he whispered. While she pulled on the pants, he slid open the door to the master bedroom balcony and stepped outside. The street below him was ten stories down. Jake looked up. A utility ladder attached to the building led to the rooftop pool. It was just to the side of the balcony. If they could just reach it . . .

"Ready," she said, at his side. Her duffel bag was strapped over a shoulder across her chest.

Jake shook his head *no,* but Kelly was firm.

"We might need it," she said. "Trust me."

There wasn't time to argue. Jake heard the pounding of a

battering ram on the front door. The FBI were starting to break it down.

"This way," he urged, pushing Kelly to the corner of the balcony and closing the door. "I'll go first."

He swung one leg over the balcony railing, reaching with his foot for the ladder. When he touched metal, he hooked his foot around the side rail and, holding on to the balcony edge with both hands, whipped his other leg to join the first, forming a bridge with his body between the balcony and the ladder. He did his best not to focus on the street below.

"Go across," he ordered Kelly.

As lightly as a cat, she leaped up onto the balcony railing and, using the building wall as a support, sidestepped across Jake's back until she reached the ladder. As soon as her hand touched the rail, she pulled herself onto it and scrambled up.

"Keep going," grunted Jake. "Wait for me up there." He couldn't see, but he could hear her disappearing up the ladder. With extreme concentration, he looped his feet around each other, the ladder rung between them. He took a deep breath and then pushed off with his arms as hard as he could, tucking his head down to his chest. The momentum carried him toward the ladder while his feet held. He grabbed the first rung he could and hung there for a moment, upside down, his feet still looped around the rung and his hands holding on several rungs down. Quickly, he straightened himself around and shimmied up the ladder.

Kelly was waiting.

"Amazing," she murmured as he grabbed her hand and led her around the pool. A door next to the elevator opened onto a staircase. Jake led her down eleven flights of stairs, into the basement. Slowly he opened the door into the parking structure. Through the slit he saw two FBI agents standing next to his car. Carefully, slowly, he closed the door again.

He ran up the stairs and peered out onto the main floor. Only one FBI agent was standing next to the big potted palm tree by the elevators.

Jake barely had time to think. Relying on the animal part of his brain, instinctively following what it told him to do, he pressed his keys into Kelly's hand.

"When the guys by the car leave, drive it out of the lot. The gate opens automatically. Meet me at Second and California. Drive East on California." Kelly nodded and dashed down the stairs.

Jake waited until he was sure she was in place. Then, steeling himself, he burst through the door into the main lobby. Sprinting across the tiles, he barreled toward the agent, reaching out to push over the palm tree as he passed. His strength and momentum toppled the tree, and the sound of its crash reverberated throughout the lobby. The agent was surprised, but as Jake sped out the front doors he heard the man call on his radio, "He's here! I need backup in the lobby."

Jake didn't look back. He vaulted over a planter and ran as fast as he could, praying that the guys in the parking garage would respond to the backup call. He ducked into an alley and ran down between the Dumpsters, listening for footsteps behind him. As he zigzagged through the neighborhood, he tried not to think of what would happen if they caught Kelly. His career might be in shreds, but her whole life was on the line. So as he crept under an overgrown camellia tree on the southwest corner of Second and California, and heard the familiar rumble of his Mercedes coming up the street, he was both relieved and grateful.

When Kelly pulled the car to the side of the road, he jumped in, and they sped off toward the freeway.

* * *

The Grande Colonial in La Jolla had beautiful suites. Tiled bathrooms, luxurious beds—it was the destination of choice for Californian lovers who wanted to spend a weekend pretending they were at an old-world European mansion.

That was not the type of accommodation Jake and Kelly found themselves in. Watching them arrive, disheveled, at close to five in the morning, the hotel clerk had assigned them a crummy room down a long flight of stairs on a hill below the hotel. The carpets smelled of mildew; the bed lacked a headboard. Jake and Kelly didn't care. They locked the door, pushed a bureau in front of it, and climbed under the covers, falling into two hours of exhausted sleep.

When Kelly woke, Jake was sitting up in the bed next to her, murmuring into his cell phone. He smiled at her and stroked her cheek. She smiled back. He said good-bye to the person on the phone and hung up.

"Joyce says Kevin and Libby are fine. They miss you, but they know you're coming back and that you love them. Of course Holly is still with them."

Kelly simply said, "Thank you."

"She also says I'm in a lot of trouble," he grinned. "Law Boy is having a shit-fit."

Kelly was nonetheless concerned. "That can't be good."

"It'll be okay," said Jake in a nonchalant tone that didn't fully reveal how he felt. "*We'll* be okay. I've been thinking about what we've got to do. Gillis is a major sponsor of a residential group home for foster kids, but there's no way he's suddenly become an angel. Something must be up with that place."

Kelly nodded.

There was a knock at the door.

"Room service," said a man's voice.

"I thought we both could stand to eat something." Jake looked through the peephole before sliding aside the bureau and opening the door.

"No, that's alright, I'll take it," he said to the bellhop, handing him a five-dollar bill and closing the door firmly behind him. He set the tray in the middle of the bed and removed the covers from the plates.

"Now eat," he insisted.

Kelly obeyed. The food tasted wonderful. They ate in companionable silence.

When they were done, Jake squeezed her hand. "Let's get down to business. I've got a friend who runs a charity that sets up foster children with mentors. She's the real thing—ethical, principled. Works tirelessly for those kids. I thought we could call her and see whether she has some ideas on how to find the weak points in Gillis's nonprofit records."

Kelly nodded. Jake dialed the number and put the phone on speaker. When he got through, she heard a woman's voice, warm and friendly.

"Jake, darling, how have you been?"

"Same as always. Trying to keep the justice system on its toes."

"It's a little early for that this morning, isn't it?"

Jake chuckled. "Sorry to call so early, Deanne. I have a friend on the line who is researching the foster care system in the United States. She's committed to exposing the truth to the media. I hope you don't mind." He raised his eyebrows questioningly at Kelly, who smiled and nodded.

"Hello, Deanne," said Kelly. "I'd be grateful for any help you could give me. Basically, I'm looking at the reasons that the federal government, state government, and various Child Protective Services departments are on a mission to reduce the number of kids included in the foster care system, while the number of kids in trouble with the authorities and on probation is on the rise."

"Right. Well, one problem is that even in the best residential group homes, there's a revolving door of staff. To the kids, everyone telling them what to do is a stranger. They know that everyone is paid to be there, and they trust no one. The idea was to place as many kids as possible in kinship care.

"But it's a business on the back of kids. Those designated level 5 through level 14 bring in $5,000 to $14,000 per month. Taxpayer dollars. Once a kid is placed with a family member, the costs are reduced and there is more chance for permanence. But support services have been cut, and many kids fall back into the system, more damaged and hopeless than before. That's why some resort to committing felonies.

"What my foundation does is match foster children with mentors, people who pledge to be a stable part of the child's life for as long as that child is in the system. In an ideal world, these relationships lead to adoptions, and sometimes they do. But mainly we try to put one caring adult, a constant presence, in these children's lives—a person who is not getting paid to spend time with them.

"Our screening program for mentors is rigorous: It requires background checks and interviews and a written application. We want to make sure people are doing this for the right reasons. In addition to regularly scheduled meetings, we sponsor group outings for the mentors and mentees—trips to baseball games, amusement parks, et cetera. The most important part is the bonding time. The mentors need to be consistent in their involvement—need to be like clockwork, because they're often the only stable, predictable thing in the child's life."

Thinking about how a program like that might have helped her as a child, Kelly felt her eyes sting. She pushed the feeling back. "That's all quite interesting, Deanne," she said. "Let me ask you about funding. Does your state-funded system accept money from the private sector?"

"Well, that's another of the problems with the system as it's currently run. Because the state's money goes to reward foster parents for taking on the most difficult cases, rather than toward preventing those children from ending up there in the first place, and because there is never enough money, there is room for people with a lot of money to throw it at the broken system. Some people use the platform and become spokespeople on behalf of the voiceless children who suffer most in our community. They receive a great deal of attention because the story is appealing to the media."

"Have you heard of Todd Gillis?"

"Of course I've heard of Todd Gillis. He puts millions into the child welfare system."

"What do you know about him?"

"Well, as I said, a lot of people get into the foster child business because they can get favorable press. The more kids they 'help,' and the more 'difficult' those kids are determined to be, the more kudos these donors get from the community. Especially politicians—saving kids pulls on the public's heartstrings. It means political capital."

"Are you saying you know Gillis personally?"

"No. But he has several PR companies pushing his kid-loving image. On the surface it's all on the up-and-up. But in one of the group homes he supported, there was a scandal a few years back. A couple of the girls called the rape hotline, claiming they had been raped. They described a Gillis look-alike as the rapist."

Kelly thanked Deanne for all the information and her time.

Then she sat still, staring into the corner of the room, her mind racing, as Jake exchanged a few more pleasantries before saying good-bye.

After he hung up, Kelly turned to him, a triumphant smile playing on her lips. "I have an idea. Here's the plan for today . . ."

CHAPTER 27

KELLY LICKED THE RIDGE OF FOAM FROM THE inside edge of the paper cup and touched her lips with a napkin. Through the window she could see the waves silently beating the rocks, puffing up spray. Fog still hung offshore like a ratty window sheer, making everything appear limp and gray. Kelly stuffed the napkin in the cup, gathered her three small shopping bags, and rose.

In a conservative, pale blue Escada suit, she was an utterly different Kelly, yet no more the real Kelly than Marilyn Monroe or Lydia Haines. She was all polish—exquisite and sleek, untouchable.

La Jolla's business district was a tumble of quaint seaside streets boasting galleries and shops that catered to the very rich. Kelly walked a short block and a half and entered a branch of American Capital Investment Bank, leaving on her sunglasses so she could look around while her eyes adjusted to the softer light. Two tellers were on duty behind the bulletproof window. An accounts manager was behind his desk on the floor. Two elderly customers were at the windows, and a surfer in board shorts was in line.

Kelly walked over to the accounts manager and spoke in a low, firm voice.

"Could you call your manager, please, Mr. . . . ?"

"Fox," said the man, pointing to the sign on his desk.

"Pleased to meet you, Mr. Fox," purred Kelly. "And the day manager is—"

"Lee. John Lee. I'll just . . ." Fox trailed off and Kelly turned to see what he was looking at. A tall Asian man in a black suit and red tie had materialized behind her. His thick hair was short on the sides and brushy on top. His cheekbones carved two ridges out of his smooth skin.

"Can I help?"

Kelly looked him in the eyes. "Mr. Lee. I'm Mrs. Todd Gillis."

The man's jaw slackened while his eyes flicked back and forth between Kelly and the door of the bank.

From the corner of her eye, she could see the word spreading across the floor that the big boss's wife was visiting the bank. If they asked, she had her credit cards and ID in her wallet, which still bore the Gillis name. But she knew they wouldn't ask. Her acting and attitude were too good. The manager tried to regain his balance.

"What are you doing . . . uh . . . what can we do . . . Is Mr. Gillis here too?"

Kelly didn't smile or give him any relief. She knew how to wield power over employees. Rule number one: Don't put them at ease.

"May I show you around, Mrs. Gillis?" Lee offered when she didn't answer his other questions.

"I need to use a private office for a few minutes," stated Kelly, ignoring his hospitality.

Lee recovered quickly and started acting to help, falling all over himself, as she knew he would. "Of course. Is that all? You can use mine." He swiped a plastic card through a reader and pushed a code into a wall lock. The door buzzed and he held it open for Kelly. "This way."

A short hallway led to his office. It was lined with framed photographs of the bank's management: Mr. Lee himself, regional managers, national VPs. In the center of the hall was a larger portrait of Gillis, handsome, tan, in a white French shirt and dark jacket and tie. Kelly looked in his eyes as she passed the painting, and they seemed to follow her. To the right of the portrait was a photo of Gillis shaking hands with the president of the United States. Below hung a photo of Gillis shaking hands with Congressman Dennis Cardoza. Kelly saw Lee glance at the photos, but he didn't look back at her.

Lee's office was absolutely free of clutter. Not a single sheet of paper was lying around, nor were any Post-it notes stuck to the computer. This was going to be harder than she thought.

"Thank you, Mr. Lee. I need to make a few phone calls and check my e-mail. Do I dial nine to get out?"

"That's right. Let me get you into the computer system. This is the code the managers use. Put it in at the prompt." He wrote down the successive numbers *12345*. Kelly paused, amused at how many people traded off security for easy recall.

"Mr. Gillis wanted me to check into a few things. I'll need to get into some of our accounts." Kelly arranged her shopping bags on the desk as she spoke—the small blue Tiffany's bag in front—and purposely did not look at Lee. Rule number two: Make extraordinary requests in the most mundane way possible.

Lee hesitated, caught in the limbo between deference to the boss's wife and upholding the bank's security rules. "Well, uh, I don't have Mr. Gillis's password—"

"I have that," Kelly snapped, "of course. But this code gets me into the system, right?"

Lee nodded.

Kelly purred, "If you could just allow me some privacy, then." Turning to the computer, she slid her hand surreptitiously into her purse.

"Certainly, of course, Mrs. Gillis." Lee nervously tapped the keys, and a series of screens flashed by on the monitor.

Kelly pressed a button on her cell phone, and it rang in her purse. Lee stepped away discreetly.

"Hello?" She didn't turn away, didn't signal to Lee to continue working, didn't acknowledge him at all. Rule number three: When someone works for you, they don't exist until you want them to. "Yes, darling. No, I'm here right now. A Mr. Lee"—she smiled enchantingly at Lee, who grimaced in return—"is helping me. I don't know. Twenty minutes? The plane can wait, can't it? Alright. Love you, too." She folded the phone and dropped it back in her purse. "Are we ready now, Mr. Lee?"

"Just about." Lee leaped back to the keyboard and clicked away. He left it with the cursor blinking in an empty rectangle labeled PASSWORD. He closed the door soundlessly.

Kelly took a deep breath and typed in *12345*. The screen flashed, the hard drive hummed, and the system opened. She typed quickly, calling up the account information on Gillis's charity sponsorships. The list was huge, but two caught her eye. One was the Juvenile Diabetes Research Foundation, to which Gillis had donated several million dollars. She knew there would be something fishy about that money. The connection to Libby's diabetes was a giveaway. Nothing about Gillis's dealings with her or her children was ever straightforward.

The other sponsorship she noticed was Casa de los Niños, a

group home Gillis donated to personally, through the Gillis Foundation, in addition to professionally, through a joint sponsorship with
his own bank.

She searched for files having to do with Casa de los Niños and
opened the first one. A long column of numbers scrolled down the
screen. Kelly scanned it, looking for anything she could use. She knew
she didn't have much time. Looking around casually, even though she
was in an office with a closed door, Kelly slid a flash drive out of her
purse and popped it into the computer's USB port. She downloaded
everything from the Casa de los Niños accounts.

When she was done, Kelly moved her fingers over the keys
again and opened up a file labeled CONTACTS within the Casa de los
Niños folders. Listed there were the names and numbers of the orga-
nization's office staff and board members. Kelly scrutinized the list
as she downloaded it. She focused on the name of one of the board
members, Louise Orlean, noting that she lived in Rancho Santa Fe,
about an hour's drive north toward Los Angeles.

She tabbed through each information field on the other board
members, paying close attention to the *Spouse* entry. Each person
had a name listed under *Spouse,* until she reached the name *Theodore
Henckle.* She did a double take. *Theodore Henckle?* He was a Nevada
senator, the right-wing conservative against whom Porter had been
running—and who would now face Porter's widow, Suzanne, in the
election. Senator Henckle was campaigning as a widower who had
lost his wife to breast cancer. It got him some mileage with women.

For Henckle's entry, instead of a full name in the *Spouse* field, the
word *Goldy* appeared beside the politician's name. Kelly smiled. She
knew Gillis too well for his own good. It fit perfectly with his motto:
The man with the gold makes the rules. She didn't know why Henckle
was on the list, but she knew she had gotten what she needed.

When John Lee knocked on the door twenty minutes later,

Kelly had her phone pressed to her ear, pretending to give orders to her housekeeper. She thanked Lee with a smile and, still talking on the phone, strode out of the bank into the lifting fog.

* * *

Two hours later Kelly and Jake were astride horses, urging them gently through the sage-scented chaparral of the mountains of Orange County. Jake, in the lead, held up his cell phone, periodically snapping pictures of the landscape and of Kelly with the camera. Mostly, though, he kept the camera trained on the rider about twenty-five yards ahead of them, a woman in her early fifties guiding a bay mare along the trail.

The woman was Louise Orlean, and she was a Gillis Foundation board member. After leaving the bank in La Jolla for Ms. Orlean's address in Rancho Santa Fe, Kelly and Jake had followed Ms. Orlean's Range Rover from her home to the Henderson Corral and Riding Trail. They'd waited in Jake's Mercedes until Louise had, after much flirting with the stable hand, saddled up and headed up the mountain. Then they had approached the groom themselves and lied about Louise Orlean having invited them to go riding with her that morning. The young man looked doubtfully at their clothes— Jake was still in jeans and Skechers from the night before, and Kelly was in Jake's old T-shirt, her own scruffy jeans, and one of his sports jackets—but he seemed to change his mind after he saw Jake mount and walk a horse. Even Kelly was impressed by his grace and power in the saddle and his gentle yet firm way with the animal.

They'd been riding about five minutes along the trail Louise Orlean had taken when Kelly called quietly up to Jake.

"Can I add 'private eye' to my résumé now? I'll put it just below 'bank robber.'"

Jake grinned. "If you ever wanted to make that a profession, I'd hire you on the spot. I don't know anyone who has a better feel for it." He snapped a few more clandestine photos of Louise Orlean, then pulled up to let Kelly pass him.

"You go ahead, get a better view. Stay out of sight, though."

Kelly prodded her horse to ascend the trail, flashing her smile at Jake as she went by. He had been thinking of little else besides Kelly Jensen for more than a week, but the sight of her on that horse, with the sun in her ponytail and on her lean, straight back, nearly undid him. He smiled back.

It had also been fascinating to watch her work. They'd been waiting outside Louise Orlean's gated estate. The minute Louise had pulled out of the driveway in her Range Rover, Kelly had begun to meticulously catalogue things about her.

"Late forties, early fifties. Fit. Nervous driver. Probably not from California. Trendy sunglasses. Trying to act younger than she is. Most likely has teenaged kids or is worried about her husband's wandering eye. Her hair will be easy. I've got a wig I can comb just that way. I need to see her walk."

Later, seated in the Mercedes at the Henderson stables, Jake had watched Kelly while she studied Louise, mirroring the older woman's head and hand movements as she flirted with the stable hand. Kelly was like a caricaturist working in three dimensions, quickly sketching the outlines of Louise Orlean's personality, desires, and look with her own body and voice.

Back on the trail, Jake watched as Kelly pushed her horse harder up the hill. As she neared the top, he could see that Louise had stopped and was looking around at the view. Kelly was getting too close; any closer and Louise would see her—possibly both of them. But suddenly it occurred to him that this was just what Kelly intended.

"Not so close," he hissed, knowing Kelly wouldn't hear

him—or wouldn't listen. "Giddyap," he murmured to his horse, tapping it lightly on the flanks with his heels. The horse moved faster up the hill.

When he reached the two of them, Jake had to smile. What was it about women that allowed them to seem as close as sisters after a chance encounter? Kelly and Louise were deep in conversation about riding boots. He didn't know that they'd already discussed manicures, chemical-free sunscreen, the latest high-protein diet, and men's need to control everything.

"Jake!" beamed Kelly as the horseman guided his sorrel mare alongside hers. "I'd like you to meet my new friend, Louise." Jake reached his arm across Kelly to shake Louise's hand.

"A pleasure," he said. "Beautiful day for riding." He thought he saw the look of recognition in Louise's eyes.

"It's so nice to meet *you*," she purred in an Americanized European accent. He could see her delight to be adding Jake Brooks, celebrity lawyer, to her mental Rolodex.

The women chatted amiably about everything and nothing for a while longer as Jake stood by, trying to place the woman's accent. It sounded like she'd come from France, but many years before. It was a pleasant voice that matched the well-groomed woman who possessed it. Louise Orlean appeared to be a little taller than Kelly. She wore a pink baseball cap over straight, shoulder-length black hair. She was handsome rather than attractive, with a strong jawline, dark (but professionally arched) eyebrows, and a long, aquiline nose that bisected her face, not unlike a dorsal fin. Sunglasses covered her eyes, so it was impossible to see how all her features came together.

Jake tried to keep from smiling when he heard Kelly's next question: "By the way, Louise, I have been looking for those exact sunglasses. Do you mind if I try them on?" Unable to resist Kelly's childlike manner, Louise took them off immediately and handed them over.

"They look so cute on you!" she squealed. Jake mentally rolled his eyes, but he watched with admiration as Kelly gazed rapidly over Louise Orlean's face, memorizing her features and plotting how to mimic them. Even squinting against the sun, Louise's eyes were striking—glinting green, the color of dollar bills.

Finally, Kelly handed the glasses back. "I'm sorry, but we have to be somewhere. We've been out since this morning."

"Oh, you can't go. You must finish the trail with me. Then come back to the house. It's not far."

"That would be wonderful, but today's really not the day," said Kelly sorrowfully. "Another time, perhaps?"

Even on horseback the two women found a way to kiss cheeks, promising to meet again. Louise called to Jake that her husband would love to meet him. Jake gave a wave and headed back down the trail.

It took all they had not to urge their horses to run down the hill. The ride that had seemed so short on the way up was interminable on the way down. At the stable, Jake gave the stable hand a tip while Kelly waited in the Mercedes. When he finally started the engine, he looked over at Kelly.

"Did you get her voice?"

"Darling," said Kelly in an astonishingly accurate mimicry of Louise Orlean's accent, "you take care of the driving. I'll take care of the impersonating."

Jake smiled and pulled out of the parking lot. Well out of sight of the stables, they dissolved into a fit of laughter.

CHAPTER 28

WHILE THE REAL LOUISE ORLEAN WAS AT HER
private Pilates lesson, Kelly, disguised as Louise Orlean, entered the
offices of the Gillis Foundation.

"Good morning," she cooed to the receptionist, in Louise's trans-
atlantic accent. "It's my turn to complete the audit and report to the
board. Could you set me up with the accounts?"

The receptionist, like most receptionists in offices all over the
world, was used to unquestioningly carrying out the wishes of higher-
ups. She knew Louise Orlean was a board member; she also knew
that the quarterly board meeting wasn't for another two months and
that this woman, in particular, never prepared her audits more than
a few hours before they were due. She knew that the paperwork for
the audit was always sent to the board by messenger; it was extremely
rare for any board member to visit the office.

But above all, the receptionist knew not to probe for details
about Louise Orlean's unusual request. She led her down a short

hall to a cubicle outfitted with a computer and a telephone, opened
the computer to the foundation accounts, provided Kelly with coffee
and a bottle of water, and walked unobtrusively back to the reception desk—where she immediately picked up the phone and began
reporting the incident in a hushed voice.

Sitting inside the cubicle, Kelly could not see the front lobby
door, but she could hear the voices of everyone around her: the receptionist fielding calls, someone on the other side of the fabric panel
soliciting donations for a silent auction. Kelly went to work quickly.

She took from her purse a key ring in the shape of a sea
anemone–sized pink puffball made of rubber. With nimble fingers,
she unscrewed it at its base and shook something out into her hand.
It was another flash drive, like the one she had used in La Jolla. She
slipped it into the computer's USB port and began downloading
account information. As a nonprofit, the foundation was required
to make its financial books open to the public, but Kelly wanted to
look at the working files. She knew that eventually she would need a
password—a password she now had, thanks to what she'd found out
in Mr. Lee's office at the bank in La Jolla.

She was progressing through the information when she felt,
more than heard, the lobby doors open.

"Hello, Cynthia," came a suave male voice greeting the receptionist, not even trying to conceal the tone of flirtation. The hair on
the back of Kelly's neck prickled.

Todd.

She heard the rumbling of another male voice. There was no
escape route. Every way out led past the front door.

"Good morning, sir. I didn't expect you this morning. Isn't the
Executive Committee meeting this evening at the Las Vegas office? I
just arranged the plane and the car."

"Thank you, Cynthia," Kelly heard Gillis murmur. "And Senator Henckle will be joining us as well."

Kelly froze. Senator Henckle again. He wasn't just a big name Gillis kept on the board. They seemed to have a relationship. She remembered the password she had found in the *Spouse* column on the computer at the La Jolla bank: *Goldy*.

Kelly heard the receptionist continue, "I tried to reach you . . . left a message. Louise Orlean . . . quarterly audit . . . a space down the hall." She heard the men moving down the hall toward where she sat and realized she was really trapped.

She inhaled deeply to calm herself. She could not get out of the cubicle without being seen, and she knew Gillis would not pass up the chance to appear to be legitimate in front of a board member. In another instant he was standing in front of her, pouring on the charm and the elegance she had witnessed so many times before.

"Louise."

Kelly plunged herself into character, pushing down her fears.

"Todd Gillis," she said in Louise Orlean's formal accent. They kissed on both cheeks.

"How's that fine husband of yours?"

"He's well. Very busy. And you? I trust you're well."

"Extremely well," said Gillis with such enthusiasm that Kelly double-checked to see if he was looking at her funny. But he was looking at his companion. "Louise, this is Rodney Farse. He's one of my oldest friends."

The other man stepped up, and Kelly had to keep herself from recoiling. She had met Rodney Farse on many occasions. He was a despicable creep, and she had always hated him. He had come on to her once when she and Gillis had first been married. She never told Gillis about it, but she wondered if he knew and had threatened Farse in some way, because the man had never tried it again.

"Louise's husband is Roland Orlean. The developer," continued Gillis.

"Pleasure to meet you," said Farse, shaking hands.

"Getting an early start on the audit, Louise?" Gillis said, his eyes twinkling. "Finding everything you need?"

Again Kelly cautiously searched Gillis's eyes for recognition but found none.

"I was just finishing up," Kelly said.

"Make sure you let Cynthia know if you need anything. Good to have seen you again. Give my best to Roland."

"You must come to dinner soon. He'd love to see you," said Kelly melodiously, the French lilt adding richness to Louise's words.

The men moved down the hall toward Gillis's office, and Kelly quietly sucked in her breath. He didn't seem to have recognized her, but her alarm bells were clanging nonetheless. She wanted to run out of there, but there was something else she needed to know. What was the Executive Committee? Why did it need to meet in Las Vegas? Kelly knew she should drop it, but every instinct was telling her this was important.

Quickly, she worked the computer keyboard, and without any trouble found a file labeled EXECUTIVE COMMITTEE. A prompt for a password blocked her entry. Sending a silent prayer to the god of computer passwords, she typed *Goldy,* and bang, she was in. Surprisingly, the file contained only one document: a short list of names—all men from the foundation board, including Roland Farse and Theodore Henckle—and an address under the heading *Las Vegas Headquarters.* The address was in an area of town on the outskirts of Las Vegas. This struck Kelly as particularly odd. She knew that Gillis's bank had an office in Vegas. Why not meet there?

Kelly memorized the address and copied the file onto her flash drive. Then, as fast as she could, she closed the file and shut down the computer. She popped out the flash drive and, looking around her, slid it back into the pink keychain. Dropping the pink rubber puff into her purse and swinging it onto her shoulder, she stood up and headed for the front door. Gillis's voice rumbled down the hall from his office.

Taking a deep breath, and using every ounce of willpower she had, Kelly strode away from the front door, toward Gillis's office. The door was ajar. She knocked twice and nudged it open.

"I'm off. I just wanted to say good-bye."

Gillis raised a hand in a gallant, yet dismissive, gesture. "Lovely to see you, Louise. Regards to Roland."

Kelly nodded and ducked out of the doorway, trying not to walk too quickly, duplicating Louise's stride. Ahead of her she saw Brigante, Gillis's bodyguard, lounging on Cynthia's desk and showing her something on his video iPod. Cynthia was smirking.

"Done so soon?" the receptionist asked as Kelly put her hand on the doorknob.

"Just off for a bite," said Kelly, and pushed out the door.

"'Bye," said Cynthia, her voice a singsong.

* * *

Kelly struggled to walk calmly up Cañon Drive toward her car. She couldn't shake the feeling that Gillis had seen through her disguise, although he'd given no concrete display of recognition.

"I'm Louise Orlean. He didn't see me," she breathed to herself, just as she had that night when, dressed as Marilyn, she had worried that he'd found her performing at Shrake's bar. The night she had met Jake.

It was early for lunch, but shoppers and tourists crowded the sidewalks. Kelly dodged one couple ambling along cluelessly, arm in arm. As she did so, she happened to glance across the street, and there, reflected in the glassy wall of the office building, she saw Gillis's bodyguard. Brigante averted his eyes, but in that instant, Kelly knew: Gillis must have suspected her. The game of cat and mouse had begun in earnest.

If she'd had more time to think, she might have made a different choice as to what she did next. Instead, she grabbed the first opportunity she saw, right in front of her. The wrought-iron-and-ficus-shaded entrance to Spago.

She had heard enough conversations among the face-lift-and-lipo crowd to know that Spago was still the reigning power-lunch spot in Beverly Hills. She wondered what sort of clout Louise Orlean wielded there. The hierarchy of tables was strictly controlled by the maître d', who looked Kelly over *sans* expression as she glided in the door. Kelly knew that the tables outside, under the umbrella, were the social equivalent of seats on the Supreme Court; the CEOs, agents, producers, celebrities, power wives, and international significant others who were seated there had to possess a combination of power, connections, and financial backing. Even beauty didn't count here the way it did everywhere else in Los Angeles.

The tables inside were a rung or two down the ladder, although the booths were considered the most desirable if rain made dining *alfresco* impossible. The truth was that to get a reservation at all was a status symbol, although as far as Kelly was concerned, the distinctions among the places one's ass rested during a meal were as meaningless as the machinations of the Spanish royal court in the fifteenth century. She just needed to know the code so she could use it to her advantage.

Kelly-as-Louise-Orlean held her new spring-line Louis Vuitton handbag in such a way that the huge fake diamond on her finger flashed at the maître d'. She engaged him in light conversation while she folded a fifty-dollar bill discreetly into the palm of her hand and slipped it to him invisibly. Fifty dollars was an amount worthy of attention, even in a restaurant like this. Her husband had taught her the art of gaining an instant power image, and proper tipping was an integral part of it. It worked like a secret code. Kelly looked anxiously over her shoulder. Brigante was not there. Either he hadn't seen her slip into the restaurant or he was lurking outside, maybe even waiting for Gillis to get there. When she turned back around, the maître d' was leading her to a prominent inside table decorated with a ball of peach and pink roses in the center of the white tablecloth.

The waitstaff, each as polished and pretty as a sitcom actor, swooped among the tables like swallows in their wrinkleless white shirts and black aprons. Kelly ordered mineral water and held the menu in front of her face, scanning the restaurant over the top of it.

Just as she brought her Perrier to her lips and took a breath, her antennae suddenly clanged a red alert. Bearing down on her, like a killer whale darting toward a seal, was a woman in a cherry-colored Versace suit.

"Honey, I didn't expect to see you in town today!" the woman drawled unenthusiastically, brushing Kelly's cheeks with lips the color and texture of dried blood. Kelly paused no more than a fraction of a second, but her mind felt like it was blowing a gasket. Who was this woman? A real friend of Louise Orlean? An opportunist wanting to glean some of Louise's conferred power and status?

"Last-minute plan," Kelly murmured softly and smiled minutely. She hoped she hadn't overdone the accent. Gillis's training and her own sensitive nature had taught her to respond to the unexpected with tiny gestures, conserving strength and surprise for when they were necessary.

"Join you?" said the woman, and without waiting for a reply she arranged herself in the chair opposite Kelly with a maximum of shifting and fluttering. She draped one skinny leg over the other for the benefit of the two men lunching at the next table—unshaven models or actors, in thin leather jackets, cashmere T-shirts, and expensive jeans. They didn't look over.

"I swear to God, the traffic in this town," the woman began. "Takes twenty minutes just to . . . I was flying out the door and Lupe had to stop me for some long conversation about a week off in June, her family in Guatemala, blah-blah-blah . . ."

The woman stopped abruptly and looked at Kelly as if really noticing her for the first time. Her eyes registered the surprise that her Botoxed forehead could not.

"Since when do you drink Perrier at lunch?"

Oh, shit. Kelly inhaled.

"I have a scratchy throat," said Kelly, barely above a whisper.

"Your voice does sound strange," the woman said, peering at her. "Something else is different." Kelly's heart ticked. The woman looked closer. "Your skin looks *great*. Arabella?"

"Yesterday," said Kelly, praying Arabella was a facialist.

"Ashley gave me the greatest stuff after my massage yesterday. It's this powder from Mexico. Supposed to keep you from getting sick all year."

Kelly shook her head and said hoarsely, "I'll just stick to my zinc and C."

Her companion cackled. "You and Dr. Klein. Call it whatever you want, honey. The rest of us know what it really is." She wriggled pleasantly and flapped the menu in front of her face. "Are we getting the usual?"

Kelly just smiled, waiting for more clues. For the next five minutes, every cell in her brain worked overtime as the woman droned through a monologue about her difficulties with choosing the tile color for her pool house. Kelly kept an eye out for Brigante and tried to appear interested in her companion's story despite the woman's distracting movements. She had a way of brushing her reddish, blow-dried hair out of her face with the backs of her thin hands, ending the gesture with a distinct flip of her fingers. Discreetly, Kelly scanned the room, plotting her escape and hoping the woman didn't notice her shifting eyes.

After an eternity, the waiter alighted at their table, putting his weight on one hip while Kelly's lunch date flirted with him. Kelly ordered a shrimp salad. The woman's eyes sparked with surprise in her otherwise expressionless face.

"Is that also doctor's orders?" the woman bellowed. "Since when do you eat shrimp? What about cholesterol? Mercury?"

"Change of pace?" Kelly vamped.

The woman pounced. "Are you telling me you're seeing Antonio again?" she whispered, leaning forward so excitedly that the waiter was unable to extricate her menu. He discreetly faded away.

Kelly slyly looked into the bread basket and dug out a pale-pink biscuit the diameter of a quarter. *To butter or not to butter?* She looked at her companion and saw that she was waiting for Louise to answer her.

"Well, not exactly," Kelly hedged. She lifted up her knife and moved it toward the butter ramekin. It hovered there for a moment as she watched the woman's face. Kelly was unsettled by how hard it was to read.

"Spill it, Louise," said the woman. "Now." Her tone was jocular but had an edge, the gossip's dread at being the last to know.

Kelly hooked some butter onto the knife and was about to reply when, over her companion's shoulder, she saw the impossible. Entering the restaurant in a flurry of manufactured tardiness was Louise Orlean! Her dark hair swung in the identical long bob of Kelly's wig; the nose and the eyebrows were indistinguishable from Kelly's artfully crafted ones. In a flash, Kelly dropped the knife into her lap. It hit her lapel on the way and clattered upon hitting the tile floor.

"*Merde!* Look at that!" She pulled a long face of dismay and brushed at the grease stain darkening the light fabric. The real Louise

Orlean was leaning into the maître d', who suddenly whirled around. In one controlled yet quick motion, Kelly grabbed her purse and jumped out from behind the table.

"I'll be right back, sweetheart," she said to the woman, and hurried toward the back of the restaurant. She passed the women's powder room and pushed through the swinging doors into the kitchen. The prep cooks looked up.

"*Salida?*" she asked, and one of them pointed to a door. Running now, Kelly shot a glance back through the window in the kitchen door and saw the headwaiter arriving at the table with the genuine article in tow. The other woman jumped up, her hands grasping her cheeks in a mask of surprise. Kelly tore off the wig and scrambled out the door. The alley looked empty. She tossed the wig and putty nose into the Dumpster as she ran past, shaking out her blonde hair. Stepping into a doorway, she peeled off her suit jacket and undid her crimson blouse another two buttons. Hidden from view, she turned the waistband of her skirt over a few times to shorten it and untucked the blouse to cover the fix. The restaurant door banged open.

"*Sí, sí,*" said a man's voice. "This way."

Kelly pressed herself into the doorway, snaking one hand out behind her to try the knob.

"You go that way."

Kelly recognized the voice of the maître d'. She heard footsteps, and then he burst around the corner. They stared at each other. Kelly kept her expression blank and tried to keep the fear out of her eyes. The man kept staring, registering recognition at some level, but trying to reconcile the blonde in front of him with the society wife from the restaurant. Kelly held her breath, knowing better than to speak. Did he remember her fifty-dollar tip from thirty minutes before? Would it matter? Her hand found the doorknob just as the maître d' stepped back toward Spago.

"Nothing down here," he shouted. "She must have gone the other way."

Kelly wrenched the doorknob and threw herself inside. She was in the storage area of a children's shoe store. She heard voices in the front of the store.

"Use your words, Ceylon. You're unhappy about something."

Kelly ditched her pantyhose and the suit jacket in a trash can and whipped a tissue out of her purse. She rubbed off the red lipstick and the dark eye shadow on her brows.

"Ceylon, it's not okay to throw things when you're angry. It's okay to *be* angry, but it's not okay to hit. Ceylon? Ceylon!"

Kelly dropped the fake diamond and the big earrings into her purse. She rolled her sleeves up above her elbows, raked her fingers through her hair, and then emerged into the shop. The salesman looked up from the floor where he was wrestling with a toddler's foot.

Kelly smiled ingratiatingly and spoke, still using Louise's accent. "I am trying to get to the valet for the restaurant. I get confused with all the doors in the alley. Is it this way?"

The salesman's mouth opened, but no words came out. Ceylon's mother broke into a huge smile.

"That happens to me all the time," she gushed. "Just go out here and to the right."

Kelly mouthed *thank you* and blew the woman a kiss. As she hurried out the front door, she heard the salesman ask, "Who was that?"

"The new Estée Lauder face," replied the mother confidently. "She's Parisian but has a house in Beverly Park."

Kelly slipped on a pair of oversized sunglasses as she passed through the door and melted into the streams of shoppers on Cañon Drive. She heard a police siren start up a few blocks away. She was careful not to look around too much. She didn't see Brigante and wondered whether he was still looking for Louise Orlean. She continued on for one block, then turned east. Her car was where she had left it, although the meter had run out and a Beverly Hills ticket fluttered on the windshield.

With relief, Kelly slid into the driver's seat, started the ignition, and pushed the gearshift into drive. At that moment, the passenger's door jerked open. A man's left leg came into view, and even before she saw his face, Kelly recognized the shoes. They were black Bruno Maglis.

"Go ahead and drive a little," smiled Gillis. "This'll be fun."

CHAPTER 29

KELLY CHECKED THE REARVIEW MIRROR. SHE SAW another police cruiser heading down Cañon Drive toward Spago. *Can't go back there,* she thought as she pressed on the accelerator.

Gillis's palm landed on her hand. "Would you look at yourself?" He moved his eyes from her shoes to her hair. "You're as beautiful as the day we met, Mrs. Gillis. Well, maybe not the *day* we met." He chuckled.

Kelly turned right onto Crescent.

"About as talkative, too." The leather made a shushing sound as Gillis lounged back in the seat. They drove in silence for a minute. Kelly's brain became a MapQuest of routes. Better to stick to commercial districts or head for residential neighborhoods? Get on the freeway or stay on surface streets? Head toward the west side or the rough-and-tumble east side, with its increased public transportation options? Simply circle Beverly Hills, with its orderly grid of streets smudged by double parkers, pedestrians, diagonal crosswalks, and elderly drivers? Kelly was as alert as a rabbit in an open field, but even so, the encounter had an air of familiarity—and inevitability—to it.

Gillis clasped his hands together. "Don't you want to know what tipped me off this time?"

Kelly knew well the tone of the third-grade boy in his voice—a combination of wanting to defy and wanting to please. She also knew that her husband required of her a maternal response, stern yet affirming. Too wimpy, and he would become instantly enraged by her weakness; too critical, and he would sulk, erupting into a geyser of payback later on. Kelly had but a split second to choose her words.

"I was afraid you'd outsmart me eventually," Kelly murmured, slowing at a yellow light. "How'd you find me?"

"Back at the foundation, Louise Orlean turned me on," crowed Gillis. "And that's when I knew it was you. No way that old bat could do it for me for real."

"How interesting," Kelly said neutrally. But her mind was spinning. *How long has he been just one step behind me?* She felt her fingers tighten around the steering wheel and tried to relax them before the knuckles went white. She could not let Gillis see her getting scared.

He ran a finger down her cheek. "Do you think Michelangelo ever forgot one of his statues?"

Kelly moved the car forward again and didn't respond.

"You were perfection in there," he said.

"I had a good teacher," Kelly replied, still playing kiss-up. She slowed behind a Hummer that was looking for a parking spot and signaled left to move around it. "Where are we going?"

"I have some ideas," said Gillis. "But first, why don't we just go for a walk. A normal, friendly husband and wife strolling in Beverly Hills. A promenade." He stressed the last syllable, rhyming it with *odd,* curling his lips ironically.

Kelly caught her breath. It was the kind of thing Gillis used to say before forcing her into some public humiliation. She made a desperate plunge.

"Todd. Is this about striking a bargain? Because here's the deal: You lay off the kids, and I"—she smiled at him provocatively—"and I lay off you." She hesitated for emphasis. "And your banks."

Gillis just grinned. "Pull over right here." He flicked his fingers toward a side street, and Kelly turned left off Wilshire and parked in front of one of the residences. "Funny you should mention a bargain." Letting his words hang in the air, Gillis grabbed her purse and started pawing through it. "What have you stolen from me this time?" he muttered.

Kelly kept herself calm and averted her eyes from the pink rubber puffball dangling from the ignition.

She looked out the window and considered her options. Ahead of her and on either side were long blocks of detached houses: Beverly Hills houses, with their security systems and housekeepers. If she ran for it, would anyone answer the door? What would she say? That she was running away from her abusive husband, the man sitting in the car over there, wearing the four-thousand-dollar suit and the thousand-dollar shoes? The man who looked like the CEO of a Fortune 500 company—which, in fact, he was? Who would believe her? She considered her other options.

After a moment, Gillis laughed and tossed the handbag on the backseat. "What did you take from my office, little Natalie?"

Kelly pressed her lips together and shook her head.

Gillis shrugged. "Well, it doesn't really matter, because once I turn over what I have to the LVPD, you're going to be toast anyway."

Thinking clearly, she said, "I have no idea what you're talking about, Todd."

"The knife that went missing from the crime scene. The

knife that has your boyfriend's blood on it. Or should I say your *ex*-boyfriend? You've already found yourself a new one, haven't you? You always did work fast."

Kelly tried to play for time. "I'm sure the investigators will be glad to have a murder weapon to close the case."

Gillis looked her in the eyes with a sincere and concerned expression. "But this knife has some fingerprints on it, too. The fingerprints of someone near and dear to you. In fact, you."

Kelly shook her head. "I used that knife to cut a lime. I made a drink."

Gillis snorted. "I know that, and you know that, but thanks to my dear old homicidal friend, Stacy Steingart, it was also the murder weapon."

Kelly spoke softly, urgently. "Todd. Let the kids and me go. Lay off us, and we'll disappear. You'll never hear from us again."

Gillis squeezed her hand. "But I *like* seeing you. You're my naughty little angel." She tried to pull her hand away, but he held it tight and continued as if she hadn't interrupted. "Stacy Steingart. Now there's a sad case. I had to pay her a shitload of money to off your boyfriend. But I think she was quite happy to do it. It's expensive to run a survivalist compound in the desolate wilderness these days. She would have done it for less. She's been loyal to me for a long time. But I didn't feel like haggling through a long, drawn-out negotiation, so I arranged for a deposit to an account for her in my bank and—after her unfortunate demise—all that money came back to me after all."

Kelly felt the old familiar desperation start to well up inside of her. "What do you want from me, Todd?" But she already knew the simple answer: He wanted her back. He wanted to win.

"You have two choices," said Gillis. "Go away for murder—you may even be the first female execution in Nevada in a long time—or come back to me. All I want from you is to stick with me for a while. I need to look like a stable family man for a year. And then you'll be free."

Kelly knew better than to believe him. As his wife, she'd never be free.

"Besides, it will give us a chance to catch up. And you know how I love being close to you," said Gillis.

"You want me close to you like you want sand in your bed. This isn't about me. I'm just like all the other toys you have a love/hate relationship with."

"How can you think like that? You're the mother of my children."

"Surprise, surprise! You remember you have children? Having children with me was your way of making sure I stayed put."

Gillis waved his hands irritably. "Alright, alright. But as a businessman, I need a wife and family. Here's your choice. You and the kids come back to the house by tomorrow night, or a hotel clerk finds the knife in the laundry chute of the hotel where Garrett died. Take it or leave it."

Kelly nearly gasped. *By tomorrow night?* Gillis opened his door, and the car pinged gently in protest. Time seemed to have slowed. Kelly heard the elaborate, multi-pitched whine of cars accelerating, the *thwap* of tires on asphalt, the pulsing bass rhythm coming from behind the closed black windows of an Escalade. She saw an older woman and a younger one—a grandmother and her granddaughter?—passing on the sidewalk, the *click-click-click* of one's heels syncopating the *clock-clock-clock* of the other's. She saw a pigeon take flight vertically, like a Harrier jet, and she felt Gillis's breath on her neck like a sirocco. The hair follicles along her scalp tingled.

Gillis was leaning over her. His hand slipped into her blouse and curved around her breast. It was just the sort of public display he got off on. Kelly saw the two women on the sidewalk avert their eyes.

"So you see," said Gillis, pressing her nipple with his thumbnail, "it's not really much of a bargain after all."

"I see," breathed Kelly, terrified. "You want me back where I belong."

"Mmm-hmm," murmured Gillis, looking into her eyes. "You keep me intrigued."

"You win," she said softly.

"That's more like it," he murmured back, smiling as he slid out of the car. "See you tomorrow night, then." He walked swiftly away from the car as Kelly watched him in her rearview mirror. Once more, the hyena was on the trail of his prey.

Brigante got out of a Mercedes limousine parked half a block behind them and held the door open for Gillis. Kelly's heart sank. She had been so scared, she hadn't even noticed they'd been followed.

As the limo passed Kelly's car, Gillis waved from a rolled-down window.

Kelly took three deep breaths, then put the car back into drive. She focused her mind on one thought: She had to get back to Jake.

CHAPTER 30

JAKE AND KELLY HUDDLED CLOSE TO EACH other under a blanket on a couch. Besides the moonlight streaming in through the picture windows, the only light in the room came from Jake's laptop computer. Kelly pressed a few keys.

"He's taking in money from a lot of different sources, and it's going toward his portion of the funding for the group home. But look, here again is a payout to a specific family."

Jake nodded. He saw the pattern too. That the money would go to residential group facilities made sense; that Gillis would be funneling money to a few specific foster homes—on top of what they received from the state—did not.

He let his gaze drift up from the computer. On the other side of the dark picture windows, the Malibu surf pounded the sand in front of the house, the moon whitening the spray into whipping cream. Jake had been in this house many times. Porter and Suzanne had bought it after her father had died; it was their California touchstone and their getaway. It had been redecorated since Jake had last been there. Fussy window treatments had been replaced by sleek blinds, and the ornate, gilded coffee table was now a chunk of marble supporting a slab of glass. The cushy sofas had become low platforms covered in leather, while the Persian carpets had given way to rough sisal.

Although Jake had never liked the artificiality of the house before, he found that he missed it a little. It seemed as sterile as an operating room, a too-permanent reminder of Porter's absence. Porter had liked warmth and comfort, and to any situation he invited conversation and hospitality. He must have hated the coldness of this room.

Suddenly Jake heard Kelly gasp.

"Look here," she said.

Jake looked at the columns of numbers on the screen. Kelly highlighted a row. He looked across to the right of the screen and in the final column saw whom the payout had gone to: Gary Gordon. He checked the date. Six months earlier. The Gordons were still taking money from Gillis.

"Bastards," he whispered. Kelly double-clicked on their name and the record of all their payments came onto the screen. Gillis had been paying them, roughly every six months, in installments of $20,000. The records went back four years. The Gordons had received $160,000 from Gillis just in that time, not counting all the years Kelly and Stacy had been in their home.

Jake grabbed Kelly's hand. "We can do something with this," he said.

Kelly shook her head, frustrated. "I have less than twenty-four hours. This isn't going to do it. No proof of anything that can put him behind bars." She groaned, covering her face with her free hand. "What *am* I looking for?"

"Let's keep at it," said Jake with a brightness he didn't feel. When Kelly had told him what had happened in Beverly Hills, he'd felt sick. He had wanted to go with her to the Gillis Foundation, but she had insisted otherwise. She always worked alone. He would blow her cover. Jake knew that this was true, especially because he was a public figure, so easily recognizable. But now he wished he had sent one of his investigators with her. He didn't want to acknowledge the sinking feeling that Gillis could have gotten to Kelly no matter what defenses he'd thought up.

Now Gillis had imposed a deadline, and Kelly believed he meant business. Jake couldn't understand why Gillis would ever set Kelly free—but he fully understood how Kelly operated. She took things as they came. In her world, planning far ahead was a luxury she couldn't afford. She evaluated her best options in each moment, took them, and then dealt with the consequences down the road.

Right now, assuming they couldn't find something solid to incriminate Gillis in the next twelve hours, she believed that her best option was to go back to him and figure out another way to leave him as soon as possible. A wave of anger swept over Jake. That would happen over his dead body.

"We're going to Las Vegas," he said decisively. "You said Gillis has called an Executive Committee meeting. Maybe we can learn something. Something we can use. I can arrange to have a plane at Maguire Aviation. It will be ready by the time we get there."

Kelly closed the laptop. "Okay."

Jake looked at her and was surprised by the depth of the love he felt for her. She was so game, so willing to say something so outrageous in the face of terrible odds. He grabbed her shoulders and kissed her.

"It's going to be alright," he tried to assure her.

"Why do people always say that?" said an angry voice.

Jake and Kelly wheeled around.

Barely visible in the hallway, her hand shaking, stood Suzanne Garrett. She was holding a gun.

CHAPTER 31

KELLY STARED. OF ALL THE PEOPLE SHE HAD feared might find her, Suzanne Garrett was at the bottom of the list. How had she known they'd be here? What was she doing waving a gun around?

"Joyce told me where I could find you, and I knew you had a key," Suzanne said to Jake, forcing her voice to sound reasonable, while fraying at the seams.

"She wouldn't," said Jake.

"Maybe not in most cases, Guv, but it's hard to resist spilling the beans when you're staring down the hole of one of these." She flicked her wrist to indicate the gun.

"Joyce has seen enough of those to know who is—and who isn't—capable of actually firing one," said Jake. And with that, something clicked in his head. He pulled out his cell phone. Sure enough, it was an unread text message from Joyce, staring him in the face.

Kelly studied Porter's widow. Her customary sleek bob was

disheveled. She wore a black Windbreaker with jeans and sneakers. She looked shorter in the casual clothes and, as Jake was trying to get her to admit, fairly ridiculous holding the gun. But when she moved swiftly toward Kelly and stuck the gun in her face, it didn't seem quite so ridiculous.

"You're the whore who did all this. Everything was fine until you came along."

Kelly could see the rage building in Suzanne's eyes and tried to hold her gaze. Jake was moving slowly to get behind her. Suddenly Suzanne whirled on him.

"Hold it, Jake!" Suzanne backed up so she had both of them at bay once more. "You both need to listen. I don't know what you're up to, but I know it will end up keeping me out of office. And I want you to know how serious I am about serving in Porter's stead. Nothing is going to keep me out of that seat. Not you, Guv, and certainly not your little whore here." She looked them over with a derisive sneer. "Jake, you never could keep your hands off Porter's things."

More calmly than he felt, Jake reached out an arm and picked up the phone. He held the receiver in front of him.

"Suzanne, I'm ten seconds away from calling the press and telling them you just threatened us with a gun. How long do you think your political career would last after that revelation? An hour? Or you can shoot Kelly and me now, and obviously you'd be kissing your political career good-bye. Go home and play politics like a good little girl."

Suzanne looked from Jake to Kelly, with the gun still leveled at their heads, but Kelly could see that her will had already left her. Suzanne knew Jake was right. She dropped her arm to her side and collapsed onto the hard, planklike, white leather sofa.

"Jake, I've been an idiot," she said sadly. Kelly thought her voice actually sounded sincere. "I suppose I could have found a different way to talk to you. But this is your fault . . . making me crazy with your phone calls."

"What phone calls?"

"Don't do that, Jake. I've acted stupidly, but don't patronize me."

"What phone calls, Suzanne?" Jake shook his head and looked at her blankly.

"All day long I've been getting messages: 'The governor wants to know about Kelly Jensen. We know about some of the stunts you pulled.'"

Jake shook his head in disbelief. "Suzanne, why would I leave you a message like that? Was it even my voice? Or coming from my number?"

"It wasn't your voice, no. But you could've had someone else do it." Suzanne continued, "You couldn't stand that I'm going to pick up where Porter left off. You've never been able to handle competing with Porter, so you took or co-opted or stole everything Porter had or said or did."

Jake anger overtook him. "Why would I care if you ran for Porter's seat, Suzanne?"

"My point exactly," said Suzanne acidly. "You disappeared from the campaign immediately after the funeral. You dropped off the face of the earth. All to chase after Porter's . . . *cunt.*"

Jake looked over at Kelly to see her reaction, but saw only a distant look on her face, as if she had already checked out of the conversation. He spoke levelly. "I've been trying to find Porter's *killer.* And we did."

Suzanne snorted. "*We* did? You had nothing to do with that investigation. The only reason you were anywhere near it was because you had my permission to be there. Without me, you'd have been out on your ass faster than it takes you to pick up a hooker."

Jake clenched his jaw and looked again at Kelly. She had listened intently to this last exchange of his with Suzanne and now had a strange look in her eyes. He felt a sudden plunge of fear. Did Kelly have a stake in haunting Suzanne with these phone calls? He hated Suzanne for planting a seed of doubt. He hated himself for wondering.

Kelly was still trying to figure out what it was that Suzanne really wanted. She clearly hadn't wanted to kill them. And if she had wanted to find out whether Jake was making harassing phone calls, she could have traced the calls. That left the possibility of something more complicated going on here, something that went back a long time. Did Suzanne feel some sort of unrequited love for Jake?

Either way, Kelly also knew the likely explanation for the phone calls, and she knew she was running out of time.

"Gillis is behind this," she said quietly.

"Gillis?" said Suzanne, wheeling on her. "What are you talking about?"

"Todd Gillis," said Kelly. "He's my husband."

Suzanne laughed. "That's the best joke I've heard all year."

"It's true," said Jake.

Kelly continued, "He knows I was with Porter the night he was murdered. He knows I'd been performing a Marilyn Monroe number at a club. He knows about the blonde wig."

Suzanne's eyes turned wary, but she was curious. "Why would that have anything to do with me?" She paused a moment and said under her breath, "You little slut."

Kelly glanced at Jake and proceeded carefully. "I think Gillis had something to do with Porter's death. I think it was because he knew Porter and I were in lo—because Porter and I were seeing each other."

Suzanne glared, but Kelly pressed on.

"Gillis is capable of destroying whomever he pleases. I think he is trying to set me up and is using every available avenue. If he's calling you about the case, I'm sure it has something to do with me."

"For a gutter whore, you have an awfully inflated view of yourself," said Suzanne. "I find it hard to believe that Todd Gillis would look twice at you, much less marry you."

"Oh, for God's sake, Suzanne," bellowed Jake. "Listen to her. She's trying to help."

Suzanne recoiled. "Help? Help *me*?"

Jake held up his hands. "Calm down, Suzanne. Hear us out."

Kelly decided to put it in terms Suzanne could understand: "Todd Gillis is meeting tonight with Theodore Henckle."

Suzanne's mouth actually fell open. "But Gillis has contributed to *my* campaign."

Jake snorted. "Come on, Suzanne, you've been at this longer than that. You think you're the only candidate getting his money?"

The transformation in Suzanne's face was remarkable. The previous moment she had been fiery, angry, and openly scornful; a split second later, her look became calculating, cold, and sly.

"*Gillis* is trying to take me out of the running?"

Jake nodded. "He knows about Porter and Kelly. So that secret will be out. And he's threatening to pin the murder on Kelly. Once he makes the first link, you're on shaky ground. When he makes the second, you're toast. I can read the tabloid headlines now: *A Wife in Name Only. The Ice Widow. The Loveless Marriage of Porter and Suzanne Garrett.*"

Suzanne silently digested the scenario Jake had described. "How does he make the second link?"

When Jake hesitated, Kelly spoke up right away. "He's got a knife with what he says are my fingerprints and Porter's blood on it." She spoke forcefully and clinically, watching for Suzanne's reaction.

Suzanne's mouth opened slightly, but Kelly saw her push her mind away from the questions, the sad and gory details of Porter's death and his affair. Kelly admired Suzanne at that moment. Like a true politician, Suzanne turned around 180 degrees when shown evidence of what would suit her interests in the campaign.

"How do we get this asshole?" she said flatly.

Jake smiled. "Atta girl. Gillis is meeting in Vegas tonight with his Executive Committee. We don't know for sure what they're up to, but we think we'll find something there."

"Take my plane," said Suzanne. "It's at Santa Monica. I'll call ahead. And keep me posted."

Jake nodded. Kelly reached for her bag and the computer.

"Take my car, too. One of my security guards can drive you. I think I'll stay here tonight—at least until he comes back."

On their way out the door, Kelly turned. "I never meant to hurt you," she said. "And thank you for this tonight."

Seated on the white couch with the vast, dark windows behind her, Suzanne looked small. But when she spoke, it was like a queen dismissing a subject. "Not one more word from you," she snapped. "Just clean up this mess you've made."

Kelly glared at her for a beat, then strode through the door. Jake shut it behind them.

CHAPTER 32

THE LINE ON THE OUTSKIRTS OF LAS VEGAS
demarcating civilization and wilderness is very clear. Either you're
standing in a developed area or you're standing in the desert.
Throughout Nevada, as in other parts of the country where popula-
tions are moving in droves, civilization's edges creep ever outward,
and the bulk of the encroachment is made up of housing develop-
ments.

The address Kelly had memorized from the file at the Gillis
Foundation offices was that of a house within a new development in
the first stage of completion. The gated entrance still fluttered with
flags, inviting prospective buyers to tour the model homes. It was
an upscale housing "community" made up of McMansions—nearly
identical, behemoth houses of no fewer than five thousand square
feet, straining at the edges of their property lines. Although each
property cost upwards of $2 million, the whole place had the feeling
of a tent city—impermanent, lonely, and easily abandoned.

Some of the houses were occupied, but some were dark. Others already had FOR SALE signs in the still-unlandscaped front yards. Jake pulled into the driveway of one of these.

"He'll probably have a thug posted outside. Let's not get any closer," Jake whispered to Kelly, mulling over the brainstorming they'd done on the plane, marveling at her uncanny ability to spin, on the spot, multiple anticipated counteractions to any number of Gillis's schemes.

"It should just be around that bend up ahead," Kelly said, pointing at the map they had printed out at Suzanne's beach house. The site of the Executive Committee meeting was at the very edge of the development, next to where the second stage was slated to begin. According to the map, it appeared that ground had not yet been broken on the next stage, so Gillis's house would be sitting with a neighboring home on one side and the empty expanse of the desert on the other.

The sliver of a moon revealed an infinite scattering of stars. Kelly and Jake moved quickly, pulling black caps over their hair and zipping up black jackets.

"You ready?" breathed Jake.

Kelly nodded. She felt a sense of foreboding, but there was also the feeling that she was reaching the end of this chapter. She would soon be free—or she would be going back to Gillis to avoid being framed for murder. But either way, nothing would be the same after tonight.

They circled around at a distance and approached the house from the rear, where it backed onto a man-made lake. Standing between the lake and the back fence, they could see bulldozers parked on the empty land at the desert edge of the house, waiting to clear the way for more mansions.

The house itself looked like every other one in the development. Built in a Mediterranean style, of white plaster and exposed beams, it had an external balcony running the length of the second story. The windows were arched with paned glass, red tile covered the roof, and decorative ironwork framed the staircase that led from the balcony down into the backyard. Sacrificed to the immensity of the house, that yard was a small sliver of dirt upon which sat a wooden shade structure and some iron furniture. Terra-cotta and glazed pots stood artfully but empty around the corners of the yard, awaiting succulents and bougainvillea and climbing trumpet vines. A flagstone pathway led from the house to a stone deck along the back fence, where a gas barbecue stood.

Under the balcony ran one long picture window, which formed the back wall of the first floor. Uncovered, and with the lights on inside, the window offered Jake and Kelly a clear view of the interior: a large kitchen that held stainless-steel appliances set off by Mexican tilework. A cooking island in the center was strewn with open bottles of alcohol, bags of tortilla chips, and tubs of salsa and dips. Off the kitchen was a great room that contained a wall-sized flat-screen TV, sectional sofas, and a coffee table holding a couple of open laptops and piles of papers.

Kelly and Jake listened for a moment, controlling their breathing so they wouldn't miss the slightest noise. The far-off roar of an occasional truck along the nearby freeway was all they could hear outside. From inside came the sound of music with a fast, heavy beat. The thud reverberated just enough to be more felt than heard.

Perfect, thought Jake, *for drowning out secret conversations.*

Kelly glanced at Jake and nodded. He reached over the fence, undid the latch, and held the gate while Kelly slipped through. Once inside, they stilled and crouched low against the fence. The music seemed to be coming from upstairs. In contrast to the blazing light of the ground floor, the upstairs was completely dark—with the exception of one lighted, arched window at the corner of the house.

Jake gently touched Kelly's elbow and they crept toward the house, staying close to the edge of the fence along the desert's edge. In their dark clothing and with the blazing lights inside, they would be hard to see if anyone should look out into the backyard. Nevertheless, they were careful to stay out of the curtain of light thrown through the picture windows.

As they neared the house, they peered into the kitchen. Styrofoam take-out containers littered the island along with the liquor bottles and chip bags. A sack of ice had slipped halfway off the counter and was dripping onto the tile floor. Their gaze traveled to the great room. Men's suit jackets lay haphazardly over the backs of the sofa; a pair of black loafers had been kicked behind the couch.

Suddenly one of the suit jackets moved. Kelly and Jake shrank into the shadows at the desert edge of the yard, near a sliding door off the kitchen. The jacket shook itself out, lumbered to a standing position, and revealed its owner. Brigante.

Kelly eyed him from the safety of her lookout. His black hair, plastered to his head, looked greasy. He reached a hand out to steady himself, then weaved dangerously across the tile floor, clutching at whatever he could—a side table, the kitchen island, a barstool—on his way to the sliding door.

He's drunk off his ass, thought Kelly, as she and Jake held their breath and pressed harder against the fence in the dark. Brigante threw open the sliding door and staggered out with an animalistic moan. He took about five steps outside, opened his fly, and let loose a horse-sized stream of piss, groaning as he did so.

Kelly shook her head. "These goons are so used to blatantly doing their dirty work, they would ejaculate right in the middle of Madison Square Garden." But she saw their chance.

Flashing a look at Jake, she went first, dodging fleetly behind Brigante's back, over the threshold, and through the kitchen and great room, toward the front of the house. Jake followed, glancing around for other guards, but Brigante seemed to be the only one.

Kelly sped to the base of a staircase, wheeled around the side of it, and crouched down. In an instant Jake was next to her, catching his breath. They froze, taking in their surroundings. They were in the front entrance area, which had a soaring, two-story-high ceiling and an enormous iron-and-stained-glass chandelier hanging from above. The Spanish tile from the kitchen continued in the foyer, accented near the door by a thirteen-foot-by-twenty-foot rectangle of colorful tiles painted to look like a fine carpet. Overhead, an interior balcony encircled three sides of the upper story in a squared-off U-shape, and Jake and Kelly could see several closed doors upstairs. The music they'd heard outside was more pronounced now, a steady rock beat coming from behind one of these doors.

They heard a crash and more moaning. Brigante had come back inside.

Kelly looked around frantically for a place to hide. Would he come to the front of the house and discover them? Built under the staircase was a door—a closet, she hoped. Her body tensed, ready to spring through the door if necessary. Then she heard the squeaky rustling of Styrofoam and the clanking of a bottle. Brigante muttered something to himself and shuffled across the kitchen toward the great room. Kelly heard a pop and a loud electronic buzz, and the huge television blazed to life, blaring a commercial at full volume.

"Shit," mumbled Brigante, "fucking . . ." There were more sounds of fumbling, and then the TV quieted down. A narrator was discussing tropical birds. Brigante did not change the channel.

Her heart still pounding, Kelly reached up to grip the banister. The iron was cold in her hand. She nodded to Jake and rose to her feet. Quick as a cat she ascended the staircase, with Jake following her up the stairs just as quietly. At the top, ears straining for the slightest sound, Kelly looked around—then entered through the first open door she spied.

The room was dimly lit and smelled acrid, like burnt match-es. It was a large bathroom, with a wide tile counter set with two sinks. Jake slipped a credit card–sized flashlight out of his pocket and shone the small beam of light across the counter. Yellowish powder dusted the surface near some chunks that looked like rock candy. Razor blades and bottle caps were scattered among Ziploc bags and uncapped syringes. A glass pipe lay in the sink. Jake felt his foot touch something and shone the light on the floor. A bag of drinking straws and a box of aluminum foil. He put his mouth on Kelly's ear.

"Crystal meth," he breathed.

She nodded and indicated for him to cut the light. They moved cautiously out of the bathroom and peered along the interior wall of the balcony. There were three more doors, all closed. Two of the rooms were dark; light seeped through the doorjamb of the third, in the middle. The music seemed to be coming from the darkened room farthest away, at the end of the corridor to their right. Brass plaques, like the nameplates found on office doors, were attached to the face of all three doors.

Odd, Kelly thought. She held out her hand for the flashlight and crept toward the first door. She flicked on the light. MR. F, read the sign. She flicked the light off.

The next moment, she felt Jake grab her hand. Before she reg-istered what was happening, he was pulling her past the door and into an alcove down the hall. The small space was lined with empty bookshelves and had a skinny, arched window and a wooden chair.

As Kelly heard a door open, someone came out of the room they had just been standing in front of. She couldn't see who it was, but the person moved down the hall, into the bathroom, and closed the door.

Jake took Kelly's hand again and they slipped out of the alcove, moving swiftly toward the door of the lit room. It was easy to read the nameplate without the flashlight: MR. G.

Jake felt Kelly's hand tense. He thought for a moment. If they crossed in front of the small shaft of light coming from beneath the door, would it cause a flicker that could be seen from inside the room? Maybe they were better off taking a quick look in Mr. F's room before he—or whoever had been in there—came out.

It was impossible to tell who reacted quicker to what happened next.

There was a sudden shout and the third door slammed open.

"Goddamnit, Gillis!" yelled a man's voice. "She's tweaking!"

Moving so quickly, almost as if supernaturally, Kelly and Jake were back in the bookshelf-lined alcove. But they had both seen the man come out of the room.

It was Theodore Henckle, shirtless, carrying something in his twitching hand.

They heard the door marked MR. G open and feet move unhurriedly across the tile.

"Ted, Ted, everything's fine." Gillis spoke slowly, calmly, as though quieting a fretful child. "Talk to me, tell me what's going on."

Henckle's voice had a slight quiver. "She's bugging out. H-h-hitting. She's going to scratch me. K-k-keeps scratching herself. Fucking cat."

"Relax, Ted," Gillis said in a soothing voice. "You're okay. She'll be alright. Let's go back to your room and see what we can do."

Jake and Kelly listened as Gillis continued moving slowly along the balcony to the room at the end of the hall, soothing Henckle with his voice and words. They heard a crash and a woman's muffled cry, then silence. Kelly stood to move, but Jake kept her back. He held up a finger as if to say, *One more minute. Just wait.*

Kelly, nauseated at what she'd heard, knew exactly what Gillis was doing in there. She'd felt his fist in her own stomach enough times to know how it hurt. She knew how the cry was involuntary—pain passing through the air being forced out of your gut. She knew that next Gillis would probably tie the girl by her wrists and ankles, facedown on the bed. She remembered how his knee felt between her own shoulder blades as he held her down.

Panic rose in her throat, and she wasn't sure she could contain herself. She had to go help that girl. She had to save that girl because no one had saved her.

Ignoring Jake, ignoring everything that advised caution, Kelly ran for the bedroom door. She thought she heard Jake hiss, "Stop!" but she kept running, her rubber soles silent on the tile. When she got to the door, she stopped.

The scene in front of her was more hellish than even she could have imagined. Kelly took it all in, like a panoramic camera capturing a wide frame. A red lightbulb illuminated the room in a grotesque bath of lurid crimson shadows. On the bed lay a girl of perhaps fourteen or fifteen, naked and facedown, as Kelly had guessed. Gillis, in his suit, was fastening a cord around her right wrist, his knee on her elbow. She was twitching and crying out, but didn't seem to be struggling to get away. The skin from her neck to her thighs held a pattern of mottled blotches. In the strange light Kelly couldn't make out whether they were fresh welts or old sores. The girl's brown hair was long and matted.

To the left of the bed, by the window, were two chairs. One girl huddled in each, their vacant eyes looking rapidly around the room but seeming not to see. They, too, were naked and extremely thin, and Kelly could see raked lines on their forearms and thighs, as if they'd been scratched. The girls were silent, but their mouths and tongues were in motion, licking their lips, grinding their teeth. In the light, and in their drugged condition, it was hard to tell, but Kelly thought they could be no more than twelve or thirteen years old.

To the right stood Henckle, wearing only his suit trousers. Gray chest hair covered the front of his body down to the flabby white paunch that hung over his belt. His normally sleek, combed silver mane was sticking up crazily, and his face was blotchy. The thing in his hands was a whip with a black leather handle. His hands were trembling so violently, he could barely keep hold of it.

On the bed, Gillis pulled the cord taut and slapped the side of the girl's head with the back of his hand.

"Are you going to be a good little girl now?" he bellowed. "You little piece of shit!"

In the few seconds that Kelly had been standing in the doorway, the images and actions piled up in slow motion. It seemed to her that a lot of time had passed, in what was really less than an eyeblink. One detail that had not escaped her notice, that her brain had given a weight equal to the horror of the scene, was Henckle's stare. He was gaping at Kelly now, his eyes darting faster than was normal between her and Gillis.

Functioning on pure instinct, Kelly sprang like a tiger toward Gillis, just as the drug-addled senator yelled, "Who's that?!" She caught Gillis as he turned, and the momentum knocked him against the wall. Kelly fought with all she had. She caught hold of his ear with one hand, digging in her fingernails, struggled to reach his eyes with her other hand, and tried to get her knee to connect with Gillis's balls.

"You cunt," he grunted through his teeth, and Kelly felt his whole body tense with excitement and adrenaline. He gave a tremendous push, and she flew nearly upright, but still she had hold of his ear. With her free hand she dragged at his sleeve, but the slippery fabric evaded her fingers. She crashed into the bed on her back, the impact bouncing her to the floor. Gillis loomed over her, a fist pulled back, his faced screwed up into a demonic grimace. Kelly scrabbled her knees toward her chest and tucked her arms and head into a fetal position. When Gillis's arm tried to connect with her ribs, she would be ready.

Coiling her legs around his shoulder, she yanked him to the ground. His forehead crashed into her lip, and she felt a hot rush of blood. But once again, the element of surprise allowed her to roll out from under Gillis. He wasn't used to her fighting back like this. She cocked her leg into her chest again and let her heel fly into Gillis's solar plexus. She heard an *ooph* and saw his face contort with a mixture of pain and surprise. She flipped to all fours and was almost on her feet, ready to run, when a blinding pain crashed over the back of her head. Her vision went white, and she felt her knees buckle underneath her.

In a flash her vision returned, and as she fell she saw the half-naked, trembling Henckle standing over her, the leather-covered lead handle of the whip still hovering above her head. Her arms didn't break her fall, but she was able to twist her body so that she landed on her shoulder. Immediately she felt Gillis's iron hand on her cheek, pushing her head into the floor. She noticed that his hands were ice-cold. His voice was even colder.

"You little bitch. This is it." He grabbed her wrists and coiled her arms behind her back, lifting upward. Kelly gasped in pain as he dragged her up by her wrists so her legs were dangling above the floor. She tried to kick, but the pain from her shoulders made it impossible. So she did the only thing she could.

"Jake!" she screamed.

Gillis was panting as he dragged her toward the bedroom door.

"That cocksucker can't help you . . . *Natalie*," he said, his voice full of mockery and his lips in a sneer.

"Kelly!"

She looked up, and her heart plummeted with despair. In front of her was Jake, his strong face bloodied, his arms held behind his back by Brigante. The thug had a knife pressed to Jake's jugular vein. Roland Farse, "Mr. F," stood next to them, uselessly looking back and forth between Gillis and Brigante. Behind her, Kelly could hear whimpering, whether from Henckle or one the girls, or all of them, she didn't know.

She could feel Gillis's fury in the brutality of his grip and hear it in the forced calm of his voice.

"Take him out," he said to Brigante, jerking his chin at Jake. "Make it look like an accident."

There is a moment of clarity just before death that psychiatrists call "peritraumatic dissociation." Time reorganizes itself into slow motion. Every sense kicks into high gear and sends hypercoded messages to the brain: Vision is in Technicolor, hearing is Dolby stereo quality, and sense of smell is as keen as a basset hound's. In that moment, Kelly felt the deep thumping of the music as if it were emanating from her own heart and controlling her pulse. She could see the tiniest beginnings of stubble starting to poke out through the blood running down Jake's cheek. The acrid smell of the crystal meth and the fetid, animal smell in the bedroom became so strong, they were almost visible.

At the same time, another part of Kelly's brain started a clip-reel of her life. Decorating paper dolls with her mom. Swinging down from a high place—her dad's shoulders—in a flame-colored park in autumn. Footsteps in the hallway, her mother's screams. The judge leaning toward her, massive in his black robes. Kevin grinning, one front tooth missing. Libby somersaulting off the front porch. In that instant, she saw the truth. She and Jake were going to die. Gillis had killed Porter, and now he was going to kill them.

All this passed in a millisecond. Suddenly, Kelly zoomed back into real time.

She twisted her neck to look into Gillis's eyes. "Todd," she murmured, "you win. You own me."

Then, like a deer surrendering to a wolf, she threw her head back and offered him her neck. For a moment Gillis looked startled, then he looked amused, and finally he looked hungry. He pounced forward with his tongue and teeth, his hand reaching between her legs, releasing its grip on her wrists.

With all her strength, Kelly slammed her knee into his groin. Gillis crumpled forward with a monstrous howl. On his way down, she slammed that knee into his face, and heard a crunch.

Kelly turned toward Jake. Brigante seemed to be momentarily stunned. Jake seized the advantage and twisted out of the huge man's grasp. Brigante lunged with the knife, but Jake caught him from behind and sent him sprawling into the wall.

"This way!" yelled Jake to Kelly, holding out his hand. She sprang toward him, and they headed down the hall toward the stairs. They'd gone about ten feet when they stopped short. Standing in front of them in the hall was Farse, calmly holding a shotgun aimed at Jake's heart. He trained it on Kelly, then aimed it back at Jake.

"You always were such trouble," he sneered at Kelly.

Behind her, Kelly could hear Brigante stumbling to his feet. Gillis, she knew, would already be up, and sure enough, she heard his voice in her ear.

"You whore. You keep forgetting that you can never get away."

Kelly struggled, but Gillis grabbed her tightly from behind and pulled her toward the wall, away from the balcony railing. He gestured to Brigante, who stumbled over to Jake and, twisting Jake's arms behind him, pushed him toward the railing. Kelly screamed. A fall from the second story onto the tile below might not be fatal, but Jake would certainly be too hurt to escape. Brigante was pushing him over headfirst; the chances of Jake hitting the ground unscathed were slim to none.

Kelly continued to struggle helplessly against Gillis's unyielding arms. Farse's shotgun was still trained on Jake. On her other side, at the end of the hall, Henckle, backlit by the grotesque reddish light from the bedroom, was peeking out the door.

She became aware of Gillis's breathing in her ear and realized he was chuckling. Furiously, she screamed out again, "No!" just as Brigante folded Jake over the railing, kicking and forcing his legs out from under him. Kelly felt a sickening surge in her throat as one of Jake's legs slipped over the railing.

Later, when Kelly tried to put it all together in her mind, she realized that the next thing her senses registered was the sound of breaking glass. At nearly the same instant, she heard an explosion, and saw a blast of smoke explode from the front door.

"Police! Everyone freeze!"

A rush of men wearing helmets and flak jackets, and carrying weapons, poured into the entryway. Brigante let go of Jake and started running down the hall. Farse swung his shotgun toward the men, fired, then dropped it and ran after Brigante. Kelly rushed toward Jake, who pulled himself back from the edge and grabbed her. They stood where they were, their hands raised in the air.

Henckle disappeared into the bedroom, while Gillis simply evaporated. Kelly had felt his grip disappear when the SWAT team broke down the door, but she hadn't seen where he went.

In a matter of moments, the police had gathered up Brigante, Farse, and Henckle and were handcuffing them. Kelly heard the shouts, the swearing, the vain threats uttered as the three men were captured. Some of the team had come through the bedroom window—the breaking glass Kelly had heard—and were helping the three girls, covering them with blankets and administering first aid. One officer came up to Kelly and Jake and asked if they were okay. Jake nodded, putting his arm around Kelly and moving her protectively down the stairs.

When they emerged from the house, a pair of officers rushed forward with blankets, and after checking their injuries, led them to the curb with orders to "wait and rest." They sat there in silence, their sides and legs touching, their hands entwined. A paramedic with a first-aid kit approached them and cleaned Jake's face. The blood was coming from a cut over his left eye. Kelly's lip had stopped bleeding but was still swollen, and her wrist was twice its normal size. The paramedic gave them each ice packs and extra bandages.

"I'm sure you want to get out of here, but you need to stay around for questioning. Someone will be here in a few minutes. Drink this in the meantime." The paramedic handed them each a juice box and patted Kelly's shoulder through the blanket.

Jake was stabbing his juice box open with a straw when he heard a familiar voice.

"You two okay?"

They looked up and saw Alana Sutter. Still feeling blurry, Jake tried to rationalize her presence here. Even in his state, it didn't take long. He grinned.

"We have Suzanne to thank?"

"Let's just say she didn't know what you'd find, but thought some pictures might come in handy." Sutter held up a video camera. "And she figured it would be easier to get them with the support of a SWAT team."

"Henckle?" murmured Kelly.

"All three of them," the campaign manager replied. "But the shots of Henckle will be most, shall we say, useful." She moved her head to indicate the police car that held Henckle, still shirtless, with a blanket around his shoulders, looking wild-eyed. "The networks will be peeing in their pants when they see these pictures."

Jake, exhausted, could only smile as he accepted the cup of coffee Sutter held out to him. Kelly took one too. Suzanne would do well in the Senate after all. She was already much more cutthroat than Porter had ever been. Work on her likability factor a little, and she could be legendary. Of course, after tonight, she would skate into office. She must have used her connections at the governor's office to get the cops there on a hunch. *However she did it,* thought Jake, *thank God she did.* He knew he and Kelly would be dead—or worse—if they hadn't shown up when they did.

Jake looked around the scene. Farse, Henckle, and Brigante were each in the back of separate police cars. The three girls were being carefully helped into the rear of a paramedic's truck; a female officer with a kind expression on her face was questioning them. Some of the SWAT team was still inside, and light was pouring out of every window of the house. Bright lights illuminated the outside, too, where officers in suits and in uniform shouted to one another, spoke in small groups, and guarded the police cars. A few neighbors in bathrobes stood, dumbstruck, at the darkened fringes of the scene. Jake shook his head. How Suzanne had managed to marshal this show of force was truly impressive. What had she told the governor?

All of a sudden, Jake felt Kelly nudge his thigh under the blanket. He followed her eyes to one of the suited cops, leaning into one of the cruisers. The detective stood up; his identity was unmistakable. His white-blond hair glowed almost blue under the sharp police lights. Jake couldn't see them, but he knew if he were close enough to the man, his eyes would be pale and his eyelashes almost albino.

Sipping their coffee, both Jake and Kelly watched Cooper, deep in discussion with two uniformed officers and writing in a notepad.

From around the corner, a black Mercedes pulled up to the curb. In the commotion, no one seemed to notice it, but Jake heard Kelly gasp.

A tall and trim man in a dark suit calmly got out of the car and strode up to Cooper. Jake heard him ask, "Are you in charge of this investigation?" and saw Cooper nod. The men fell into deep conversation. Jake could feel Kelly starting to shake under the blanket.

"He's going to get out of this," she whispered.

The man was Gillis. His nose, where Kelly had kneed him, was clearly broken, but it was not bleeding. His hair was smooth; he was breathing evenly. There was absolutely no trace of the pimp he'd been just a half hour earlier in the house.

Jake leaped to his feet and marched over toward Cooper and Gillis.

"The house is rented by my foundation," Gillis was saying, "but I wasn't on the premises this evening. It was made available to some of my board members. I was in town and came out the moment I heard there was trouble."

Jake walked up to the men and stood very close between the two of them, saying nothing. He thought he saw a glance pass between them.

Cooper rolled his eyes. "Brooks, you pop up in the strangest places." He eyed the cut on Jake's face.

Jake's mind was flying, intercepting every legal trap Gillis was about to leap over.

No DNA samples because he was not physically engaged in the act.

No witnesses except for Kelly and Jake—whose testimony might not be corroborated.

The girls, when they came down from their drug highs, were the only solid link. And they were all underage—easily intimidated.

"Nice friends you keep company with, Mr. Gillis," Jake uttered. "Detective Cooper, this evening was organized entirely by Mr. Gillis. I'm sure phone records will show that. Airport staff and others could be persuaded to testify."

"Perhaps in court, Mr. Brooks, but those losers in the cars? They're getting booked tonight—pandering, possession of illegal substances, providing illegal substances to minors, discharging of fire-arms, child endangerment, rape, molestation. And yet they all insist that Mr. Gillis knew nothing about this."

"What my board does on their own time is their business," said Gillis with a maddening smile. "They don't share it with me. And they don't involve me in their sordid dealings." Jake quickly glanced over to where Kelly was sitting, her face in her hands. He was almost surprised to see her still there, half expected her to be gone.

"How'd you break your nose?" said Jake.

"Save your rhetoric for the courtroom, counselor," said Gillis with derision. Turning to Cooper, he asked, "Do you need me tonight?"

"It's late," agreed Cooper. "We're going to ask you a few more questions. But there's not enough evidence to inconvenience you tonight. You're free to go, but do us a favor? Come into the station tomorrow with your attorney."

Gillis grinned and shook Cooper's hand. He turned to Jake.

"Tick, tick, tick," he said.

Jake felt the air go out of his lungs. Gillis wasn't giving up Kelly. The deadline was still on. Jake nearly screamed in frustration; there was nothing he could do here. His power existed in the courtroom, but the crime scene wasn't his territory. He would do everything he could to bring Gillis to justice, but he knew it would be a long, losing battle. For the first time, he truly understood what Kelly had endured her whole married life. They were trapped. Gillis would play by his own rules—rules he was rich enough and smart enough to make up. Rules he could bend when he needed to get exactly what he wanted.

"See you tomorrow, then, Detective Cooper. And thank you." Gillis gave Cooper a little salute, and with a steady gait he walked back to his Mercedes, fired the engine, and drove off.

Jake's brain went into overdrive. He had to think of a legal way to get this guy off Kelly's back.

"This isn't over," growled Jake to Cooper. "And I'm bringing you down with him."

He staggered back to Kelly. The enormity of what he had just seen and experienced in that house was hard enough to bear. His realization of Gillis's reach and power further deflated him. He sank down next to Kelly and gathered her into his arms. He felt her body shudder, then her warm tears pooling on his shoulder. At that moment Jake felt as though the sole reason he had been put on earth was to find a way to protect Kelly Jensen. How many other men in her life had felt that way about her? He didn't care. He loved her.

"I'm going to find a way out of this for you," Jake murmured into Kelly's ear.

She had nothing to say in return.

They sat there holding each other while a cop came over and asked them a few questions, dutifully writing their answers in a notebook. The paramedics' van drove away with the three young girls. Finally the police cars left, too, and Jake and Kelly had nothing else to do but limp back to the driveway where they had left their car what felt like weeks before.

PART THREE

PART THREE

CHAPTER 33

KELLY, WEARING A RED BIKINI, WAS COMPLETELY in her element, as though she were a princess and Lake Tahoe were Lake Como. Her shiny hair fell in loose waves around her face as she leaned back in a chaise lounge. A book lay open in her lap, but her eyes were on her children in the water. Sunglasses shaded her eyes. Her brown legs stretched out forever.

"Come on, Mom, *throw*!" shouted Kevin, insistent and excited.

Kelly leaped up and began heaving plastic weights into the pool. Kevin noisily threw himself into the deep end to retrieve them, sending Libby flouncing out of the churning water to a nearby flower bed where she began stabbing at the dirt with a small spade. A couple of dogs raced by, nearly knocking Kelly into the water. She hammed it up, windmilling her arms until the children were shrieking with glee. She staggered over to the lawn and collapsed on her back. Kevin and Libby piled on top of her, and she wrestled them gently to the ground.

Jake watched from the house, hesitating before joining them.

He wished he could freeze this moment, bottle it for Kelly to keep in her small collection of good memories.

Eight months had passed since that night in the Las Vegas suburb, and so much had happened since then that it seemed like a lifetime ago. Senator Henckle had been destroyed by the scandal, of course. The video Alana Sutter had shot and given to the media clinched his ruin. Although there hadn't been time to remove his name from the ballot, he had been defeated soundly by Suzanne Garrett. Technically, Porter had won—his was the name still on the ballot. But after the voters elected a dead man rather than vote for Henckle, Suzanne had been appointed to the seat by Governor Glen Green. Jake had to admit that, for all her faults, Suzanne would do a good job in the Senate. He sent her a congratulatory note after the election, but they hadn't spoken since the night in Malibu. He wondered if they ever would again. They were deeply in each other's debt, but after what they'd been through, he never wanted to acknowledge it to her. He was sure Suzanne felt the same way.

Henckle, Farse, and Brigante were all still awaiting trial, but they might as well be awaiting execution. The media and public had already tried and condemned them. They would do hard time somewhere and wouldn't fare well. Jake had questioned the victims—the girls who had been prisoners in the house that night—which only confirmed Gillis's meticulous control over the incident. The girls had sworn under oath that Gillis had been their savior.

And Gillis? Jake, with Kelly's welfare foremost in his mind, had managed to box him into a corner. A small, temporary corner, but a corner nonetheless. Using every shred of acting ability he possessed, Jake had groveled at the feet of Law Boy in Los Angeles. He threw it all on the table: expense sheets of private plane trips, the lease on the Vegas house, questionable entertainment bills—the works. He had at last persuaded the U.S. attorney, the morning after the Las Vegas incident, to arrest and charge Gillis with charity fraud. It had kept Gillis off balance enough that he hadn't called in Kelly's debt. The knife had not surfaced. It had bought Kelly a few more days.

A quick arraignment gave Gillis a choice: a laughably short sentence (nine months in a minimum-security country club) or a protracted trial during which not only the FBI but also the IRS—two runaway federal agencies that operated like vicious little dogs, grabbing hold of a cuff and not letting go—would turn over every stone in his life. Gillis had decided to get the prison time over with, Martha Stewart–style, rather than face the maggots that would turn up if the law started digging too aggressively in his garden. Gillis was now seven months into the nine-month sentence. In a few short weeks he'd be out.

Jake flinched as he stared out the window at Kelly and her kids. He hadn't seen her for those seven months. After what they'd been through, they had agreed that Kelly needed time alone with her children. She'd been living at Jeanette Pantelli's estate through the winter and spring. Now it was summer, and Kelly had called Jake to come up for a visit.

Jake was uncharacteristically nervous about their meeting. Truth was, he was enticed and alert. He was glad he'd gotten Gillis out of the picture for a few months, knowing he'd bought Kelly this time to heal, but he was haunted by the look on Gillis's face when he had walked away from the house that night in Las Vegas. Getting into his Mercedes, Gillis had looked Jake straight in the eye and winked, the smirk on his lips unhidden and unashamed.

And Jake remembered Cooper's oily obsequiousness toward the powerful man. Gillis was a man totally accustomed to buying attorneys, juries, politicians, freedom. Even the cops who had led him into the van that took him to prison seemed to defer to Gillis's authority. Both Jake and Gillis knew that after a few months away—somewhere gentle—followed by a little probation and a tiny media flap, it would all blow over. This was nothing for a man of Gillis's power and reach. Soon enough Gillis would be out, ready to set up business again, ready to go after Kelly, ready for revenge.

The thought that he had gained only the smallest reprieve for Kelly brought an acid taste to Jake's tongue. He held up a hand against the sun. Kelly and her children glistened with happiness. Jake was glad they'd had these months to be alone together before he'd offered himself into their threesome as a permanent fixture. Steeling his nerves, he forced his feet outside and waited to be noticed.

Kelly looked up right away. "Jake!" she called gaily, running toward him and kissing him lustily on both cheeks. "Libby, Kevin, get your little behinds over here! Jake!"

Jake's stomach flipped hearing her smooth voice around his name again.

"Hello, Mr. Jake," said Libby in her squeaky munchkin voice.

"Hi, Jake," mumbled Kevin, looking at the ground.

Jake caught his breath. The boy was a miniature replica of Gillis. The same dark hair, the same cut jaw. Intelligent eyes. But the boy had a gentleness his father lacked, a softness that came, Jake knew, from Kelly. Completely atypically, Jake was seized with a sudden shyness in the face of this shining, happy family. He could not think of a single thing to say to these children but "Hi, guys."

He caught Kelly grinning at him and relaxed. "I'm glad you're having a good time," he uttered. His stomach flipped again at the sight of her radiance.

"Okay, *muchachos*, lunchtime!" Kelly cried. "Go see what Sera-fina's got for you. After that you can do some more swimming. I'm going to have a little chat with Jake." The children tore into the house and tumbled into the arms of a round housekeeper, chattering like baby birds. They ran off in a little group, laughing, toward the kitchen.

"You let them swim after eating?" poked Jake.

Kelly watched the children disappear into the house. "Between air pollution, global warming, terrorism—I can't imagine how low swimming after eating rates." She peered at Jake over her sunglasses. "This setting has been so great," she said, indicating the surroundings. "Jeanette has made us feel so welcome. Thank you, Jake."

Jake pulled Kelly into his arms. She was elastic and warm, like taffy, and she filled his crevices, smoothing into them like a custom fit.

"I've missed you," she said.

Relieved, Jake held her closer still.

At last Kelly laughed. "Come on, Mr. Talkative." Arm in arm they walked beyond the pool, down a little path, and through a gate toward the lake. The sun had glazed over the crystal blue surface of the water, creating a wide platter of white light. The smell of pine was strong in the air as Kelly led Jake down to the small private beach. They nestled into the warm sand, leaning their backs against a boulder, and contemplated the blue of the sky, the green of the trees, the blue-black of the water.

Jake reached out a finger and traced a meandering line from Kelly's jawbone down her throat, across her collarbone and along her arm. She tipped into him, putting her head on his shoulder, and he watched a droplet of sweat swim down her chest and disappear into the dark channel between her breasts. Jake loved nothing more than the scent of a woman. She turned her face up to him for a kiss. As their mouths moved gently together, he closed his eyes to shut out the sun bouncing off the sand. Every cell in his body wanted to be inside her, but he tenderly took her hand instead.

"We don't have long," he whispered.

"The kids are fine," murmured Kelly. "I've been with them all morning. They love Serafina."

"That's not what I meant, Kelly. I meant Gillis. I meant . . ."

Kelly shook her head. "I know what you meant, Jake. But this is our reality right now. Sun. Sand. You. Me. Kevin and Libby are safe. That could all change—in just a few minutes. Maybe you'll say something. Maybe something's out of our control. It's this minute—*this* reality—I'm interested in. I want to be with you. I want *you.*"

Jake didn't need to hear another word. They rolled over in the sand, and he dove into the warm, salty ferocity of her sea.

CHAPTER 34

KELLY WRAPPED HER ARMS AROUND JAKE'S shoulders and held on. She was grateful, of course, for everything he had done for her. He'd risked everything—his career, his reputation, his life—to protect her. After the night in Las Vegas, he'd done even more to get her away from Gillis, at least temporarily.

She pulled back for a moment and stared at Jake now, memorizing the line of his eyebrows, the cut of his chin, his penetrating gray eyes. A ruffle of wind moved through his hair. He smiled.

"Are you getting ready to impersonate me?" He laughed. "You've got that look in your eye."

Kelly smiled back. "No, just looking."

Jake—for all his intelligence, his crushing adeptness as an attorney, his power in the courtroom and over the media, the wheels of justice, and the people who came to him—seemed to her like an innocent. He saw, he experienced, he felt—for her, for his clients—but he didn't *know*. His sympathy was as acute as that of anyone she'd ever known (even Porter, she'd come to admit), but empathy was a different story. Like racism, pregnancy, the death of a parent—the experience of being abandoned as a child was something you didn't know unless you'd been through it.

She smiled at Jake again, her eyes shining with unmistakable love.

Jake pulled her back toward him, and they lay against the sand side by side, their arms flung over their eyes to keep out the sun.

A deep melancholy settled over Kelly as she thought about what she had to say, as she watched Jake lie there breathing evenly, companionably.

"This is nice," he murmured.

"There's something I want to say," began Kelly. She sensed a band of electricity run down Jake's body, but he remained motionless. She pressed on. "I'm going away for a while. With the kids."

Instantly, Jake sat up. "No," he said. "No. No. It's not okay. No."

Kelly shushed him, placing her hand gently on his mouth as though he were her young son.

"You have to listen to me," she said.

"No, *you* have to listen to *me*," said Jake. "We are going to be together. I'm not letting you go. We need each other, and you're not leaving me." He stopped abruptly, both of them shocked by his intensity. Neither pointed out how much he sounded like Gillis. How many other men had tried to possess Kelly in the same way?

Jake threw himself back on the sand, and his arm covered his eyes again. He exhaled loudly. "Alright. Continue," he said petulantly.

"You know I love you," said Kelly, keeping her voice as even as possible. "I need you too, I really do." She hesitated, wishing she could see his eyes but at the same time glad he was covering them. "My kids have always come first. I can't keep moving from place to place, wondering when their father is going to find me."

Jake grunted. "That's what I'm saying too. You've got *me* now. I—we—have ways to keep him away from the three of you." But they could both hear the truth hidden behind his words. It would always be a struggle. Jake's throat went dry. Porter had probably said exactly the same sorts of things to Kelly, even promising her the power of his office, his position as a congressman, to keep her sociopathic husband at bay. And that had done no good. No good at all.

For a split second, Kelly considered telling Jake what she knew. She wondered whether it would do them any good—either to help her leave or to help Jake save her. Because when it came right down to it, Kelly really did want to be saved. Her personal hell was her hope—she had always desperately wanted the salvation she knew would never come. But she knew she couldn't tell Jake the whole truth. What was the point? All that mattered was that she knew the truth now, knew the only way to escape it, and that was that. Her kids would never know. Jake would never know. The secret would die with her.

She had known for seven months now, but the weight of it felt like seven lifetimes. Back in November, two weeks after that night on the outskirts of Las Vegas, Kelly had gone by herself to Houston. Jake was embroiled in getting Gillis put behind a chain-link fence, and Kelly had left her children once more in the safekeeping of Frank and Holly.

As she had driven up to the house in a rental car, she could see that the place was just as she'd remembered it. The long driveway, the leafless autumn trees. She rang the bell, waiting many long minutes before the door opened. A tiny woman, her brown face wrinkled like creased paper, stood before her. A flicker of recognition sparked in the woman's eyes when she saw Kelly, her brain computing the passing of years.

"Griselda. I need to come in."

Wordlessly, the maid widened the door, and Kelly stepped over the threshold. She stopped in the entryway and glanced around. The house had never been warm, but in its abandoned state, it was in purgatory—soulless, but not quite dead.

Griselda opened her mouth as if to speak and shut it again. Kelly swept past her and climbed the stairs to the second story. In truth, the housekeeper disgusted her. This was not a reunion of similarly tortured souls who could finally break through years of missed opportunities to show a tenderness that had always existed below the surface. This was a meeting of a jail guard and her former prisoner.

Kelly felt nothing for this wizened old woman and what she may have suffered in Gillis's employ. Just fifteen when Gillis first brought her there, Kelly had blocked out so much of the daily life of the place. One thing she knew was that not once had another adult tried to help or intervene. They all knew that what was going on wasn't right. But they all owed him something. They were too afraid of him—and eventually too complicit themselves, too guilty—to do the right thing.

Kelly held her duffel bag tightly over her shoulder and entered the master suite. She didn't wait for her eyes to adjust to the darkness; she strode over to the window and tore back the heavy drapes. Diffuse light poured in through the sheers. The room, like everything else she had seen, was exactly the same. The black bedspread—surely not the same one from so many years ago?—adorned the king-sized bed. The snow-white carpeting. Kelly willed herself not to feel anything as she walked through the bedroom, past the cavernous closets, and into Gillis's study.

When she had lived here as his wife, she hadn't been allowed to enter this room. Even when Gillis was in it, she was forbidden entry.

She felt a wave of dread as she stepped into it and had to remind herself that Gillis was still incarcerated. Even with his power and the strings he could pull, he would be behind bars for a whole nine months. Still, she sensed a prickle on the back of her neck as though she were being watched, and she spun around.

Griselda stared at her, eyes narrowed.

Kelly hissed at her the way one might hiss at a cat. The little woman jumped and scurried away. Kelly moved toward Gillis's desk.

The top of the desk contained two items: a black telephone, somewhat outdated, and a chrome picture frame. Coming around the vast tabletop, Kelly saw that the frame contained a photo of her on her wedding day, looking over her shoulder as if surprised, her unsmiling face framed by a white veil. She remembered Gillis snapping the photograph. He'd ushered her ahead of him into the city hall, then called her name. Kelly felt a wave of pity for the teenager she had been, seeing the combination of expectancy and fear on her younger face and remembering all too well her feelings at that exact moment: choosing a life with Gillis as her best option for getting out of the foster system, sensing but not fully comprehending the misery her naïve choice would bring her.

Kelly brought the photo closer to her face and studied it. She could see how guarded her green eyes were, a look she'd seen in every foster child she'd known; a look she was proud to say she had never seen in her own children's eyes. Abruptly, Kelly tossed the frame on the desk. She was pleased to see the chrome corner nick the polished wood. The frame's glass trembled, too, and the photo was knocked askew.

Kelly started with the desk drawers. She wasn't surprised to find them filled with useless things: opened packs of gum, now stale; a hand-grip exerciser to tone the forearms or to release stress. The few papers she found were meaningless as well: pro forma letters from insurers, a few anonymous holiday cards from business toadies, old phone books, real estate specs, year-end reports. Kelly removed a rubber band from a stack of business cards and shuffled through them. She didn't recognize any names, but she banded them again and dropped them in her duffel bag anyway.

She shut the drawers and spread her hands on the top of the desk. Their warmth left a ghostly impression in the polish. She pulled her hands back to her lap and watched the handprints fade. Sitting back in the chair, she let her gaze travel around the room. She wasn't sure what it was she was looking for. She had come here expecting to find remnants of her past, to rescue a few shreds of her life, and, with any luck, to exorcise the memories. The moment she'd walked through the door, however, she'd realized she wanted nothing from this time of her life. It was better to forget it all than to try to memorialize it.

From the looks of things, Gillis hadn't spent much time here either. Clearly he kept his business details elsewhere. Kelly wondered why he even bothered to keep this house. The answer came to her immediately. Gillis never gave up anything that he had made his own. Businesses he bought and sold, but people, houses, these were his forever, even when he no longer needed them.

Kelly eyed a tornado of dust motes spiraling in a shaft of light thrown by the window. The constant motion, the sparkle, the minuteness of it mesmerized her. How many worlds were contained in each tiny speck of dust? How deep did their ignorance go, of the larger world that contained them, with its horror and its beauty?

Her gaze fell again upon the wedding picture on the desk. Her hand reached out and pulled the frame toward her—and at that moment she saw it. The picture had shifted inside the frame, and the corner of another picture was poking out from underneath. Turning the frame over, Kelly pushed aside the brackets and removed the back. She lifted out the other print.

It was another image of her, from about the same time of her life, at fifteen or sixteen years old. Her blonde hair hanging over her shoulders, her green eyes clear, she stared at the camera with a wide, relaxed smile. She wore a polo shirt with the collar turned up and pink pants that flared out at the knee.

Kelly stared. She didn't recognize the clothes. When had she ever worn them? She also didn't remember ever feeling as relaxed and happy as she looked in the picture. But the strangest thing was that she was sitting in a group of other teens, and they were all smiling and looking happy. A boy sat on either side of her, and Kelly had an arm draped companionably around the shoulders of each of them.

Kelly squinted. *I don't remember this picture*, she thought. She studied the unfamiliar clothes, the smiles—put on? No, the happiness on their faces seemed genuine. Maybe it was taken in one of the group homes or at a school play? But Kelly knew she had never been in a school play. She had finished high school while she was living with Gillis, but she had always gone straight to school and come straight home. She had never socialized with other children her age. She knew this scene had not happened to her.

She felt a rising panic. Had she blocked even more of her life than she knew? Had she somehow led a double life?

Kelly leaned into the picture again. The boy on her right looked familiar. His was an easy smile, his hair curly and brown, and she noticed with surprise that his hand was on her knee. The boy on the left was stiffer, his smile incomplete, his hands rigidly on his own knees. Kelly looked closer at him, and her insides turned to water.

The second boy was Gillis. Younger, in his teens, but unmistakably Gillis. Kelly's brain strained to resolve the discrepancy. This was impossible. She flipped the picture over. Faintly, in blue ink, was written, MICHELLE AND ME. Next to that was written AND MICHAEL. But MICHAEL was crossed out with the straight lines of an X.

Kelly recognized her parents' names immediately. She flipped the picture back over. A buzzing started in her ears. The girl in the center was not her. It was her mother. The boy on the right was her father. The boy on the left was Gillis.

Gillis had known her parents.

Horror washed through Kelly as she sat frozen, staring at the picture. *Gillis knew my parents*, she repeated to herself. Her vision became a tunnel.

As if moving through wet cement, she struggled to her feet and staggered out of the room. Passing the closets, she stopped. In Gillis's closet the rods were lined with suits and shirts, probably a hundred of each, abandoned. Above the closet rods was a long shelf that held rows of plastic boxes. Kelly ran to grab a chair and threw herself at the upper shelf. She tore through the contents of the boxes—shoes, sweaters, cuff links, belts—until she got to a cardboard box hidden behind the others. She pulled it to the floor and opened the lid.

She was not really surprised by the first thing she pulled out. A gallon-sized Ziploc bag, rust powder obscuring its contents. She undid the plastic zipper. In the bag was the knife, of course, the one Gillis was saving to destroy her life. But Kelly felt no relief now at having found the object of her ruin. Something told her the box contained far more sinister answers. Dropping the plastic bag containing the knife into her duffel bag, she lifted out the next thing from the box.

It was Gillis's high school yearbook. Underneath it, letters and notebooks. She didn't need to read many lines before realizing what they revealed: Gillis had been in love with her mother. He had been insanely jealous of her father. His letters to her mother were juvenile declarations of the deepest love. She must have returned them to him. The ramblings in the notebooks were teenage screeds of mayhem and murder, all directed at her father. With each page she read, Kelly felt the life as she thought she knew it unravel more and more.

All of a sudden she became aware of a movement off to her left. Wrenched from her thoughts, she spun around and saw Griselda creeping toward her duffel bag. With a yell, the housekeeper sprang forward, grabbing for it.

"Not yours! No take!"

Kelly heaved herself toward the small woman, catching her around the shoulders and rolling her backward. Griselda clawed and kicked. Kelly, bigger but matched in strength, threw herself over the woman, trying to grab her arms. Growling, the woman wriggled free.

"No take! Mr. Gillis know!" She feinted left and faked Kelly into lunging that way. Fleetly the woman grabbed the bag and slipped past Kelly. Regaining her balance, Kelly sprinted after her through the bedroom into the hall. She leaped for Griselda's shoulders and brought the woman down on the tile. Kelly heard a crack as the housekeeper's head hit the hard floor. The woman grunted, the handle of the duffel bag still gripped in her fist.

Kelly pried open the woman's fingers and then noticed the blood on the housekeeper's head. Griselda lay motionless.

Kelly ran back to the closet, threw the papers into the box, scooped it up, and returned to the hallway. Griselda was stirring. Kelly touched two fingers to her neck. Her pulse was strong. She would be alright.

Without looking back, Kelly ran down the stairs and out the front door. She threw the box and the bag into the passenger seat of the rental car and drove off to a hotel, her mind untangling her life with every mile, like a bobbin unraveling. Nothing was what it had seemed.

On the hotel bedspread she followed the unspooling thread

through more letters written by Gillis, but unsent, telling Kelly's mother that she belonged to him forever. At the very bottom of the box Kelly found the object that destroyed everything she had believed of her family's history until that moment: In a plastic sandwich bag, stuffed into the corner of the cardboard, was a small envelope. Inside it was her mother's wedding ring, the ring that had disappeared the night her mother was murdered. The meaning was unmistakable. Gillis had been there that night. Gillis had killed her mother. Gillis had been the shadow she had seen in the doorway, the voice that had commanded her not to move an inch.

> "Go back to bed," he commanded. "Don't move an inch." The timbre of his voice, deep with intensity, demanding obedience. The light from the hallway made it impossible for her to distinguish his features, but she remembered his form blocking the entire doorway, he appeared so big.
>
> She covered her head with the blanket, knowing she would never forget the guttural sound that echoed in her ears . . .

Gillis had watched from the courtroom while Kelly's father had been tried and convicted for the murder. Gillis had watched as the orphaned girl was sent into the foster care system. He had stalked her while she was in it, had lain in wait for her when she tried to escape. He had controlled every aspect of her life before she had even known him. His whole life had been about destroying hers.

Even in her wildest nightmares Kelly had never imagined a hell like this. Gillis had killed Porter. He would get out of jail eventually, and someday he would kill Jake. Kelly sat on the bed, an animal moan escaping her throat involuntarily. She was more alone than she had ever been.

That night Kelly spent hours in front of a computer at an Internet café in Houston. With the codes to the Joan Davis account she had discovered in La Jolla, she entered all the false Joan Davis accounts nationwide, transferring just under $10,000 from each fake account to a numbered account in the Cayman Islands. She was amused to discover that even though every one of them had the same mother's maiden name, no one had ever caught on. When she was done, Kevin and Libby's future was secured.

The next morning, Kelly had flown back to Lake Tahoe and her kids. The rest of her ultimate escape plan came to her on the plane.

Sitting here now with Jake, seven months later, she took the next step. She had to get him to listen. But she realized he wasn't going to.

He was saying, "I'm going to figure out a way to get him put away permanently."

Kelly decided to change her approach. "Jake . . ."

"We've got him on the charity stuff . . ."

"Jake!"

Jake looked at her as if for the first time.

"You're right. I won't go. I'm not leaving."

"You're not?"

Kelly shook out her hair. "We'll stay here for another week, if Jeanette's okay with that."

Jake interrupted excitedly. "She said you could stay here as long as you need."

Kelly continued, "During that time we can look for a place in LA where we can be near you. Not with you, not yet."

Jake felt the tension drain from his body. That sounded reasonable.

"Anything."

They held each other in a long embrace. Jake realized Kelly was right. They had this moment. In the next moment, they would go back up to the house. In the moment after that, they would play with the kids, swim, eat some more. In the moments after that, they would put the kids to bed, sit on the couch, maybe in front of a fire. They would comfort each other. Moment by moment. Jake could live with that.

* * *

And so it went until after lunch the next day, when Jake returned to Los Angeles. The phone call came that evening.

Jeanette, with a puzzled tone in her voice, asking weren't Kelly and the kids staying another week . . .

Jake's frantic but halfhearted calls to his contacts . . .

No trace of Kelly. No trace of the kids. All three of them were gone. Kelly had made herself invisible at last.

The headlines in the morning papers did not surprise Jake at all. Emancipated foster children all over the country had received substantial checks from a Mrs. Joan Davis. Reporters everywhere were trying desperately to find the identity of this mystery benefactor. But there was no way to identify her. The checks came from many different American Capital banks across the country.

* * *

Todd Gillis almost choked on his toast as his newspaper fell to the floor.

"Bitch!" he cried out. "Just you wait . . ."

CHAPTER 35

THE MERRIWEATHER MINIMUM-SECURITY PRISON
in Nevada was surrounded by a six-foot-high chain-link fence, but no
guard towers watched over the perimeters. Low, blue-roofed buildings were arranged around a central courtyard, piazza-style. The
inmates wore khaki pants and blue button-down oxford shirts. They
walked in twos and threes around the courtyard, some bent over
notebooks and binders, others clutching magazines and newspapers.
The basketball court was empty. It looked like a campus for a high-
tech company or a training school for corporate executives—which,
in a way, it was.

The inmates and guards greeted one another with nods of the
head, like colleagues in a hallway. In fact, the guards were nearly
indistinguishable from the inmates; the only differences were that
their shirts were forest green instead of blue and they wore guns
on their belts. They also wore baseball caps emblazoned with the
prison's logo.

It was July, and the afternoon sun was hot. The guard was on his usual rounds, noting who was talking with whom and who was out in the sunshine and who was staying in the shade under the overhanging roof of the courtyard.

He didn't look up at the security cameras that dotted his route, but instead kept his eyes on the ground. He cut around the back of the dormitory and entered it through the main door, unlocked per protocol. Inside were eight double bunks, with metal lockers standing beside each one. The beds were all neatly made, the blankets pulled tight. Communal toilets and showers were in a room off to the right of the entrance door.

The large room was empty except for one man. On the bottom of the last bunk, farthest away from the door, hunched over a laptop computer, was Todd Gillis. His fingers clicked on the keys as the guard approached and stood with his back to the camera that surveilled the dormitory lengthwise. Gillis looked up. He smiled.

"It took you long enough."

"I've got my own schedule," said Kelly quietly, noting that even in the guard's uniform and male makeup, Gillis had taken but a second to recognize her. "You always were the smartest man I'd ever met. What were you expecting?"

Gillis grinned, cockier than ever. "Something like this. Maybe a little sooner. Maybe out on the yard."

"You were a very good teacher," Kelly replied. "What is it you used to tell me . . . ? Memorize the topography, memorize the population, memorize times of day . . . Don't leave a speck without analyzing it."

Gillis chuckled. "You're wasting your time. I'll be out of here before you know it." He closed the laptop. "This time has been a godsend. No board meetings to distract me." He tapped the top of the computer. "I'm in pretty good shape, actually."

Kelly eyed him. She knew he was talking about payback—about the plans he'd made for revenge—but it was also true physically. His hair was grayer, but she could see the outline of biceps under his blue oxford shirt.

"I've got one question for you," she said slowly.

Gillis returned her stare, his eyes mocking.

"You knew my mother," whispered Kelly.

Gillis smirked. "That's a question?"

Kelly stared at him.

"You always were so uneducated." He tossed the laptop on the mattress. "I *more than* knew her."

"She was pregnant when she married my father."

"Yes, she was. And to this day, I don't know whose child she was carrying." His voice was deep with intent to destroy her.

"You killed her."

"I wasn't the one who got the chair for it."

"You'd been tracking me since she died. You knew the kind of life I endured in foster care."

"I didn't want you to turn out too well adjusted." Gillis grinned.

Kelly spat. "You killed my mother because she married my father, and even after she was dead, you came after me."

Gillis snorted. "Don't flatter yourself. You were six years old. Your mother was whoring around with that jackass father of yours right under my nose. After she promised to marry me. It was his money she wanted. She slummed around with me even when they were married. Don't kid yourself; you're just like her. A born con artist. And a born whore."

Kelly swallowed hard. "I know you killed her. I know you were there. I remember the first time you spoke to me. You told me to go back to bed."

"It wasn't the last time I said that to you," Gillis wisecracked, a smile carved into the mask of his face. "Let's play 'what if,' shall we? What if she and I created you? What if she made your father believe you were his baby daughter? What if it was *him* who stole you from *me?*"

Kelly shook her head at the gruesome suggestion. She felt herself slipping. She fought to take back control of the situation.

"I can play 'what if' too. What if we did a paternity test and it proved my mom loved my father, not you? Not ever you?" Even as she heard herself say the words, Kelly knew that the truth of her identity would remain buried with her mom.

The trick worked, though. Kelly saw Gillis shift uncomfortably and knew she was back on top. With that one sentence, she had erased the validity of his entire adult life. She saw his brain frying with the effort not to believe what he knew to be true. She smiled a satisfied smile.

Gillis's eyes flicked to the gun on Kelly's guard's belt.

"You loved me when you married me," he said, his voice disguising his desperation.

"I thought you were a disgusting old man. You were my escape hatch."

Gillis lunged for the gun on her belt. Kelly was fast, but he was faster. He twirled it to point at her heart.

"You won't kill me," whispered Kelly. "Because then it will all end."

She angled her body so the camera could pick up what was happening. She goaded Gillis again. "I dare you," she said.

They both heard movement outside the dorm, and Kelly prayed that her plan was on track. She watched Gillis's eyes, his brain debating between what she was saying and what he wanted to do.

All of a sudden, eight armed guards stormed the dormitory—four through the main entrance and four through the back windows. They held their guns in both hands, all eight weapons trained on Gillis.

"Easy, Gillis," shouted one. "Drop the gun."

"You're a pathetic coward," whispered Kelly, her arms up, "and your life is nothing!"

Gillis's gun exploded. Instantly the guards fired back, and Gillis flew backward in a bloody spray. The lead guard barked orders. Men ran in and out in a chaotically choreographed dance. Everyone seemed to know what to do, and each stuck to his duty.

Kelly didn't look back. She raced out with one of the guards heading for the paramedics, following him to the administration building and ducking down a side hall, out a side door. Her stolen guard's uniform was never found in the Dumpster of the Wal-Mart in the next town. She never learned whether the investigators had checked to see whether the gun Gillis fired was loaded with real bullets or blanks.

The news fed the TV outlets for weeks. A captain of industry killed behind bars. The mystery of an unidentified guard who could not be found. Talking heads suggested that the guards were overworked. Congress called for prison reform. The FBI suspected Mafia connections. Only Jake, watching the bank of TVs in his office, knew what had really happened.

He didn't know how she had done it, but he knew why. And yet none of what he understood—or thought he understood—about Kelly provided the least little clue as to where she was now.

CHAPTER 36

THE OCEAN WAS BLACK, AND THE SKY HAD GONE lavender. The sun, a red ball, was sinking into the sea, taking a few orange clouds with it. Jake watched the pageant from his apartment window, a glass in one hand, his saxophone in the other. A handful of stars were starting to come out. The sky took on its reddish Los Angeles glow. He blinked and the sun was gone.

Jake took a long swallow of his tequila and turned away from the window. The letter lay on the coffee table, its ends sticking up, as if it were trying to refold itself and slide back into the envelope. The envelope with no return address. The envelope postmarked Miami, even though the letter itself said she wasn't there.

Jake drained his glass and picked up the single sheet of blue paper.

Dearest Jake,

You know by now why I had to go. What hap-
pened was supposed to free me, but it didn't.
Please know, though, I'm safe, and so are Kevin
and Libby.

I inherited a large sum of money from Gillis,
but gave most of it away to homeless and foster
kids. I kept enough. I can always sing if I have
to—maybe you should give up the law and play
music full time. Just a thought.

This will be postmarked Miami, but that's
not where I am. It's probably best if you don't
come looking.

I remember every moment of our time
together. I will always love you. I will always
love Porter. I will never forget all you did for me.

Forever yours,
Kelly

Jake watched the letter flutter back down to the table. He refilled his
glass but didn't take a sip. Instead he shuffled over to the fireplace
and poked some kindling around. He held the lighter to the wood
chips, but they wouldn't catch. Exasperated, he grabbed the envelope,
touched the corner of it to the lighter flame, and dropped it into the
fireplace. He watched it curl and shrivel, but before collapsing into
ash, it caught the kindling. Smoke twined up the chimney from a
small, glowing spot on the wood, and he gently blew on it. The flame
grew larger and larger, and to his surprise, he had a fire. He carefully
arranged a log on the grate and walked over to the bookcase.

From *The Sibley Guide to Birds* he withdrew the picture he had hidden there. He stared at it for a moment, the unsmiling Kelly flanked by the stern Gordons. He imagined Kelly, just a child, stuck in that house full of unwanted kids, trapped by her foster parents' abuse. He thought about the risks he took for her by concealing evidence, and he knew he would do it all again in a heartbeat. In a swift motion, he fed the photograph to the fire, blowing on his sax while the paper incinerated and the image turned first to gel and then black smoke.

Jake knew better than to presume he knew anything about Kelly's plans for the future. He knew that her children would always come first and she would always do whatever she had to do in order to protect them. Her intelligence went even deeper than he'd suspected, and she was far braver than he'd known.

From early on Kelly had been a step ahead of everyone. With his help—him risking everything for her—she had gracefully sidestepped a trial after the bank scam. She'd gotten just about everyone who'd come in contact with her to bend the law for her. And here he was, destroying evidence for her, after having concealed it for months—all against the law.

Jake had decided to believe Kelly really did love him. Had he done enough for her? At least as much as Porter would have done? What if Porter had lived? Gillis would have been a reality in Kelly's life whether it was Porter who loved her or Jake. Was Jake's love for Kelly independent of his love for Porter . . . or was it part of the same ache? Would he have fallen in love with Kelly no matter the circumstances, no matter what? That was the question that lingered long after any other, and Jake had blown a hurricane of notes through his saxophone, pondering it. Either way, the answer was one he didn't think he'd ever know.

Jake was spent by the time the fire started to die, and he laid down his instrument. The letter still sat on the coffee table. Jake picked it up and started to read it again, before tossing it, too, on the embers. The paper landed at a slant and started to slip off the grate. Jake stopped it with the poker and pushed it impatiently back. A tiny firework of sparks shot out and showered into ash. At last it curled into flame. As Jake watched, his BlackBerry signaled a message. He ignored it, thinking through the words of her letter once again. They were heartfelt, he knew that, but they were utilitarian, almost anonymous in their sentiments. They could have been written to anyone. The letter fluttered and disintegrated. It was gone.

Jake put his hand around his drink and took a sip. Absently, he pulled his BlackBerry toward him and glanced at the waiting message. The subject line read: *The status of your account.*

It had been sent from an address in the Cayman Islands. Jake moved to delete it, then paused. On a hunch, he opened it.

> Your account is delinquent. Please contact us immediately regarding the state of your affairs. Sincerely yours, N. S. Brooks, CEO Wave Bank, Grand Cayman.

Jake laughed aloud. "Natalie St. Clair Brooks. CEO of a bank. And married without a license."

He e-mailed back immediately:

> Situation dire. Account languishing. Need your help. Also must discuss issue of marriage without a license. Must rectify immediately.

Her reply was instant:

> We lack only you. Come.

In one fell swoop, Kelly had allayed all of Jake's anxieties and doubts, and he let out a whoop of elation as he punched in the number on his cell phone.

"Get me on the next flight to Grand Cayman . . . No, not a round-trip ticket. This time it's going to be one way."